I0566384

CONTENTS

ACKNOWLEDGMENTS

The children who inhabit the story are real to me because at one time or another I taught someone just like them. They have made me laugh, they have made me cry and often they pushed me to the limits of my patience. In retrospect, I loved every minute. I sincerely hope I have done them justice and written a story they will enjoy inhabiting and perhaps sharing with their own grandchildren.

Grateful thanks to Welsh artist Jason Portt who gave us permission to use his atmospheric painting in our cover design.

The Pit of Shadows

CHAPTER 1

THE LOTTERY

A chill November wind tore down the valley, whined through a tangle of television aerials and charged into the marshalled rows of satellite dishes. Billy clung to the sides of the terraced houses hoping it would not notice his frail figure slip through the shadows. It must have smelt what heat was left in his scrawny body. Icy fingers tugged at his skimpy track suit searching for every slight tear and threadbare patch. Something lurked watching from the dark beyond the street lamps as he shivered his way home.

It was so cold Billy was glad he was wearing the balaclava Nan had knitted him. He had eaten his last chip and his fingers were numb. He thrust his hands as far as they would reach inside the pockets of his track suit. The street was deserted. Not just his street. Billy guessed every street in the country was as eerily empty as this one. Each given over to stray cats, dogs and kids like him.

The creature watched as Billy stopped outside his front door. It would bide its time and wait until the child was alone before making its move. Silently it slipped back into the black midnight pool of the night.

Avoiding the cluster of empty milk bottles Billy crept around to the window and pressed his face against the glass. He could see his parent's heads and shoulders, black silhouettes against the bright glare of the television screen. His breath rolled like thick fog over the frosty pane and they were gone. Billy wiped the condensation with his sleeve and lifted the soggy bottom of his balaclava over his mouth to stop it happening again. A Famous Personality with big teeth and false smile pressed the button that jolted Modred to life. A nation stopped breathing. An avalanche of balls rumbled like thunder through a million homes. Somewhere the lightning bolt of fortune was about to strike.

Any second now Dad would jump up from the sofa, curse, crumple his ticket into a ball and toss it onto the floor next to the waste paper basket. Mum would pretend not to care, tell Dad off for dropping litter and storm into the kitchen to attack the kettle wondering what life would have been like if she had married Gerald from the bank. A few more minutes and they would calm down. At worst, he might get a row for coming home late but more likely Dad would disappear down the pub to drown his sorrows.

It never happened. Billy watched as Dad got to his feet clutching the worthless slip of paper. There was something about his strange jerky movements that troubled Billy. Perhaps the disappointment had been too much and he was about to have a heart attack. For once Billy was glad he was outside in the cold. Mum would only panic and he'd end up having to give mouth to mouth. The thought of kissing his father filled Billy with horror. But wait, now Mum was doing the same thing! Mum and Dad stood facing each other hardly moving. Was he about to become an orphan? If he did would Matron let him live with Nan? If that was worrying what happened next made Billy wonder if he should call the Police.

Without warning Mum and Dad threw themselves at each other like a pair of Sumo Wrestlers long past their sell-by date. Gripping each other in a fierce embrace they tried squeezing each other to death. They stopped when it became clear neither of them had the strength to finish the job. Dad was bigger and stronger but not exactly at the peak of fitness and got short of breath very quickly, a fact Billy often used to his advantage. Mum was a completely different kettle of fish. She was smaller but wirier than Dad. If the fight went the distance his money was on Mum.

Suddenly the struggle took a new turn. Mum and Dad did something Billy had never seen before, not even in the school yard. Without releasing their grip, they began to jump up and down and round and round. Billy guessed they must be trying to unbalance one another. This didn't work either. Hulk Hogan had nothing to fear from 99 *Amelia Terrace*.

In his excitement Billy let the balaclava slip. The epic struggle disappeared behind a silver film of frosted mist. Hurriedly he rubbed a small peep hole. The room was empty. Mum and Dad had vanished, or had they? Perhaps they were lying behind the sofa locked in a last embrace, bulging eyes staring at the nicotine stained ceiling. Should he knock for the neighbours? But what would he tell them? All they would see was an empty room. Worse, what if Mum or Dad answered when they rang the bell? They would both go ballistic. There was only one thing for it, Nan!

Billy always wanted a tree house. A secret place where he could hide from the world below. Whenever his parents lost their rag he would clamber into its welcoming branches and gaze up at the distant stars until the storm passed and he was forgotten once more. But there were no trees near where he lived, only the pathetic scattering in the local park, hardly big enough to hold a doll's house. Besides, after dark, others claimed the territory. Youths with dark haunted eyes who slouched and staggered about the deserted playground and gathered in groups among the shadows. Billy might not have a tree house, but he did have Nan!

Something brushed against his legs. He looked down and Buster, his huge scruffy Ginger Tom looked right back up at him through his one good eye waiting for Billy to make up his mind. The window had clouded over again. Billy shivered. With Buster loping alongside stride for stride he ran down the empty pavements, spindly legs flashing like knitting needles under the street lights.

CHAPTER 2

THE BEST ASSEMBLY EVER

'The Hollies' was once a Baptist Church until the members got old and died. The building was sold and re-opened shortly afterwards as an Old People's Home. Up and down the valley chapels and churches closed at regular intervals to resurface months later as nursing homes or bingo halls. At the last count nursing homes had nosed ahead. Billy often wondered where they would find enough old people to fill them.

"They'll fill them all in time, don't you fret," his Nan told him before dissolving into fits of laughter. Billy hadn't understood but his Nan was always laughing at something. That's the way she was and one of the reasons Billy loved her.

By the time he reached 'The Hollies' Billy was gasping for breath. The cold air burnt his lungs as he gulped, bent double, hands on knock-knees. Nan's room was on the ground floor around the back. A low privet hedge bounded the lawn that stretched up to her window. Buster sniffed the long grass for signs of intruders. Billy stooped down, picked up a handful of gravel and flung it at Nan's window. It clattered against the glass echoing down the narrow streets. Billy half expected to see the Four Horsemen come charging out of the night just like the Visiting Speaker had told them about. Lots of children suffered nightmares for weeks after. Mr. Meredith didn't ask him back. Pity, it had been much better than normal assemblies, especially when Kayleigh Williams started to cry.

It began just like any other boring assembly except for one thing, Elder Stoker. He stood beside Mr. Meredith smiling a saintly sort of smile from beneath a wiry beard that seemed to have grown out of control and run amok all over his head. Behind thick lenses his eyes swam like pebbles in a deep pool. He reminded Billy of an owl hiding in a bush. Mr. Meredith beamed as he introduced the Guest Speaker.

"You'd think he was introducing the flipping Stereophonics," whispered Ryan Bottomly.

Billy knew he was being set up. Ryan Bottomly was one of Ellis Kinsey's 'toadies'. There was nothing Ellis liked better than dropping somebody in it. Billy's reputation as a giggler was legendary. He felt it coming and tried to stifle it but like pop from a shaken can it squirted through his clenched teeth exploding with sheer joy as it escaped into the musty air of the school hall. A space opened around Billy leaving him red-faced and alone. They might as well have pointed an accusing finger straight at him.

Mr. Meredith eyed Billy in a way that spelt trouble. Billy's nails dug into the palms of his moist, clammy hands. He was not going to cry. He hoped Mr. Meredith didn't shout too loudly.

Then it happened. Fate stepped in just as Billy realised how a rabbit must feel cornered by a bad-tempered stoat. Not only did Fate step in, it placed a firm hand on Mr. Meredith's startled shoulder.

You could tell Mr. Meredith was not pleased. Next to the Queen everyone knows the people you just don't touch are those with horrible infectious diseases and head teachers. Mr. Meredith's face looked like an over ripe tomato about to burst its seams. Elder Stoker ignored the outraged Mr. Meredith and to Billy's great delight followed up by putting both feet even further in it.

"Suffer little children Headmaster, suffer little children . . . And suffer they will!"

He spoke so forcibly that Mr. Meredith's expression changed from anger to alarm as swiftly as a cloud passing across the sun. Elder Stoker raised his eyes to the ceiling. Everyone, including Mr. Meredith, looked up. There was something in the way he stared at the polystyrene tiles that sent shivers down Billy's spine. Elder Stoker was doing that thing Miss Price had told them about in Science. Elder Stoker was metamorphosing. One thing for sure, Elder Stoker was not turning into a butterfly. Perhaps he was a Werewolf or something worse like the thing Billy had seen prowling in the shadows outside the park. He did have a lot of hair for a Christian.

Elder Stoker slowly raised his arm and pointed a chubby finger at the ceiling where a large section, sodden with rainwater, bellied overhead. Had an angel warned him the tiles were about to collapse on their up-turned faces?

"Can you see them?" he said in a loud squeaky voice.

A disappointed Billy realised Elder Stoker probably wasn't changing into a werewolf.

Mr. Meredith began to mumble something about the 'Authority' and 'Financial Constraints' and how it was 'Perfectly Safe' provided no-one stood underneath for too long. Ignoring the flustered headmaster floundering around the stage like a beached halibut Elder Stoker raised a hand.

"Listen!"

He cupped an ear. A hush fell.

Eat your heart out Mr. Meredith. Even Brooklyn Hopkins stopped chewing. Everyone strained to hear whatever it was Elder Stoker was listening too. Nothing! Ross Tudor hiccupped loudly but he always hiccupped when he was nervous.

"Can you hear the distant thunder of hoof beats?" said Elder Stoker his voice a strangled falsetto.

Mr. Meredith was showing signs of panic. It wasn't only Mr. Meredith, some of Year One began to snivel. Billy wondered if grownups developed acute hearing as they grew old to make up for losing their teeth and stuff. He looked out of the window expecting to see a herd of buffalo charging through the yard. All he could see was Mr. Huggleston the caretaker picking up stray crisp packets that had escaped from the overloaded bins. Even old 'Huggy' would break into a trot if a herd of stampeding buffalo were galloping towards him. Billy watched for a few more seconds never having seen anyone trampled to death by a herd of buffalo before. Still nothing.

On the stage things were hotting up. Mr. Meredith was struggling to get himself in front of Elder Stoker but Elder Stoker was having none of it. For a few moments, the children watched spellbound as they jostled for position like a pair of slippery ballroom dancers. Mr. Meredith was fast running out of puff. He paused to draw breath and Elder Stoker saw his chance.

"They are coming!"

Elder Stoker turned to Mr. Meredith wearing such a ferocious expression that Mr. Meredith stepped back and nearly fell off the stage.

"Woe to you in authority who fail to warn these little ones. The Four Horsemen draw near. Their time is at hand."

Billy turned to Ryan Bottomly, he knew all the latest groups, but he simply shrugged his shoulders. Whoever the Four Horsemen were Elder Stoker seemed to be expecting them any minute. They would have to be good to beat this for entertainment, thought Billy. Elder Stoker teetered on the edge of the stage waving a big black book above his head still ranting about the Four Horsemen. Perhaps he was their agent. Meanwhile Mr. Meredith was struggling to resist the urge to push Elder Stoker off the stage. Mr. Meredith must prefer male voice choirs.

Miss Perry, the Deputy Head, stood open mouthed by the hall door. Mr. Meredith waved his arms at her as if showing a jumbo jet where to land. His antics eventually caught her eye but it took some time before she decoded the message Mr. Meredith was desperately trying to send. Nodding her head so violently Billy was sure it would come unstuck she disappeared through the doorway. But all this had taken time and Elder Stoker made the most of it.

The children listened wide-eyed as Elder Stoker ranted in gory detail about the Four Horsemen. Their music might be rubbish but they were definitely worth seeing. They all rode on stage in horses dyed a different colour. Billy couldn't help thinking Elder Stoker was going over the top with his publicity blurb. It made heavy metal sound soothing. There was a lot of talk about swords and conquering and slaying and famine and things. Just like the Evening News.

"Cool!" whispered Ryan Bottomly when Elder Stoker described the last member of the group.

He rode a pale horse and called himself Death and Hell. That was when the fire alarm went off and everybody rushed for the doors except for Kayleigh Williams who stood there crying. Billy stood there too but for an entirely different reason.

Outside where the playground should have been was open countryside. Rolling hills dotted with white flecks, that Billy thought must be sheep, stretched away to a horizon turned scarlet by the setting sun. Three riders, not four, were fast approaching along a dusty road winding its way through the hillsides. The road led directly towards the large window set in the school hall. Billy watched as the riders loomed ever larger. He'd heard other kids talk of 3D movies they'd seen. This is what it must be like but better because you didn't need those special glasses.

The horsemen were getting closer. Billy could hear the thunder of their hooves and see clouds of dust billowing in their wake. Elder Stoker must have gone to a lot of trouble. Pity Mr. Meredith had been such a spoilsport. Just as it looked as if they were about to smash through the window the horsemen wheeled to the left giving Billy a grandstand view.

Mr. Groucutt had been teaching them about the Civil War where the king got his head chopped off. The first rider looked just like one of the people who fought for the king. He wore a wide brimmed hat with a plume and his long dark hair streamed behind him. Most of his face was covered in a thick black beard.

Try as he might Billy could not remember what the second rider looked like but the third rider he would never forget. He was a big man hunched forward in the saddle. The hood of a monk's black cowl covered the upper half of his face further shadowed by a wide brimmed hat. As the first two riders disappeared the third stopped and turned to face the window. Billy had an uncomfortable feeling that although he could not see the rider's eyes they were staring straight at him.

"Kayleigh Williams, Billy Jenkins, into the school yard now!"

Mr. Groucutt's voice echoed across the hall.

The horse reared and wheeled and in an instant the rider was gone.

"Hurry up Jenkins," barked Mr. Groucutt.

Billy blinked. The grey playground had replaced the green fields. How awesome was Elder Stoker? That assembly was the best.

CHAPTER 3

MATRON

"Ninety-nine . . . one hundred!"

Nan should have opened the fire-door by now. Billy stared across the tiny patch of moonlit lawn he imagined stretching away to infinity and beyond. The instant his feet touched the forbidden earth he expected the tell-tale strangled scream of sirens to betray him. Searchlights would hunt him down and out of the darkness a monstrous, gargantuan shape would loom casting a giant shadow over the valley. MATRON!

Matron and Billy were natural enemies. To begin with he was a child. In Matron's eyes, the only good thing to be said for children was they would one day grow old. Billy was a particularly disgusting example. A spindly, scruffy streetwise urchin. His very presence lowered the tone and was the reason several clients suffered a sudden change of heart about offloading unwanted elderly relatives into Matron's tender care. More than once she had been met by the troublesome child whilst showing them around the antiseptic corridors. His dark eyes would gaze at them and they would look away. Afterwards they made hurried excuses and shuffled off never to return. She cursed the day his grandmother had been admitted for with her, like a shadow that haunted her dreams, came Billy.

Matron lived upstairs in what had once been the attic. Rumour was that when Matron walked in the spiders packed their bags and walked out. Billy often thought about hiding under Nan's bed, sneaking out when it got dark to climb the stairs that led to Matron's lair. Billy was an expert on Vampires and knew Matron was one of their evil brood. Not the kind you saw Buffy slaying on TV that sucked your blood and hated the smell of garlic. Matron was, as Nan would say, 'The Real McCoy'. Yet whenever the chance came Billy's courage failed and he trudged home under the weight of his weakness, unable to look Buster in his one good eye.

Ever since Nan had been resident in 'The Hollies' Matron slowly sucked the life out of her. Helplessly Billy watched her ebb away like the tide. Bit by bit Nan was leaving him and he dreaded being left alone on the empty beach that was his life. She hardly ever laughed now. The sparkle gone. Her bright blue eyes faded like old paint ready to peel away from the walls of an abandoned house.

Billy hated Matron with a passion too big for a little boy. A passion that sometimes frightened him. He watched as she pretended to talk to Nan while ignoring her completely. She might have been talking to her own reflection in the mirror, only vampires don't have reflections. Billy burned as he listened to Matron speak to Nan as though she were a small, helpless child. He was sure she did it even more when he was there because she knew how much it upset him.

"Come on now Missus," she would say in that sharp matronly way of hers. "Eat up your breakfast like a good girl or there'll be no elevenses mind."

Billy bit his lip to stop tears welling up. Nan was the wisest person in the whole wide world, not a silly old woman whose marbles were missing. His bottom lip quivered when he tried to speak. The last thing he wanted was for Matron to think he'd gone soft. Instead he just glared at her plotting the revenge that one day he determined would be his.

Like black clouds that hid the sun Billy's thoughts raced across his mind as he waited for Nan to open the fire-door. She must have crept up while he was deep in his own darkness. One minute she was in his head and the next she was standing over him. Billy braced himself. There was no telling what she might do. Funny things vampires at the best of times and two hours after sunset was not one of them. Should he try making the sign of the cross or simply scarper? Matron moved closer. Billy's legs ached from the effort of running so, seeing there wasn't a sharp stake handy, he shut his eyes and silently recited *The Lord's Prayer* that Nan had taught him.

Billy felt a large, meaty arm wrap itself around his shoulders. He wondered if vampire bites hurt, or did they inject you with anaesthetic like at the Dentist? He was about to find out. Gritting his teeth and scrunching his eyes he told himself no matter what happened he would not give Matron the pleasure of hearing him scream. Billy was totally unprepared for what came next. Instead of the stench of Matron's hot breath on his neck he felt her arms around him. Only then did the full horror dawn upon him. Matron was giving him a hug. Billy squinted up at her. It was worse than he imagined, she was smiling at him. Now Billy was really afraid.

"Billy, what luck!" she warbled reminding Billy of the Famous Personality with the big white teeth. "I've been trying to get in touch with your parents all evening, but there's no reply."

"That's because murdered people can't answer the phone," he muttered under his breath.

"Pardon?"

Matron's new-found friendliness slipped a little. She stared down at Billy as if he were a deadly infectious germ on the other end of a microscope for which there is no known cure.

"You're quite a little comedian, aren't you?" she said. "Actually, I wanted to speak to them about your grandmother."

Suddenly Billy was more frightened than he would have been in a graveyard full of ghouls. He opened his mouth but the words refused to come because if he didn't ask the question he was aching to ask everything would stay the same.

"Perhaps you'd better come inside with me young man. I'll try phoning your parents again."

Her voice was firm and her arm around his shoulder tightened forcing his unwilling feet over the frozen grass.

The entrance, lit by a garish fluorescent light, loomed ahead. The gateway to a nightmare realm from which he might never return. The empty corridors seemed to be expecting him and even the shadows stood watchful as he passed. Billy had only ever felt like this once before, the day he had accidentally smashed Mr. Meredith's windscreen the only time Mr. Meredith had parked his car in the school yard. Mr. Meredith was furious and Billy had been summoned to the Office. A hush fell on the playground. Children moved aside to let him pass. Someone whispered.

"Dead man walking."

There had been cruel laughter. There was no laughter now, just the sound of Matron's heavy tread on the thin carpet.

CHAPTER 4

THE GREAT GARDNER-ALLEN FIASCO

Matron had secretly longed for this moment ever since the 'Great Gardner-Allen Fiasco'. The Gardner-Allen's were the wealthiest family in the county. They lived in a large house with its own indoor swimming pool on 'The Croft', a cluster of posh houses perched on top of a hill overlooking the valley. The Gardner-Allen's wealth was the result of years of hard work by the 'Gaffer'. A small business selling china urinals had blossomed into a multi-million-pound industry.

Much to the Gaffer's displeasure his son moved the business into the space-age with spectacular success. The new Gardner-Allen urinals were fitted with automatic doors that swung open whether the user was ready or not. Much to the delight of Billy who hung around with his friends in the hope of spotting someone they knew. As a result, they were only ever used by desperate strangers. This made them very popular with local councils who made huge savings on cleaning bills. There was hardly a town or village anywhere in the country that did not boast a Gardner-Allen patented 'bog-house' lurking on a street corner like a discarded Tardis.

For the Gardner-Allen's life was sweet but storm clouds were gathering and taking shape. That shape was the spitting image of the Gaffer.

Mr. and Mrs. Gardner-Allen first became aware there was a problem when a group of angry men from the local Allotment Society turned up on the doorstep one Sunday morning. They demanded the Gaffer's head and any other bits of him they could lay their hands on.

The Gaffer explained he was a member of the Chicken Liberation Front, the only member to date in fact, and where better to begin liberating chickens than in your own back yard. Mr. Gardner-Allen offered to pay for the pampered fowls. The offer was greeted with outrage. How was he to know every chicken had its own name? When news of events reached the Pigeon Fanciers Association armed guards began patrolling the most expensive pigeon lofts.

It was when the Gaffer's attention turned to inanimate objects that the problems began. 'The Chicken Liberation Front', was quickly forgotten and 'The Garden Gnome Liberation Front' was born. One-day Mr. Gardner-Allen came home from work to find the living room knee deep in gnomes of every size and description. There were gnomes sitting on toadstools, gnomes fishing, gnomes reading books and even gnomes doing things that should not be done outside of one of Mr. Gardner-Allen's patented urinals.

Every night for a week Mr. Gardner-Allen, clothed like a member of the SAS on a night mission, would return the gnomes to their owners. Unfortunately, he returned many to the wrong homes. This happened so often startled gnome-owners became convinced supernatural powers were at work.

Experts in the paranormal flooded into the valley making it the U. K.'s version of 'The Bermuda Triangle'. Corn circles and U.F.O.'s were forgotten as the world's Great Minds advanced their own pet theory. One Great Thinker announced that garden gnomes had been replaced by alien life forms which only became active at night. Unused to their surroundings they lost their bearings in the dark and ended up in the wrong gardens.

Things were getting too hot. It was only a matter of time before someone sent for Mulder and Scully. Then, to Mr. and Mrs. Gardner-Allen's relief, the Gaffer said he was disbanding the Gnome Liberation Front because the ungrateful creatures kept going back.

Sadly, for the Gardner-Allens', it proved to be the calm before the hurricane. A chance remark was all it took to set off the dreadful chain of events. One foggy, wet March evening they were sat around the television watching the golf from sunny Florida when Mrs. Gardner-Allen spoke the words that would haunt her forever.

"I almost feel sorry for those golf balls the way they bash them all over the place."

The Gaffer leapt to his feet and glared at the television set just as a large man in a tartan sweater was about to smash the ball another 300 yards down the fairway. He turned off the television and stormed out of the room. They listened as his feet stamped up the stairs. His bedroom door slammed. Slowly they turned to look at each other.

"What?" bleated Mrs. Gardner-Allen.

Mr. Gardner-Allen shook his head.

The Meadow Vale Golf Club was the poshest in the County. Being rich didn't get you in, you had to know Someone. That Someone would put you forward for membership and after that it was mostly plain sailing. Mr. Gardner-Allen met his Someone selling a batch of hi-tech urinals to a city council. The Someone did very well out of the deal and Mr. Gardner-Allen was invited for a round of golf. Two more invites followed and it was hinted by the Someone that membership would soon follow.

So, that fateful Sunday morning Mr. Gardner-Allen set out for the Meadow Vale Golf Club like a donkey chasing a carrot. Not once did he wonder why the Gaffer had got up so early and not returned from his morning ramble. Even less did the thought to check the drawer where he hid his black combat kit enter his head. The sun shone and on the horizon, the promise of Full Membership beckoned.

As Mr. Gardner-Allen was about to tee off on the third hole when he glimpsed a figure lurking in a copse of trees that lined the fairway. Taking his eye off the ball he sliced it badly and it flew like an arrow towards the self-same trees.

"Don't bother looking for it old boy," said the Someone, "you'll never find it in there. It's like the bally Amazon."

The Someone reached into his bag and did not see Mr. Gardner-Allen's ball come hurtling back like a guided missile from where it had only just landed. The last thing Mr. Gardner-Allen remembered before everything went black was the distant sound of someone shouting, "Bullseye!" in a very familiar voice.

When Mr. Gardner-Allen came around he was sitting in one of the large armchairs in the clubhouse. He was not alone. The lounge looked like the casualty ward at the local hospital. Members sporting lumps and bruises dotted its four corners.

"Thank goodness you're all right old boy," said the Someone.

"Was it an explosion?" mumbled Mr. Gardner-Allen.

There was a lump on his head the size of an egg.

"Absolutely not!" replied the Someone. "It's some Nutter. Sounds like he could be ex SAS. Highly strung those boys you know. When they snap, anything can happen. Anyway," he said staring out of the window, "looks like the police have collared the blighter."

Memory came flooding back. The figure in the trees dressed in black, the ball hurtling towards him, the familiar voice. The clubhouse door burst open and two burly policemen appeared holding tight to an old man dressed in black. He was holding a balaclava in his hand.

"He says one of you can vouch for him," said the policemen.

There were gasps of horror and everyone shook their heads. Almost everyone.

"Hello son," said the Gaffer.

Three weeks later Mr. and Mrs. Gardner-Allen and the Gaffer were sat in the back of a chauffeur driven limousine parked outside 'The Hollies'. From his hiding place behind the rhododendron bushes Billy watched with growing interest as the Gardner-Allen's got out. They stood on the forecourt like shipwrecked sailors setting foot on an unknown island. Billy noticed the old man was refusing to take another step. Very sensible of him thought Billy, there's worse than cannibals inside there. The man and woman were trying to coax him round. When that didn't work, they'd stop pretending to be nice and use force. Billy knew the rules of that game very well.

"Come on Dad, please."

The younger man with the large lump on his head sounded near to tears.

"Just give it a try for a week."

The old man clamped his lips and shook his head.

"If you don't like it we'll come and get you on the weekend," said the younger man.

Billy could stand it no longer.

"That's what they said to my Nan," he said stepping out from behind the bush, "that was ages ago."

Billy's appearance was so sudden and unexpected that a startled Mrs. Gardner-Allen screamed and dropped her handbag. Mr. Gardner-Allen stooped to pick it up, fumbling around for its contents on the grass. Billy and the Gaffer looked at each other and winked. It was the strangest feeling, as though they recognised one another but from a great distance where time didn't matter.

"Is he your boy?" asked Billy curiously.

The Gaffer nodded.

"He's not a bad lad. Bit slow on the uptake."

Billy nodded, the Gaffer could be describing his Dad.

Mr. Gardner-Allen couldn't believe his ears. Right in front of him his dotty father and some scruffy kid were discussing him as if he were the nine-year-old.

"And who are you?"

Mr. Gardner-Allen tried to sound stern but the lump on his head made him feel slightly silly. If he'd known he was going to be talking to some cheeky little school kid, he would have worn a hat.

"Billy Jenkins. Are you going to dump your Dad in there?"

The question, and the way the child fixed him with his dark eyes made Mr. Gardner-Allen very uncomfortable.

"I'd hardly say *'dump'*," said Mr. Gardner-Allen.

He felt himself turn a bright, guilty red. This was ridiculous, he was being cross examined by a nine-year-old.

"I would," said Billy.

There was an awkward silence. Mr. Gardner-Allen felt like an ageing boxer caught on the ropes desperately trying to fend off a younger, stronger and quicker opponent. The child's gaze did not waver. Mr. Gardner-Allen blinked, the lump on his head was beginning to throb. At that moment, he was saved by the bell.

"Mr. and Mrs. Gardner-Allen!" Matron's voice boomed. "What a pleasure. I've been expecting you."

She launched herself across the forecourt hoping the little brat had not done too much damage. She had been awaiting the arrival of the Gardner-Allen's all morning. Fresh flowers had been placed in the entrance hall and the doors to every room locked to ensure they did not bump into one of the residents wandering around the corridors like untidy ghosts. The whole event had been planned like a military operation. Matron had thought of everything, everything that is, except Billy. What was he doing here? The child must have a sixth sense. She forced a smile. It could not have been very convincing because Mr. Gardner-Allen flinched. She prayed her eye did not start twitching.

"I see you've met Master Billy."

Her voice trembled as she tried not to stare at the large egg-shaped lump the size of a small mole-hill poking out of the crown of Mr. Gardner-Allen's head.

"Oh yes. We've met."

Something in the tone of Mr. Gardner-Allen's reply warned Matron all was not well. Her hands itched to wind themselves around the child's scrawny neck. She forced another smile. It was a mistake. The strain proved too great and her eye began to twitch.

"This is Matron," said Billy to Mr. Gardner-Allen who was finding it impossible not to stare at Matron's twitch, "she's a vampire."

"You little . . ."

Matron's face twisted into a mask of fury, all that was missing was the serpent hair-do. It didn't seem to matter as Mr. Gardner-Allen might as well have been turned to stone already. He could only watch as the creature known as Matron lunged at the little boy. Thankfully the child dodged nimbly to one side.

". . . little monkey!"

This time Matron did not even attempt a smile. The mask had slipped completely.

"He's such a . . . such a . . ." said Matron trying to speak and control the twitch at the same time.

She watched Billy race across the forecourt and leap over the boundary wall before vanishing around the corner.

"Would you like to come inside?"

Spittle covered Matron's quivering lower lip. Between her eye and her lip Matron's face was taking on a life of its own. Mr. Gardner-Allen took a hasty step backwards.

"Ah no," he stammered, "we, that is, my wife and I, well, we've . . . um, changed our minds. The Gaffer, Dad is not going into any nursing home. Dear me no, unthinkable! Thought we'd come and let you know in person, so to speak. Well, you must be very busy with all your inmates . . . patients . . . whatever. Good day."

Matron gaped as Mr. Gardner-Allen turned on his heel and ushered Mrs. Gardner-Allen and the Gaffer into the limousine. There was a squeal as the sleek black saloon lurched forward and sped down the road leaving in its wake the shattered dreams of rich clients beating a path to Matron's open door. Lifting her eyes to the heavens she mouthed a dark and dreadful oath in which the name Billy was repeated several times. Overhead thunder rumbled behind the darkening skies.

P S Rowlands

CHAPTER 5

A STROKE OF LUCK

Now her 'prayer' had been answered. She led the poisonous little creature through the dimly-lit corridors.

"Sit here a moment while I ring your mother and father. They must be worried sick about you."

Billy sat in the chair opposite Matron's office. The door shut and he was alone. He waited a few seconds until he heard Matron's muffled voice pretending to talk into the telephone. Billy was not fooled, he knew this was the chance she had been waiting for. She was probably sharpening her fangs. Any second the door would burst open and Matron would stand there staring at him through red eyes. Only it wouldn't be Matron but something worse, much worse.

Slipping off the chair and into the shadows he tip-toed down the corridor. Matron's words replayed in his head.

"I want to speak to them about your grandmother."

Why had Matron been trying to ring his parents? She only ever did that to complain about him or . . . Billy tried to stop the thought getting into his head but it refused to go away and he did not have the strength to keep it out.

The corridors seemed longer and less familiar. He recalled a story Nan had told him about this ancient Greek bloke called Percy who ended up getting trapped in an underground maze with a monster half man and half mad cow breathing down his neck. Behind one of the doors someone coughed. Billy's heart moved into overdrive. If he could have the choice of who was chasing him he'd take the mad cow any day.

He turned a corner and stopped to listen. It was difficult to hear anything above the pounding of his heart. Nothing! Gnawing at his bottom lip he peered back around the bend half expecting Matron to leer at him through blood red eyes, her lips drawn back revealing yellow fangs. Still nothing! Billy abandoned the idea of becoming a vampire hunter.

Nan's room was the last on the left. What if it was locked? Where could he hide then? He reached for the door handle and was surprised by how wet and slippery it was. He rubbed his hands down his track suit and tried again. It was stiff but it wasn't locked. Billy hesitated, suddenly he no longer wanted to open the door. What was he afraid of? It was only Nan on the other side. Why was it so quiet? She must be sleeping, but then he would hear her snoring. Nan had a tremendous snore.

If Billy thought he'd been afraid as he slunk down the corridor expecting to hear Matron's heavy tread close behind he had been wrong. This was real fear. A fear he could not name and it waited for him on the other side of the door. But, so did Nan. Summoning his courage, he turned the handle, opened the door and stepped inside.

"Then you will come over later? Good, and once again, congratulations!"

Extraordinary! What a stroke of luck. Matron laughed at the pun, and her laughter was the sound of wind blowing across a stagnant pool. If she played her cards right she could be rid of the child for good. She opened the door. The chair was empty. As expected the boy had slipped off for a chat with his precious Nan. What a shame! Best give him a little time on his own. Time to come to terms with what had happened. Time to suffer. She turned down the corridor towards the staircase that led to her attic flat. There was no danger the boy's parents would rush over. They had more important things to think about than an unwanted old woman and a disobedient little brat. She fumbled for the keys with trembling hands. Behind the door it waited patiently for her.

A bedside lamp was the only dim light. It took a few seconds for Billy's eyes to adjust. A large figure loomed over the bed blocking his view of Nan. Billy reached for the door handle ready to bolt, heart pumping. The sudden surge of blood to his stomach made his head swim. His legs felt distinctly wobbly. If he cried for help who would hear him? Only Matron. Plucking up courage he released his grip on the door-handle and turned to face whatever monstrosity dared threaten his Nan.

He had once seen this old black and white movie. Some men dug up a tomb in the middle of the desert. The stone coffin stood upright which Billy thought a bit strange. They opened it and got excited when they found a body all wrapped in white bandages. Whoever his doctor was he couldn't have been much good.

That night one of the men stayed in the same room as the Bandaged Man writing in a diary. As he wrote the man in bandages began to move jerkily, arms outstretched. The man bent over the desk didn't hear a thing. It was only when the shadow fell across him that he turned around and screamed. Billy had been too frightened to scream. He still had the odd nightmare. The figure standing over Nan's bed reminded him of the Bandaged Man. This was not good. Billy stood his ground as it turned its head. The loathsome creature smiled at him.

"Hello Billy boy, come to visit grannie, have you?"

Ryland's words crawled across Billy's skin like scarab beetles. As he spoke he heaved his massive body away from the bed.

Ryland was Matron's henchman. When he lumbered through the corridors in his crumpled blue uniform the residents hid in their rooms.

There they waited in hope his heavy footfalls would not stop outside their door. When they did, the unfortunate occupant would walk around sporting a huge bruise on his arm for weeks.

"Old people bruise easily," Ryland explained when Billy asked him about the one on Nan's arm. "Sometimes it's difficult to find a vein."

Billy thought that was probably because Matron had got there before him.

Something was terribly wrong. However poorly Nan felt she always managed to raise herself up and smile when Billy visited. This time she did not move. Her head was turned away from him. He inched towards the bed as though it were a wild beast that might awake at any moment and lunge at him.

For the first time Billy noticed the tube in Nan's hand. It was attached to a large clear plastic pouch suspended from some metal contraption. The bag was half full of a clear liquid that flowed through Nan's veins. He stared in horror.

"It's a saline drip," Ryland said. "When patients are unable to eat or drink it provides the fluids needed to keep them alive."

He smiled.

"What do you mean *keep them alive*? What's happened to Nan?"

Icy fingers curled around Billy's throat squeezing out his voice in sharp spurts. He leaned over and looked at Nan. She was not sleeping. Her eyes were open but not fixed on anything.

What frightened Billy most was the way one side of her face was pulled downwards by invisible hands.

"It's a stroke caused by a blood clot. The clot stops oxygen getting to the brain."

Ryland's tone was as cold as his eyes.

"Will she die?"

It was a question Billy did not want to ask but he desperately needed to know.

"Not, unless she suffers another in the next week or so. You can never tell with strokes," Ryland said, sowing seeds of doubt, "they're such sly things. We don't know yet if there's been any lasting damage."

Billy clutched Nan's hand. It was cold. As fragile as the injured bird he had once discovered in the park.

"Nan, Nan, it's me Billy." Her eyes flickered feebly. "I know you can hear me. You're going to get better. I promise."

Something warm and wet struck his hand. Billy was crying. Billy never cried. Not even when Ellis Kinsey beat him up in the school yard. This was different. It hurt more than anything a hundred Ellis Kinsey's could ever do. He buried his head in Nan's pillow so Ryland could not see his face.

"I'll leave you two alone for a while. If you need me for anything press the buzzer."

The door closed.

Billy waited a few seconds then lifted his head. Nan was still unaware he was there. She gazed out towards a distant horizon only her eyes could see. They reminded Billy of a summer spent pond dipping in his secret pool. Every time his hand reached down the still water turned murky and it was impossible to see what lay beneath the surface. Something similar had happened to Nan but it was only a matter of time until the water became clear again.

Something caught Billy's attention. Buster was leaning against the window pawing at the glass.

"Go home Buster!" Billy shouted before burying his head back in the pillow.

CHAPTER 6

BUSTER

Buster appeared out of nowhere. One morning Billy opened the front door and there he was. A great big scruffy Ginger Tom staring up at Billy through one good eye. He made such a fuss rubbing against Billy's legs that the milk bottles scattered like nine-pins. The noise brought Mum to the door armed with dustpan, brush and a very sour expression on her face. The sight of Billy struggling to lift the most enormous cat she had ever seen in her life stopped her dead in her tracks.

"Whose cat is that? Put it down at once."

Billy's mother was not an animal lover, she was sort of neutral. Billy put the cat down. It brushed against him purring loudly. Billy was smitten. His mother was not. Gripping the sweeping brush, she thrust it at the enormous stray.

"Shoo! Go on, shoo," she shouted.

To Billy's delight the cat arched its back, hissed and spat. Billy's mother took a step backwards.

"Raymond, get out here!"

From inside the house Billy heard a newspaper rustle impatiently.

"What's the matter now?"

Dad hated to be disturbed when he was reading the newspaper. Then Billy heard the familiar sound of slippers slapping sulkily against the passage floor.

"It's just a few milk bottles for goodness sake. WHOA!"

Billy could tell Dad was impressed the way the blood drained from his face.

"Well, do something Raymond. Make it go away."

Billy remembered something Nan had told him about a Rock and a Hard Place. He guessed that was where his Dad was now. Billy bent down and petted the creature. It nestled against him purring. Emboldened by the cat's display of affection Dad moved closer to Billy.

"You'd best leave him to me son," Dad said in that voice he used when he wanted people to listen to him.

Big mistake, it never worked at the best of times. Dad reached out to take hold of the cat. What followed made a big impact on Billy who was never normally impressed by anything his Dad did. He reminded Billy of the Red Flash who could move faster than lightning. Though the Red Flash never yelled as loudly as Dad.

"Aaaaaah!"

Dad yanked his hand away to avoid it being savaged by one of the cat's massive claws. At the same time, he stepped backwards once more scattering the unfortunate milk bottles while treading on Mum's foot. She gave Dad a hard whack with the brush.This seemed to satisfy the cat who settled down at Billy's feet.

"Are you going to get rid of that thing?"

Mum's face was bright red. This was not good. Dad never argued with Mum when she was that colour.

"Can I keep him Dad?" he pleaded.

The cat glared at Dad through its one good eye.

"Certainly not. He probably belongs to someone," said Mum. "Has he got a collar or something?"

"No," said Billy. "Can I please Dad?"

"I. . . er. . . um . . ." Dad stuttered still stumbling around between the rock and that other place.

Dad's hesitation was the only invite the cat needed. It plodded past Mum and Dad tail erect. Dad and Mum flattened themselves against the passage wall and watched it stroll past.

"Be good for Billy to have a pet," said Dad.

Mum gave Dad a look that suggested he had better hide behind that rock for a few days.

She did smile when they entered the living room and found the cat curled up on Dad's armchair. Dad gingerly picked up his newspaper and sat on the sofa. Mum charged into the kitchen to bully a few pots and pans into submission. Billy knelt by the armchair and stroked his new companion behind the ears as he imagined all the adventures they would have together. Billy had no idea!

Buster settled in without any bother. The same could not be said for Mum and Dad. They discovered very early on it was they who would have to make changes. The armchair was an immediate flashpoint. Dad and Buster engaged in a sort of Cold War over ownership. Dad took to getting up early to stake his claim. Buster used a different tactic. He would lie on the carpet and wait until Dad went to the bathroom. As soon as Dad left the room Buster reclaimed the armchair as his own.

As for Mum, she was sunbathing in the garden one afternoon in late Summer when a blood-curdling scream shattered the silence. It sounded uncannily like her next-door neighbour Mrs. Pryce. But that was impossible, Mrs. Pryce was much too posh to scream. In fact, according to Mrs. Pryce, she was much too posh to perform any of the embarrassing bodily functions essential to the health and wellbeing of the rest of the population.

Curiosity overcame Mum's fear that something terrible had occurred over the garden wall. What if a maniac in a mask and a chain saw was running loose in Mrs. Pryce's garden? She thought about calling Dad and imagined him holding a rolled-up copy of the Western Mail as he came face to face with a chainsaw wielding maniac.

"Oi, what do you think you're doing with that chain-saw?"

Most likely the last words he ever spoke.

Best not disturb him. Cautiously she moved towards the wall that bounded Mrs. Pryce's garden.

Mrs. Pryce's garden was unlike any other in the street. Mum had been invited there once for a grand tour. She spent an uncomfortable half hour squeezing between nymphs and centaurs not to mention the occasional cherub. There was even an ornate fountain squashed between a couple of unhappy satyrs with a few gnomes thrown in for good measure. There were certainly plenty of hiding places for crazed killers if they weren't too large or allergic to stone statues. Looking on the bright side there wasn't much room for a homicidal maniac to wield a chain-saw in anger.

Mum leant against the wall and listened. Nothing, all she could hear was her heart pounding in her chest. Was the Mad Slasher crouched on the other side doing the same thing? What had become of Mrs. Pryce? Gory pictures flickered across her mind like a sick horror movie. Unable to stand the tension any longer Mum stretched on tip toes and peeped over the wall. A forest of statues stared back at her. Nothing moved. It didn't look like anyone was lying in wait with murder in mind. Perhaps the Crazed Killer was working his way down the street, or maybe his chain-saw needed oiling.

Then she heard it. An animal whimpering in pain. It came from the patio area at the top end of the garden. Mum slowly turned her head wary of what she might face. Mrs. Pryce stood next to an enormous hutch that housed Flopsy, the Pryce's precious giant rabbit. If it wasn't for the fact she was trembling and whimpering at the same time Mrs. Pryce could have been mistaken for one of her statues. Her raised arm pointed down the garden towards a large growth of shrubbery. Perhaps the maniac was lying in wait in the bushes thought Mum.

"Look! There it goes!"

Terror dripped from every word like bat's droppings.

Mum's eyes followed Mrs. Pryce's shaky finger but there was no sign of a Masked Maniac dodging through the maze of frozen figures. Instead she glimpsed the rear end of a large ginger cat disappearing into the shrubbery.

"Did you see it?" shrieked Mrs. Pryce.

"I think I may have seen something," said Mum.

Suddenly the Mad Slasher would have been welcomed with open arms.

"I'm not really sure," she added. "What's the matter with Flopsy?"

Flopsy sat on his haunches in the centre of the hutch. Mum had never seen a rabbit caught in the glare of a car's headlights but she supposed this was pretty much how it would look. Wild eyed and open-mouthed it too stared at the shrubbery.

"My poor darling," cried Mrs. Pryce suddenly reminded of her petrified pet. She stooped down and lifted the rabbit out of the hutch rocking him back and fore in her arms. Flopsy's expression did not change and Mum wondered whether it had suffered some permanent psychological damage.

"That dreadful creature was about to eat Flopsy alive!"

"Did number forty nine's pit bull get loose again?" inquired Mum.

"No, it was much, much worse. When I came out the thing was crouched on top of Flopsy's hutch staring in. If I hadn't arrived when I did poor Flopsy would have been . . ."

The end of the sentence dissolved into more hysterical sobbing and Mum wondered whether she should give Mrs. Pryce a hard slap. Mrs. Pryce must have noticed the glint in Mum's eyes because she stopped crying and blew her nose.

"It probably escaped from a wildlife park somewhere. It was like a cat only a lot bigger."

"You go inside and I'll pop over and make us a nice cup of tea," said Mum as she cast a backward glance down the garden hoping the creature was at this moment snoozing on Dad's armchair.

CHAPTER 7

A CAT'S GOT TO DO. . .

Tonight, Buster had more important things on his mind than giant rabbits. Crouched in the shadows he considered what he should do next. The Enemy had made its move and Billy was in the eye of the storm. He decided to wait in case Billy needed his help. Buster carefully selected a fork in the branches of a large horse chestnut tree that dominated the garden Matron had not gotten around to having the tree cut down although its days were already numbered. Every Autumn the garden was infested with hordes of children squabbling over its prickly fruit like rats in a rubbish dump. Hidden in its branches Buster waited and watched.

He did not have to wait long. There was a squeal of tyres as a car stopped outside. Mum and Dad tumbled out of the battered old Ford Cortina and skipped hand in hand up the gravel path. Hand in hand! Buster's suspicions were well and truly aroused. The only sign of affection he had ever noticed was when Dad once put his arms around Mum while she was washing up. She elbowed him sharply in the ribs. Now, laughing and smiling they paused at the main doors.

Humans were an odd species but the way Billy's mother and father were behaving was downright peculiar even for them. They might have been wearing masks from some ancient Greek tragedy as they rang the bell for attention. The door opened and Buster guessed Matron had been lying in wait on the other side. Neither Matron nor Billy's parents seemed able to decide whether they should frown or smile. Their expressions changed so often their facial muscles had difficulty keeping up. Matron ushered them inside and they were gone.

More information was needed before he could decide what to do. Buster leapt down onto the frozen lawn at the exact moment Bella, the toy poodle, tripped into view. During her nightly 'walkies' Bella always deposited her calling card beneath the horse chestnut tree. She was startled by the sudden appearance of the largest cat she had ever seen in her life. She growled a warning and bared her teeth. The cat did not budge an inch. Instead it glared at her and crept forward back arched. Bella's growl died and with a howl of terror she turned tail and ran.

Her owner, who had been guiltily enjoying a sly cigarette, stared in horror as Bella shot past chased by a creature that resembled an impossibly large and ferocious ginger cat. He could only gawp after the fleeing Bella in disbelief. Roused to life by the lighted end of the cigarette singing his fingers he set off in pursuit.

"Bella! Here girl!"

He tried to whistle but the effect of jogging and smoking left him panting and breathless.

Truth to tell he would be happy if the dog disappeared for good. The only reason he took her out after dark was because he was ashamed to be seen walking the pathetic creature in the day. If he returned without her his life would not be worth living. Besides, Bella's nightly walk was the only chance he had for a peaceful smoke. Gritting his teeth, he jogged on.

Buster loved a good chase and this was a very good chase. The dog proved surprisingly swift. Tiring rapidly the frantic Bella turned into an alley branching from one of the rows of terraced houses. It was a dead end.

For a moment Bella stood shivering as she stared in horror at the brick wall barring her way. Behind her something heavy padded slowly down the alley. Bella was only a toy poodle but she was still a dog with a sacred duty to uphold the honour of her kind. She turned to make her last stand.

A cold full moon hung over the rooftops directly opposite the alley. Splashes of silver lapped at Bella's paws like the incoming tide. Less than fifty yards away a monstrous silhouette was framed against the distant orb its one good eye lit by the reflected glow of moonlight. There was nowhere to run or hide so Bella stood her ground. The alley was suddenly brightened by a rectangular patch of light from an open door. An elderly lady struggled outside dragging a bulging black bin bag. She glanced at Bella and was about to speak when she glimpsed the hideous shape in the shadows. The door shut, darkness returned, and Bella was alone again.

Having seen the rear end of the Cat-Thing turn down the alley Bella's owner forced his aching body forward. Up and down the street doors were opening and closing like clockwork as householders dumped dustbins and black bags on the pavement. One or two paused to stare at the stooped figure staggering home from the pub. His attempts to warn them of the wild beast roaming their street were met with a shake of the head or the occasional "tut-tut" and the sound of a door being slammed. He reached the entrance to the alley knowing he would have to face the creature on his own.

"Bella! Come on girl! Bella!"

Curtains parted as residents strained to get a look at the drunk making such a row. He no longer cared he just hoped Bella would come bounding out of the alley and they could both escape being mauled to death.

"Bella! Here girl!"

An upstairs window on the opposite side of the street opened and the tattooed torso of an angry muscular individual leaned out

"Oi Mate, shut it! Some of us have got work in the morning."

"It's my dog, she's being chased by a monster."

"There's only one monster you'll have to worry about if you don't CLEAR OFF!"

The tattooed man closed the window and a few seconds later the bedroom light went out.

Bella's owner paused, as if preparing to dive into a deep pool of icy water, before plunging into the alley. The sight that greeted him sent shivers rippling down his spine colder than an Arctic blizzard. Bella stood at the far end of a blind alley teeth bared. Facing her was the creature who might have been a cat if cats grew to such a ridiculous size. It was slinking towards Bella the way domestic cats do when about to pounce on a mouse.

"Bella!" he shouted. The creature spun around to face him.

The word echoed in Buster's head.

"Bella . . . Billy!"

Buster's heart sank. He must get back to Billy as quickly as he could. One great bound took him within a few feet of Bella's startled owner who quickly stepped backwards and collided with a large aluminium dustbin. It toppled over with a crash like a medieval knight unseated in a joust. The bedroom light in the street opposite came on. Leaving chaos in his wake Buster vanished into the night.

Bella's owner looked up expecting to see dripping fangs and baleful eyes staring down at him. Instead he saw a heavily tattooed man burst from the house opposite like an enraged wrestler.

Relief at escaping the jaws of the beast was replaced by visions of forearm smashes, pile-drivers, drop kicks, power slams and other moves too horrible to even contemplate

"I fell over the bin," he explained.

"You don't say," said the tattooed man grabbing Bella's owner by the lapels of his overcoat. "Well guess what, now you're going to fall over a few more!"

"Grrrrrrrr!"

The Tattooed Man, startled by the sudden appearance of a snarling toy poodle let go of the lapels sending her owner crashing back into the bins.

"Good dog, stay."

Bella bared her teeth and snapped at the outstretched hand. After what she had just been through nothing would ever frighten her again. Her owner watched in amazement as the Tattooed Man backed away never for an instant taking his eyes off Bella. Only when the door slammed shut did she stop growling and rejoin her astonished owner.

"Good girl Bella, good girl."

Bella felt her head being ruffled. Strange, she thought, he's never done that before.

"Come on girl let's go home."

Bella trotted beside her proud owner down the silent street. This time she really was going home.

CHAPTER 8

FAMILY SECRETS

Billy sat in the back of the car scuffling empty cans of Coca Cola with his feet, his mind a whirl of mixed emotions. The engine spluttered and coughed but stubbornly refused to fire.

"This bleeding car . . ." began Dad.

"Never mind love," interrupted Mum, "you'll soon be able to drive a Rolls Royce."

"When I do," he said slamming his hand against the steering wheel, "you're off to the scrap yard."

"Who me?" said Mum.

They burst out laughing.

"What about Nan," came a small voice from the back seat, "are you going to send her there as well?"

The uncomfortable silence was broken as the car burst into life. Dad quickly shifted into first gear and began to pull off.

THUD!

The car stopped. Mum was pitched forward her head making painful contact with the windscreen. The engine stalled then died.

"What the heck!"

Dad stared in disbelief at a large creature straddling the bonnet of the car eyeballing him through the windscreen.

"It's Buster!" said Billy.

"Who else?" Dad replied. "That cat, or whatever it is, needs certifying."

"He could have killed me," said Mum rubbing her forehead. "Billy don't you dare let him in."

Buster leapt into the car through Billy's open door. He settled himself on the back seat, curled up, and pretended to fall asleep. If only he hadn't chased that stupid mutt, he would perhaps know what was going on and what the enemy's next move might be. Billy began to tickle him gently behind the ears. Whatever he did he must stay alert.

"Is Nan going to die?"

Dad parked the car outside the house and was about to get out when Billy's question stopped him.

"Nan's a tough old bird. She'll pull through."

Dad was finding it difficult to talk.

"Why are they taking her to hospital then?"

In Billy's mind hospitals and graveyards were much the same thing.

"She needs to have some tests done love," explained Mum.

"Like in school? Spelling and stuff?" said Billy.

"No, they'll give her a blood test and most likely a scan."

Mum knew that Billy, though a child, was tougher in many ways than his father. She would tell him the truth.

"What's a scan?" he asked.

"It's a sort of x-ray."

Billy knew first-hand what x-rays were.

"They'll look inside Nan's brain to see what damage the stroke has done."

Dad opened the car door without saying a word. Mum and Billy watched him disappear into the house.

"What sort of damage?"

Billy's imagination was running riot. Was Mum talking about the kind of damage his ball had done to Mr. Meredith's windscreen. Mr. Meredith had shouted and carried on a lot but the windscreen was as good as new the next day. Or did she mean the sort of damage the fire had done to the stolen car on the bypass last summer. Its scorched shell had lain on the side of the road until it had been removed. Billy watched it burn.

"Well," said Mum, "she might find it difficult to talk, walk or write. But we just have to wait and see."

Billy could not think of anything worse than Nan being unable to speak.

"Let's go inside in the warm. We can talk more if you want to," said Mum before Billy could ask another question.

Lost in his thoughts Billy followed Mum indoors. Dad had been busy making a cup of tea and a hot chocolate. Billy knew that something very serious had happened. Dad only made cups of tea at Christmas and on Mum's birthday. Billy and his mother sat by the kitchenette table. Dad stood drinking tea with his back to them.

"Thing is love, we've had some good news tonight as well."

His mother was smiling now and that made Billy sad. How could any news be good when Nan was lying on some hospital bed unable to speak? Mum must have noticed the disapproval in Billy's eyes.

"We've won the lottery Billy. Do you understand what that means?"

She spoke louder, like Mum always did when she got excited about new shoes or something. Billy shrugged.

"It means we're rich. We'll never have to worry about money again," said Dad.

Dad spoke without turning to face them but he didn't sound excited like Mum.

"Will it make Nan better?"

Billy's question was met with silence. Mum was the first to recover.

"It means we can make sure she gets the best treatment possible before she returns to the nursing home."

If Mum thought her answer would satisfy Billy she was wrong.

"You can't send her back to that place. Matron's a vampire!"

Billy's mother rolled her eyes. Where did Billy get these ideas from?

"Is there anything you'd like love?"

"Can I have a new tracksuit please?"

Mum did not answer. She got up and stood behind Billy. For a moment she gazed at him as though noticing for the first time the flimsy replica tracksuit with its threadbare patches. She opened her mouth to speak but the words would not come. Instead she threw her arms around her son and hugged him tight. It was Dad who answered.

"Course you can son. Course you can."

Buster woke with a start he was lying in the back of a car shivering. It was not just from the cold. That dream had been much too real. He closed his eyes and once again he was back on the high bleak mountains of Ska his freezing body flattened against an icy outcrop of rock. Something was crawling down the barren slopes towards him. He listened for the slightest movement that would give it away. All he could hear above the shrieking wind was the cry of karks threading dark patterns between the mist shrouded cliffs like weavers of doom. Far below lay the bones of the dead. Some had slipped on the icy surface and fallen to their death. Others jumped rather than fall prey to the hideous beings that infested this forsaken place. Picked clean by giant birds of prey they were a grim warning to weary travellers. Buster opened his eyes. Billy was staring in through the window. Billy! Oh no, Buster had done it again.

"Sorry Buster," Billy said, "we forgot about you."

Buster slunk out of the car knowing he had messed up and was no nearer discovering the Enemy's plans than he had been before he fell asleep. That was the problem being a cat. When you weren't chasing things, you slept a lot. He followed Billy into the kitchenette. Dad and Mum sat by the table. Mum glanced up as Billy and Buster shuffled into the kitchen. The cat hung its head and dragged its tail. It looked a little like Billy whenever he'd been up to mischief and got found out.

"You could have left him out there a bit longer," said Mum.

"It's cold," Billy protested.

"I wouldn't worry about Buster. He's got enough fat on him to last a couple of winters," said his father.

Buster narrowed his eye and glared at Dad.

"Look who's talking," he thought.

Why wasn't Dad sitting in the armchair anyway? Something was wrong. The dream had spooked him. The Enemy was at work. They were getting stronger which meant someone was getting weaker. He guessed who.

"I think I'll phone the hospital," Dad said.

"They said they'd ring us if there was any change," Mum reminded him.

Dad punched in the number on his mobile.

Billy desperately wanted to reach out and grab the phone from Dad. Instead he waited as time slowed to a trickle just like it did during the dreaded spelling lessons with Miss Perry. There were lots of, "Uh huh's", and "I see's" before Dad slipped the phone back into his pocket.

"No change but the next twenty-four hours are critical," he said.

Mum looked at Dad and rolled her eyes towards Billy whose bottom lip was beginning to quiver.

"She's a tough old bird," Dad said for the second time that night. Dad made Nan sound like one of Mum's Christmas dinners. There was an awkward silence.

"Perhaps I should let Auntie Vera know," said Dad.

"It can wait till morning."

Mum spoke with the voice she used when she wanted to change the subject. Like when Dad asked her how much her new shoes cost.

"I suppose," Dad replied. "I'm off to bed."

Dad disappeared through the door like a troubled ghost.

"Who's Aunt Vera?" said Billy, he had never heard her name before.

Mum sighed and Billy guessed it was a subject she didn't want to talk about. This made him determined to find out more. Even Buster seemed curious.

"Ah well you'll have to know sooner or later."

Billy was totally unprepared for what came next.

"Aunt Vera is Nan's twin sister."

Billy stared at his mother open-mouthed like a fish on a supermarket slab.

"Nan's got a twin?"

It wasn't a question. Billy was trying to get his head around what Mum had just told him. There were twins in his school. Billy couldn't tell them apart. He kept calling them the wrong names. Billy wished he was a twin. He and his twin brother could pretend they were one person and that way they could have every other day off school.

"Does she look like Nan?"

Mum smiled.

"Would you like to see a picture?" she asked.

Billy nodded. Mum left the table and Billy listened to the sound of her footsteps on the stairs.

Twins? Buster had only ever seen Nan through the window of her room in The Hollies. It was never particularly clean but she reminded him of someone. Now he knew why.

CHAPTER 9

THE ALBUM

It was old. Anyone could see that, even if Mum had made a better job of brushing off the dust and cobwebs. The cover was brown leather, dark and mottled with age.

"Is it a book of spells?"

Billy imagined the scuff marks that pitted the surface having been caused by long curved nails.

"Not exactly," said Mum smiling, "though there may be a picture of a witch inside."

She pushed the book towards Billy.

For a long moment Billy sat very still as it lay on the table before him like an ancient doorway beckoning him to pass through if he dare. It smelt of mould and decay and Billy hesitated to reach out and touch it. He wondered from what creature the leather had been skinned. Probably dragon's underbelly he guessed.

"Are you going to open it or are we going to sit here all night?"

Mum was getting impatient so Billy took a deep breath and reached out.

Once, when Billy suffered with a very sore throat, Mum brought home a disgusting bottle of medicine from the doctors. She'd spent a long morning in the waiting room fending off a variety of germs propelled her way by spluttering patients. Mum made sure Billy finished the medicine to the very last drop. Touching the cover made Billy feel exactly as he had when he took the first sip of that awful medicine.

It was warm and he was sure it had responded to his touch like a living thing. He withdrew his hand quickly and let the cover drop.

"It won't bite you," said his mother but Billy was not so sure.

"Look," she said, pointing to a faded sepia photograph on the first page. "I bet you can't guess who that is?"

A stern gaunt man stared at Billy from a frozen distance in time. He wore a flat cap and crumpled baggy trousers. A long jacket covered a sort of vest. His dark eyes and hooked nose reminded Billy of a hungry watchful sparrow-hawk. A long drooping moustache made him look miserable, as if he had just missed a kill. He could certainly do with a good feed. Billy couldn't imagine anybody messing around if he was headmaster. He was covered from head to toe in what appeared to be black dust.

"I expect he's just had a row for getting dirty," said Billy, "and that's why he looks so sad."

"He's a miner," laughed Mum, "they used to work underground digging for coal."

Billy thought that was something he might like to do. He couldn't believe you got paid for getting dirty.

"There used to be lots of coal mines but that was a long time ago."

Billy's dream of becoming a miner died almost before it had chance to take breath.

"They say the valley is riddled with old tunnels deep underground."

Billy was alarmed. What if the tunnels collapsed under the weight of the houses above them? Suddenly the world didn't feel a safe place anymore.

"You still haven't said who you think is in the photo," said Mum.

"It's not Nan's twin sister any way," replied Billy.

Mum smiled.

"No, it's Nan's father, your great-grandfather."

Billy stared at the photograph and the piercing dark eyes stared straight back at him. It didn't look like his great grandfather shared Nan's sense of humor.

"What was his name?"

"Glyn. That was the last photo he ever had taken," said Mum.

"Why? Couldn't he afford to pay?"

Billy hated the days when the school photographer visited. He always took a note asking to be excused and watched while classmates in their best clothes were called one by one while he sat at his desk and pretended he didn't care. Mum placed an arm around his shoulders and when she spoke her voice was deep and husky.

"He went to work that afternoon and never came back. Just disappeared. There was no explosion or roof fall. They said he just turned a corner and vanished. He became a bit of a legend. He had already survived an explosion that killed four others just after they were first married."

"How old was Nan when he left?"

Mum stared at Billy for a moment wondering why he had chosen to describe great-grandfather's disappearance as if he had simply caught a bus somewhere.

"Tragic really. It happened a few months after Nan and her sister were born. She never knew her father. Molly, your great-grandmother brought them up on her own."

Now Billy understood why Great-Grandfather Glyn looked so sad. He knew something bad was about to happen. For weeks before Nan's stroke Billy had sensed something hanging over him like black storm clouds heavy with rain. Nan never talked much about her father. She told Billy he left when she was young and that made Billy think he had run away to join a circus or something.

"Excuse me a minute, love. I just need to check on your father."

Mum stroked his hair as she got up from the table. Billy wondered why Mum was being so nice. He turned back to the album and was about

to turn the page when something caught his eye.
It wasn't possible! How hadn't he noticed it the
first time? An extremely large scruffy ginger cat
sat at great-grandfather Glyn's feet, Billy could
almost hear him purring.

"Buster!"

Buster plodded over and placing two massive
paws on the kitchenette table peered over Billy's
shoulder at the album. Billy felt the cat's great
body stiffen as if he too could not believe what he
was seeing.

"Buster, that's you, isn't it?"

At that moment Mum returned. Billy leapt off
the chair and ran towards her.

"Mum, look at this quick."

He took his startled mother by the hand and
dragged her towards the table. Buster dropped to
the floor and slunk off to the farthest corner of the
room.

"What is it love, what's the matter?"

She bent over the album.

"Look there!" Billy said.

"What am I looking for?"

His mother was clearly puzzled and Billy
noticed her eyes were red and puffy. He stood
beside her and pointed at the gigantic one-eyed
ginger tom who sat at great-grandfather's feet.
There wasn't one! Buster had vanished, just like
great-grandfather. What was going on?

Billy turned to look at Buster. Buster lay his
head on his paws and closed his one good eye but

not before flashing Billy the guilty look that meant some poor bird would never again return to its nest.

"Have you found Nan yet?"

Billy shook his head. His mother turned the page. An old-school photo took pride of place in the centre of the next page. It was black and white and the image was still sharp. The first thing Billy noticed was that all the boys wore shorts and knitted cardigans or jackets, many with patches on the sleeve. No one stood out wearing the latest designer gear or not. The girl's dresses were long with big collars. They all wore ankle socks and sandal type shoes.

Sat in the front row either side of a boy who squinted into the sun were twin girls. Billy looked at his mother. She nodded. Which one was Nan? Billy didn't take long to decide. Nan was always smiling so she must be the one on the left. The smile apart they were identical. Both had black curly hair and deep blue eyes but Nan's sister stared into the camera fiercely in a way that reminded Billy of Great-Grandfather Glyn.

"That's Nan?" Billy couldn't imagine Nan ever being as young as him. "So that must be Auntie Vera?"

"Yes, that's her," Mum said.

"You don't like her much, do you?"

"She's an interfering old hag."

Mum took a sip of tea and made a face as she forced the lukewarm liquid down her throat.

"Is that why Nan never talks about her?"

Billy could not believe Nan had kept her twin sister a secret from him. Why?

"They had a massive quarrel years ago and haven't spoken since," said Mum.

Billy was surprised. Nan just didn't quarrel with people. She always looked for the good in everyone, though even she struggled to find any in Matron.

"Auntie Vera must have done something terrible!"

"The worst," said Mum.

Billy recalled a time in school when the twins had quarreled. That had been bad. One of them told the rest of the school his brother was an evil clone planted by aliens to suck the eyeballs out of other kids while they were asleep. Everybody avoided the 'alien' twin for the rest of the day and kept making the sign of the cross any time he came near. The plan backfired badly because the next day the twins came to school in matching clothes and no-one was sure which one was the 'alien' so they avoided them both. In the end the real evil twin had to come clean and admit he had been lying. Lots of children kept well clear of them though, just in case.

"What's the worst thing?"

Billy was not going to let this go. Mum begun to wish she had left the album upstairs.

"She stole Nan's boyfriend," said Mum as if describing an event too terrible to talk about. Billy was disappointed.

"Nan had a boyfriend?"

There was an awful lot about Nan he didn't know.

Mum placed a finger lightly on the boy sandwiched between Auntie Vera and Nan still squinting into the sun.

"That's him?" said Billy. "He's only a kid."

Mum smiled and turned the pages of the album. A pretty, dark haired young woman was posing arm in arm with a young man. They were gazing at each other. The young man looked very familiar.

"Did he marry Auntie Vera?"

"No, she soon lost interest and dumped him. It nearly broke Nan's heart."

Although Mum was talking about Nan she had that faraway look in her eyes she always had when she spoke about Gerald in the bank.

"Why did she dump him?" said Billy.

"She lost interest. She only wanted him because he was Nan's boyfriend. Anything Nan had she took just for the sake of it."

Auntie Vera did not seem like a very nice person.

"Serves her right though," continued Mum, "he went on to become a millionaire. Just like us!"

"Did he win the lottery as well?"

"No, he started a business selling urinals. Everybody laughed behind his back but he took no notice and after a few years he'd made a fortune. People stopped laughing. His son runs the business now the Gaffer has retired."

Bells were ringing in Billy's head. He closed his eyes and once again he stood outside *The Hollies* where a man with a large lump on his head was trying to persuade his father to go inside. The Gaffer had looked at Billy as though he knew him.

"You must be tired love, I think it's time for bed."

"Can I have five more minutes please?"

Mum stood behind Billy and placed her arms around him.

"Five more minutes while I check on your father," she squeezed him tightly and whispered, "I'm so sorry love."

Billy wondered what Mum was sorry about. He was drawn back to the album. How many more secrets did it hold? He flicked back the pages and once again gazed down at his great grandfather. There was no sign of Buster just those fierce sad eyes gazing up at him.

"What happened to you?" he asked, but great grandfather Glyn said nothing.

CHAPTER 10

GREAT GRANDFATHER GLYN

The light from the candle played across the faces of the babies nestled side by side in the rough wooden crib. Enfolded by walls of wood and love they slept the trusting sleep of the innocent. In the darkness outside their dreams a being with evil in its heart sniffed and prowled.

He leaned over the cot and reached out to touch their faces one last time. One of the babies curled her tiny fingers around his own but did not wake. The other opened her eyes and stared at him as though she read his thoughts and was not pleased.

"I only wanted to protect you," he whispered.

The baby's dark blue eyes forced him to look away. She knew he had lied. Now the only way to keep that promise was to leave and never return. He turned away. Molly stood facing him. She had been silently watching him.

"What is it Glyn cariad? Is something wrong?"

He did not want to lie to her any more but it was too late for the truth now.

"Nothing wrong, I just wanted to carry the memory of the girls with me through the shift."

Molly did not smile.

"I spoke to Mrs. Evans earlier."

"What did that old gossip want? You need to take what she tells you with a pinch of salt."

"Why? Did she not tell me the truth?"

"About what?"

Why couldn't that old busybody keep her nose out.

"She saw you in town today coming out of the photographers."

Glyn looked down at his worn boots.

"How can we afford to have our photographs taken, we can barely feed the children?"

She was angry now. Still he said nothing.

"Don't I deserve an answer?"

She deserved far more but he could not tell her.

"I wanted you to have something to show the children in case . . . "

"It's the explosion, isn't it? You've never forgiven yourself for being the only one who survived have you? It changed you Glyn. You came back a different man."

He almost smiled at how close to the truth she'd come.

"But what if I was never meant to come back Molly? What if it should have been my time?"

"How can you say that," hurt in her voice, "if you hadn't come back the girls would never have been born!"

Vera began to bawl. Molly picked her up and gently cradled the tiny bundle in her arms. The baby still fixed him with eyes almost black in the twilight shadows. He reached inside his pocket and took something out, handing it to Molly in one quick movement. She held it between her fingers as she rocked the baby to sleep. From the photograph, he looked up at her through stern eyes.

"You could have at least smiled."

"What," he joked, "and break the habit of a lifetime."

He wanted to smile. To leave a memory of someone who had known happiness. But he could see the future and a smile would have been another lie.

"Do you have to go in today?"

The question took him by surprise. Had she guessed something was wrong? He thought he had been so careful.

"Only if you want food on the table tomorrow."

The baby had fallen asleep in Molly's arms. She placed her back in the cot alongside her sister. Without speaking Molly crossed the room and embraced her husband laying her head on his broad chest. He stroked her hair once then turned away.

"I have to go or I'll be late."

She watched him slip through the door into the shadows.

Outside, lights appeared in the darkness. The village was coming to life. Men grumbled as the cold early morning air erased the memory of their warm beds. Soon they would stumble onto the streets and make their way through the winding terraces to the pit head and the endless coal face night.

He dare not look back for fear she would be standing at the door waiting to wave a last goodbye. It would take all his strength to complete the short journey he had made so many times before. The pithead wheel loomed ahead like a gigantic iron memorial to the dead. The day he staggered choking out of the dense black dust cloud everyone believed four men had perished. Only he knew there had been five. As far as was possible it was time to right a terrible wrong.

He couldn't remember getting into the cage with the other miners. When he did the joking and grumbling stopped. Since the accident people fell quiet in his company. He still remembered the shocked astonished faces as he walked out unharmed. Many still shook their heads in disbelief. In the local chapel the minister declared it a miracle. In the pubs men muttered darkly the Devil looks after his own.

As the cage descended he kept his gaze fixed upon the layered seams of coal and rock ignoring the sly glances and whispered comments. The cage jerked to a halt and the men spilled out. The coal face was half a mile away and as they walked the men split into smaller groups, chatting and laughing. Great-Grandfather Glyn lagged further and further behind until their voices were lost in the distant darkness. No one seemed to notice his absence or if they did no one cared. He had become a bad omen. The man who cheated Death, only Death would not be cheated.

Afterwards, when asked to describe the events that followed, men could only speak of a bright light. A light that with a sudden fierce brilliance lit up the darkness and blinded their eyes. It lasted only moments. Eerily, there was no sound that would have warned then something was wrong. The canaries still chirped in their cages. No creaking wooden props sounded a grim warning of disaster. When they turned towards the light Glyn was gone.

Somehow Molly knew the knock on the door was bad news even before she opened it and saw the little group of men shuffling their hobnailed boots. Not one looked her in the eye. One of the twins began to cry. Molly guessed it would not be Vera.

"What's wrong?"

The men looked at each other waiting for someone to speak.

"There's been an accident hasn't there? Where's Glyn?"

"I'm sorry Mrs. Jenkins."

"Sorry for what?"

She fixed the man with her eyes but he turned towards his friends like a drowning man seeking help.

"What's happened to my Glyn?"

A short stocky older man pushed his way to the front and laid a gentle arm on her shoulder.

"He's gone love."

She was determined not to show any weakness in front of them, she knew what they thought of Glyn, how they treated him.

"What have you done with his body?"

This time no one answered.

He stepped through the portal into the dazzling pure light and something Molly once said as she nursed the twins to sleep slipped between his dark thoughts.

"I'm so happy you survived the explosion Glyn. Then I feel guilty because of those other poor women. Every morning I wake up I'm afraid it was all a dream and you really are gone."

Now he was.

As his eyes adjusted to the light he saw figures moving towards him through the shimmering brightness of their being. The flaming swords they held in their hands marked them as Warrior-Guardians. For the first time, he felt the sharp edge of fear keener than his shame. It was not fear of what would become of him. The fear that gnawed at his bones was for Molly and the twins, those innocents he'd left behind in the world of men. Warrior-Guardians only appeared in perilous times. Their presence was an evil sign. He knelt before them, bowed his head and shut his eyes. He would make no excuse.

Whatever punishment he received he would embrace like a long-lost brother who would help ease the guilt that weighed him down. He waited the solemn silence screaming in his ears.

"Was being a man all you hoped it would be?"

He looked up into the face of Rowan the Guardian but could not hold that searching gaze longer than a few heartbeats.

"All I hoped and feared and more."

"Those you left behind are in great danger."

The words struck him like stones.

"I will do anything. . ."

"You have done enough!" said Anselm thrusting forward his eyes black as the night. "The veil is torn and many will suffer."

"What is done is done."

The authority and sadness in Rowan's voice caused him to bow his head. Anselm's angry eyes burned into him like hot coals.

"What will become of them?" he asked.

"The Realm of Mortals is in danger of slipping from our grasp. The Enemy grows ever stronger."

Rowan's eyes searched his face.

"But it is not Mankind of whom you speak?"

"No! He thinks only of his own."

Anger sharpened Anselm's words and Thorn felt them pierce his heart. There was no shield against the truth.

"Your fates are linked."

Rowan's voice was grave while Anselm simply snorted.

"The woman will follow you. She will discover the portal and pass through."

"What about the twins?"

Even as he spoke he realised he was thinking like a man, like Glyn, limited to the boundaries of Space and Time.

"See, he is more Mortal than Angelis. I say we banish him forever.

Anselm smiled as he spoke. A smile without warmth that chilled Thorn to the core.

"That is not our decision," said Rowan and Anselm's face darkened.

Rowan turned to Thorn.

"Did you think we would leave the children unprotected? Your task now is to wait for her and take her back."

"How do I find her? There are many Realms and worlds without number." Even as he spoke Thorn knew he would search for eternity across the Realms and within the countless worlds they held to find the woman for whose love he had abandoned everything.

"Have you forgotten she is Mortal? One realm only is open to her. That which Mankind calls it's past."

As Anselm spoke a vision of Molly bending over the twins as they slept in their wooden cribs slipped into his thoughts. He heard her soft husky voice whispering a lullaby as he stood by the door and watched her for what he believed was the last time. Now hope rose like the dawn in his heart.

Rowan drew Thorn aside. Anselm glowered.

"The bond between you cannot be broken."

Rowan's voice was low and urgent.

"Do not fear, she will be drawn to you once she enters the portal. Love is a more powerful touchstone than the ancient stones themselves."

Rowan's words soothed Glyn's fearful thoughts that strained like wild horses to break free.

"But how will she find the portal?"

Rowan did not answer but his aura blazed so fiercely Thorn was forced to shield his eyes. The sky was filled with shooting stars that burst across his vision. A vast whirlpool of light growing in power drew him towards its dazzling centre. He cried out and felt strong arms grip his own as he fell headlong into the swirling brightness.

Billy closed the album and Great Grandfather Glyn was once again entombed within.

"I expect we'll never know eh Buster?"

Billy looked across to where Buster lay. He was sure Buster had been watching him out of his one good eye. He must have been mistaken for Buster was dozing on the kitchen floor.

When Mum came in to tell Billy to go to bed he was slumped across the table fast asleep.

The Pit of Shadows

CHAPTER 11

REVELATIONS

Buster watched Mum struggle to lift Billy in her arms. She soon gave up and ran to the foot of the stairs.

"Raymond, get down here and help me get Billy to bed."

The old wooden staircase creaked beneath Dad's heavy tread. He must have been awake already Buster thought. Apart from the Archangel's last trump the only thing likely to wake Dad was the smell of bacon sizzling in the frying pan. Normally Mum would be angry which ended in the usual argument followed by Dad's sulky retreat but tonight was different.

"Couldn't sleep?" asked Mum.

Dad shook his head and stepped into the kitchenette. He looked down at Billy as though seeing him for the first time. Very gently he lifted Billy up in his arms and carried him carefully out of the room. He reached the foot of the stairs when the doorbell rang.

Dad froze.

"It can't be anyone from the hospital," said Mum as she saw alarm spread across her husband's face like a mountain fire.

They waited for what seemed an age. It rang again.

"Stay there," Mum said.

Dad lay Billy down on the sofa and watched his wife disappear down the darkened passageway. Muffled voices drifted back towards him fading like early morning mist before he could grasp what was said. As he strained to hear the voices were raised.

". . . Imperative I speak . . ." Unknown voice.

". . . upset him any more." Mum

". . . not about Raymond . . . your son." Unknown voice.

Dad knew with dread certainty who the speaker was and what had brought her to their door at midnight. The conversation was replaced by footsteps in the passage. He glanced down at Billy overcome by a desire to protect him from what lay beyond their front door. It was too late now.

Mum entered first her face as dark and threatening as thunder clouds.

"A visitor for you Raymond."

The way Mum said 'visitor' made it clear she meant *unwelcome guest*. She stepped aside and Aunt Vera swept into the room like royalty. Her eyes surveyed the humble lounge before settling on Billy curled up on the sofa.

"Is this the boy?" she asked.

"If you mean Billy," said Mum her feathers well and truly ruffled, "our son, yes it is."

Mum perched herself on the edge of the sofa next to Billy's feet. Aunt Vera's mouth curled upwards at the edges in a grudging smile.

"I suppose you have told your wife nothing?"

Though her question was for Raymond, it was Mum's eyes she held in an icy stare.

"What's she talking about Raymond? What haven't you told me?" said Mum.

Raymond shifted from one foot to the other, a sure sign he was hiding something. Like a lobster caught in a pot, squirm as he might, there was no way out. His head turned towards the kitchenette as though directed by some unseen force. Through the open door the family album lay in plain view on the table. Vera saw it.

"Well?" demanded Mum.

Had Mum been fitted with a temper gauge the needle would now be hovering in the red zone.

"Are you going to tell me what this is all about or do I have to drag it out of you?"

Dad hung his head but said nothing. He was rescued by Aunt Vera who strode into the kitchen.

"Where do you think you're going?"

Mum was suddenly unsure who she should focus her rising anger and frustration upon, the rude visitor or her hapless husband. Vera returned with the family album before Mum could make up her mind.

"It's time you told her the truth Raymond."

Dad appeared unable to speak. He stared down at his slippers. Mum was also finding speech difficult.

"It's all in here."

Aunt Vera patted the album.

Mum looked at her as though she'd carried a venomous snake into the room.

"All *what's* in there?" said Mum.

Fear dampened Mum's anger. Dad slumped down in the armchair. The springs groaned.

"How old is Billy?" inquired Aunt Vera.

"Nine, he'll be ten next month," said Mum, completely wrongfooted by the question.

Aunt Vera glared at Raymond.

"So little time. You know he is the third generation."

Mum's head was spinning. What was the old witch talking about? *So little time* for what, and what was that nonsense about *the third generation?*

"I thought you came to ask about your sister. You do know she's in hospital with a stroke?" said Mum steering her way to solid ground.

"No, you thought I came because of the money," said Aunt Vera.

Mum gaped. She looked across at Raymond who shook his head.

"How did you know?"

Mum was growing more certain by the second Aunt Vera was an actual witch.

"It doesn't matter and I have already seen my sister. She is safe for now."

"Safe?"

Mum was struck by Aunt Vera's odd choice of words. She also noticed that Raymond's posture had changed. He was sitting upright and leaning forward his eyes fixed on Aunt Vera, hanging on her every word.

"Billy is the reason I am here. He is in grave danger."

For Mum this was the final straw. The woman was clearly looney. It was little wonder she lived alone in that big crumbling old castle with only the mice to keep her company. Mum leapt to her feet.

"That's it! I want you out of my house now!"

Mum's patience hadn't just snapped it splintered into a thousand pieces. Aunt Vera gazed at Mum through the depths of her icy dark blue eyes and let the storm break over her.

"Raymond! Get rid of this woman."

Whenever there was trouble Dad's favourite tactic was flight. If flight proved impossible he would find the nearest fence and sit on it. His response was the most unexpected and shocking moment of the evening.

"Valarie, for once in your life shut up and listen!"

It was unmistakeably Raymond's voice but never had it sounded so hard and stern. Mum sat down and gazed at her husband.

"There is something I have to tell you. Something I should have told you long ago," he paused like a weight lifter about to attempt a lifetime best, "my family is different."

"You can say that again!"

"I mean Vera, Nan, me. . . Billy."

He stopped but Mum said nothing. Her hands gripped the sofa. She sat poised at the crest of a gigantic roller coaster ride she wished she had never got on. Knowing it was too late to turn back she stared wide eyed and waited for the headlong plunge, into what? Outside the wind rose and storm clouds spat huge globs of sleet against the window pane.

"What do you mean *different*? Some kind of hereditary insanity?"

She was surprised how small and lost she sounded, like an echo in a vast cave.

Dad sighed and looked across to Aunt Vera. She handed him the album.

"I'll make us all a strong cup of tea."

Aunt Vera disappeared into the kitchen.

This time Mum did not protest. Dad tapped the arm of his chair and Mum perched herself upon it. She looked down at the album Dad had opened and watched him turn the pages as Billy had done earlier. Had it been just this evening? It seemed a lifetime ago. She sensed this time it was she who would discover hidden secrets. Suddenly her mouth was dry and she could hear her heart pounding against her chest.

Dad paused when he reached the photo of his grandfather. Glyn looked up at her from within the mottled pages and for the first time she noticed a deep sadness in great grandfather's eyes. Raymond was staring at her trying to read her thoughts. She was suddenly struck by the likeness between the man in the photo and her husband. Dad was flabbier and not so fierce looking but there could be no doubting that they both climbed out of the same gene pool.

"It's your grandfather, Billy's great grandfather," said Mum.

"My grandmother's husband died in an underground explosion, two years before this photo was taken."

Mum's eyes narrowed. What did Dad mean by *my grandmother's husband*? It was an odd way to describe your grandfather. Was this a practical joke? She knew it wasn't. Her husband would never play childish pranks while Nan lay ill on a hospital bed.

"Twins!" The answer struck her like a lightning bolt. "You're right Raymond, I probably would have said *no* if I'd known there were so many of them on your side of the family. I would have married Gerald instead."

Mum smiled and a wave of relief washed over her. So, that's what all this was about. She listened to Billy's muffled snores and thought, *"It's a bit late to worry about that now. Talk about shutting the stable door."*

"Aunt Vera and Nan are the only twins in my family," said Dad.

Dad held her gaze as he spoke and fear returned creeping slowly back up her spine before wrapping its cold fingers around her throat so she couldn't ask the question that was taking shape. Outside the sleet turned to hail striking the window in spiteful volleys. They punctuated the phrase that kept repeating itself over and over in her head, *". . . he . . . is . . . in . . . grave . . . danger."*

"Here we are."

Aunt Vera appeared from the kitchen carrying two steaming mugs. Mum took one and sipped the warm brew rather too hurriedly. She gasped as it splashed against the back of her throat.

"Is there a question you want to ask?" Aunt Vera said once Mum had taken a couple of mouthfuls.

Only the hail stabbing the double glazing broke the silence.

"Who is the man in the picture and what has he got to do with my Billy?"

Mum spoke slowly, the words coaxed from between pinched lips.

"That's the thing," replied Aunt Vera, "the person in the photograph is not Great Grandfather Glyn. He's not strictly speaking, a man."

CHAPTER 12

A DREAM OF ZOMBIES

Billy knew it was a dream but couldn't wake up no matter how hard he tried. He didn't like this place, it smelt like the dentists' and that was his least favourite place in all the world. He hated sitting in the waiting room listening to magazines rustling as everyone tried to ignore the high-pitched whine of the dentist's drill. Besides, it was nothing like a waiting room, it wasn't even a room at all.

He was standing in a long corridor bathed in the harsh glare of fluorescent light spilling down from a high ceiling. The antiseptic smell meant it couldn't be the nursing home but it was something similar, a hospital. Yet this was no ordinary hospital. To begin with, the corridor was impossibly long stretching away towards what looked, from where Billy stood, like the entrance to a cave. It couldn't be a cave of course, hospitals don't have caves.

Billy's feet had taken on a life of their own. They refused to turn and run in the opposite direction which was what the rest of Billy's body was desperate to do. Something waited for him, something he knew he should run from as fast as his legs would carry him if only they would listen to his brain. His footsteps echoed down the empty corridor as though there were an army of Billy's marching to some distant battlefield.

Nan once told him that whenever he felt afraid the best thing to do was make a loud noise. Billy pursed his lips and blew. At first nothing happened, his dry tongue simply stuck to the roof of his mouth. He tried a second time. Instead of a cheerful whistle a shrill screech bounced off the corridor walls and ceiling like a startled flock of angry seagulls. Just as Billy thought it wasn't such a good idea his feet stopped moving and he found himself standing before a large steel door, a lift. Nan's advice had worked. Now he could escape whatever was lurking in the shadowy depths of the cave. With each step, it yawned wider and Billy felt it waited to swallow him whole like the whale did to Jonah. That story always made Billy feel sick. Imagine being inside a whale's slimy stomach. Billy didn't like the smell of fish at the best of times let alone when you were splashing around inside it's digestive organs. He stood by the door and was about to press the button when he noticed it was already climbing. How Billy knew it was going to stop at his floor he could not say. He just knew. I suppose in dreams you just knew stuff.

Something was very wrong. Most hospitals had just two floors. His mouth dropped open as he gazed at the lift's control panel. There were too many buttons. The red light kept moving up and up lighting each one in turn. Billy guessed the hospital, if that's what it was, must be taller than the Empire State Building where King Kong made his last stand. Without warning another thought crawled into his head that made him think being inside the belly of a whale was not such a bad place to be after all

What if the building did not go up like a skyscraper but down into the earth like the old mine shafts Nan had told him about? What if the lift was filled with the ghosts of miners horribly killed in some terrible underground disaster? Worse, what if they were not ghosts but zombies with dark haunted eyes and a taste for little boy's intestines? Nan had once taken him to see a male voice choir in the local chapel. She had told him they were all ex miners. It had been a scary experience a lot of them looked more than half way to being zombies already. Imagine what they would look like if they really were dead?

Any second now the doors would slide open and a choir of zombies with mottled skin and stained red jackets would burst into song. They would begin shuffling towards Billy with outstretched arms and a deep hunger in their dead eyes. There were just four buttons waiting to be lit before the zombies reached his level and Billy guessed they wouldn't be carrying flowers.

He stepped back from the lift and once more his feet turned towards the cave. At least it would be dark in there and zombies don't have good eyesight. Behind him he heard a metallic click as the lift doors slid open. Try as he might Billy could not force his feet to move any quicker than they did when he was called to Mr. Meredith's office. Hopefully what awaited him was nothing worse than the usual stern warning about his unacceptable behaviour followed by a boring lecture on how to control his temper. Anyway, Mr Meredith was a fine one to talk he lost his cool more often than Paul Bailey lost his dinner money.

Some *thing* was following him down the long corridor. Billy had never felt this afraid even when he'd been kept waiting for ages outside the Office door. There was something familiar about the sound it made but Billy couldn't quite place what it was. Then it came to him. It was like the squeaky trundle wheel they used to measure the school hall during practical math's lessons. The wheel kept falling off so in the end he and Ronald Lloyd had simply guessed. Mr Groucutt was not happy, he said that according to them the school hall was only slightly smaller than the deck of the Titanic. Billy argued that it was a very big hall and as he listened to the steady rhythmic squeak he knew that this must be a very big trundle wheel or something much more sinister. Maybe the Zombies were so old they needed Zimmer frames and it was their synchronised squeaking he could hear as they shuffled along the corridor. There was no way he was going to turn around and find out. Some things it was better not to know about and this was one of them.

Billy gritted his teeth and walked towards what was not the entrance to a cave but a darkened room with the doors gaping open wide. The increased tempo of the squeak meant whatever was following was getting closer with each step. As he approached the threshold of the darkened room Billy could see a bed. Pale shafts of light like prison bars lay folded across the sleeping patient. It was Nan.

Then, like a sharp slap around the ear, Billy remembered. Nan was in hospital with that stroke thing, but this was only a dream hospital so that couldn't be Nan in the bed. Still, a dream Nan was better than no Nan at all. Nan lay with her back to him which meant if he wanted to see her face he would have to move around to the far side of the bed. It also meant he would have to face whatever followed him. Billy was afraid. More afraid than when the 'alien' twin had threatened to suck out his eyeballs if he didn't swap his Darth Vader card for a Storm Trooper doubler. Billy resisted then, even though it meant sleeping with the bedroom light on for a week, and he would resist now. His Nan was far more valuable than a whole pack of Star Wars stickers. Besides this was just a dream, even if it was more real than any nightmare he'd ever had before and he'd had plenty of them in his short life.

He moved as quietly as he could even though the thing must know he was there. It was probably looking at him through blood red eyes at this very moment. Keeping his gaze fixed firmly on the bed he reached the far side and sat down on a small hard chair wedged between it and the wall. Nan looked peaceful. If Billy hadn't known Nan was seriously ill, he would have thought she was just sleeping. Slowly he lifted his eyes. Opposite was another bed but Billy could only just see its base as curtains were drawn around three sides. Nan was not alone. Perhaps other visitors would arrive to keep him company. The thought snuggled up to him like Barney his battered old teddy bear he refused to abandon even though he was not a little kid any more. Then the squeaking started up again.

Billy was torn. Should he look up and discover the dread source of the squeak or duck under the bed and hope he had not been seen. He was not a wimp, except when it came to blood sucking vampires, werewolves, zombies and big black hairy spiders. Billy hated fighting, he never hit back when Ellis Kinsey and his gang bullied him. Nan told him it took a stronger man to walk away and so he did, not because he was afraid to fight back but because he was afraid of what might happen if he did. Besides, Ellis Kinsey and his gang had given him a very wide berth since the incident with Ross Tudor's conker.

P S Rowlands

CHAPTER 13

THE GREAT CONKER CONFLICT

They had been playing conkers in the school yard surrounded by a crowd of wide eyed spectators. Ross Tudor was undisputed conker champion. He possessed a wickedly accurate downward swing that smashed his opponent's conker into several large chunks scattered across the playground to loud cheers from enthusiastic supporters. On the rare occasion he did miss he never failed to whack his opponent squarely across the knuckles with a sickening thud. They left the playground nursing swollen knuckles but at least with their conkers intact vowing to return to fight again another day. Most of them never did.

Some of the more bitter victims of Ross Tudor's conker wielding wizardry claimed it was a deliberate tactic to disable his most feared opposition. Others even dared suggest Ross Tudor cheated by soaking his conkers in vinegar overnight and then baking them in the oven. This Ross always denied with a hurt expression and a solemn oath sworn on the life of his pet guinea-pig. Billy often wondered about that because Ross Tudor was allergic to fur. Legend had it Ross Tudor's conker had been handed down from generation to generation. It's victims now numbered in the hundreds. Ross boasted his great grandfather had been one of King Arthur's knights and that his conker wielding was so deadly he could unseat a man on horseback at a hundred paces with a long stretch of string.

It had been a sunny day in late September and the conker season was already in full swing. Billy and Ross Tudor, encircled by an excited crowd of children, eyed each other warily. Hector and Achilles preparing for battle before the glistening walls of Troy could not have had a more eager audience. Billy recalled the gasp of astonishment that greeted one of the rarest events ever witnessed at Valleys County Primary School. Ross Tudor missed with a downward swipe. Billy could barely believe his eyes. Not only had Ross missed but Billy's knuckles were still intact. At first Billy thought it was just the numbness before the sharp throbbing pain kicked in forcing him to flee to the safety of the toilets where he could run cold water over his mangled fingers. Ross Tudor gaped in disbelief as Billy's conker dangled unharmed from one of his old shoelaces. Like all true champions Ross Tudor was first to react.

"You moved your conker!" he cried as tears of frustration began to mist his glowering eyes.

"I never!" said Billy.

It was the truth, Billy had not moved his conker but move it did. Billy felt the shoelace twitch in his hand, a bit like the grass snakes he caught up the mountain each summer. No wonder Ross Tudor was mad.

"You're a cheat," cried a loud voice.

A gap opened in the circle of spectators as Ellis Kinsey elbowed his way to centre stage with two of his cronies by his side. He snatched the conker out of Ross Tudor's hand and pushed him to the floor. Ross got up and wiped his eyes before scampering away, already yesterday's news.

"Am not!" said Billy, hoping no one would notice the quaver in his voice.

"Hold it out," barked Ellis Kinsey.

Billy did as he was told. Nobody argued with Ellis Kinsey and his crew.

"Keep it steady wimp."

Try as he might Billy could not keep his hand from trembling.

"Grab him before he wets himself."

Ellis Kinsey's cronies advanced towards Billy with mean smiles. Billy prayed he really did not wet himself. One caught Billy's free arm and twisted it behind his back with spiteful force. Billy yelped. The other gripped the arm that held the conker so Billy was unable to move. Ellis Kinsey sniggered but that was the only sound that · broke the silence. Many of the watching children knew exactly what it was like when Ellis Kinsey came calling and what would happen to them if they dared interfere.

"Don't think the bell will save you wimp boy, it's Friday remember."

Billy's heart sank. Friday meant long play times while the teachers drank coffee and pretended to enjoy the same stories Mr Meredith had told a hundred times before. Children had been known to drop with fatigue before the bell sounded and they could crawl back to their desks.

Then he noticed Brooklyn Hopkins edging her way towards the back. She caught Billy's eye and winked. At that moment Billy thought Brooklyn the most beautiful girl in the world. He knew she had a crush on him so he avoided her whenever he could but she still managed to squeeze next to him at dinners. That girl had a homing device like an Exocet missile. She would watch him chew every mouthful through her big blue Barbie eyes. It was no point asking Mum if he could have packed lunch because Mum would only say they couldn't afford it. So, he was stuck with free dinners and Brooklyn Hopkins. As she winked and edged her way to the school Billy couldn't help but smile back. It was a big mistake.

Ellis Kinsey glanced around to see what could possibly have made Billy smile just as Brooklyn was about to make a dash for the staff room.

"Get her!" he yelled.

A large girl called Mavis Trott caught hold of Brooklyn's blonde pigtail and gave it a hard yank. Mavis Trott was also sweet on Billy and seized the chance to hurt her prettier rival. Brooklyn screamed and struggled but it was hopeless and as Billy watched his heart sank.

"Ready?" said Ellis a sly smile breaking across his face.

He lifted Ross Tudor's conker aloft and prepared to deliver the fatal blow. Billy shut his eyes tight and clenched his teeth, bracing himself for the pain. He wished Mr. Groucutt had not told them that story about the King who got his head chopped off after quarreling with the Prime Minister. Now Billy knew exactly how he must have felt as he waited for the axe to fall. All he could hear was a loud swishing sound as Ellis Kinsey swirled the conker about his head just like the executioner must have done to the king. Swoosh! The conker sliced through the air and as the crowd gasped someone cried aloud in pain.

At first Billy thought it was his voice screaming in agony. Slowly the truth dawned. Ellis Kinsey had also missed. Billy thought he knew why. This time he was sure he hadn't deliberately moved the conker. How could he when Ellis Kinsey's henchmen held his arms? But the conker had moved, he felt the shoelace twitch just like one of Matron's facial tics. Brooklyn Hopkins told him afterwards it was the funniest thing she had ever seen. Ellis took an almighty swipe, completely missing Billy and the conker, and whacked himself squarely on the knee. Everybody laughed but Ellis didn't see the funny side.

"I said hold him tight you stupid losers," he yelled as he rubbed his knee.

The only other person not laughing was Billy. Ellis was mad now.

"That was just a practice swipe," he said as he glared at the spectators daring anyone to call him a cheat.

No-one did. Up close Billy could see just how mad Elliot was. Red blotches appeared on his face and his breath came in short gasps. It was not a good sign. Billy wondered how long it would take him to learn how to use his left hand. If it was badly mangled perhaps he could get it replaced with a hook? Someone began to cry. Billy guessed it was Brooklyn. To be fair, she wasn't a bad sort for a girl. This time Billy was determined to keep his eyes open whatever happened. I expect the King kept his eyes open as he watched the axe fall because that's what kings did. If the King could do it so could he. Besides, an axe would probably hurt a lot more than a conker. As he watched Ellis Kinsey swing the conker above his head, his twisted face a mask of focused fury Billy began to think the King had got off lightly. He was not going to apply for the job when he grew up.

What happened next passed into the folk lore of Valleys County Primary School. Billy watched the conker swirl above Ellis's head. If it made contact Billy's conker was history. On the positive side if Ellis was aiming for Billy's knuckles he would probably get at least a couple of days off school depending how bad the break was and what mood Mum was in. This time Ellis Kinsey didn't miss. Ross Tudor's conker sped straight towards Billy's which hung limp and lifeless as it gloomily awaited its doom.

Days afterwards children were found whispering in corridors and cloakrooms about the weird events they had witnessed but still could not quite believe. Ellis Kinsey had been deadly accurate with his aim and caught Billy's conker flush in the centre. It should have shattered into a thousand pieces like the wicked queen's mirror. It never flinched. Neither did the shoelace from which Billy's conker hung. Instead Ross Tudor's conker swung back towards Ellis Kinsey and struck him with such force on the nose that blood began to trickle down his chin splattering red tears all over his white T-shirt. Talk about the biter bit! Fate had just taken a big chunk out of Ellis Kinsey's trousers.

But that was not the end or the strangest part of the whole incident. Having struck Ellis Kinsey's nose the conker wrapped its string several times around Ellis' neck.

Ellis clutched at the string trying to loosen its grip. He was sobbing from the pain in his nose and yelling in panic as he clawed at his neck. It reminded Billy of a Tarzan film where the Lord of the Apes fought to the death with a giant snake that looked a bit rubbery. Tarzan had won but Billy wasn't too sure if Ellis Kinsey would get the verdict in his epic struggle with Ross Tudor's conker. Ellis' cronies released Billy but no one moved forward to help the stricken Elliot. Like the stone statues in Mrs. Pryce's garden children stood frozen as Ellis Kinsey writhed and wriggled on the floor, terror twisting his bloodied face.

"What an earth is going on here?"

Mr. Meredith's voice cut across the playground. The spell was shattered. Like startled meerkats children turned their heads towards the headmaster. Judging by his colour Mr. Meredith looked as if he had just had a near miss with a dangerous reptile himself. Everybody stepped back a pace including Ellis Kinsey's cronies. One of them managed to push Billy forward so he stumbled over the crumpled form of Ellis who now lay on the floor bleeding and sobbing. Billy noticed that the string was now slack around his neck. Mr. Meredith's eyes widened as he caught sight of the unfortunate Ellis.

"Are you responsible for this outrage boy?" he thundered glaring at Billy. Secretly he believed Ellis Kinsey had at last got what was coming to him.

"I dunno sir," replied Billy realising how pathetic he sounded.

"You don't know?"

Mr. Meredith repeated Billy's words slowly leaving Billy in no doubt as to whom he believed was the culprit.

"Is that the best you can do boy?"

Mr. Meredith turned his attention to Elliot who was sitting up rubbing his neck between sobs.

"We'd better take you inside and get you cleaned up," he said.

Mr. Meredith spoke more in hope than expectation. The boy looked as though he had been caught in a combine harvester. He wondered what possible explanation he could give the boy's parents.

"The rest of you make your way to the hall when the bell rings and wait for me. As for you my lad, outside my office in ten minutes."

Mr. Meredith surveyed the sorry mess that had once been the school bully and then turned his gaze back to Billy. Surely not? Shaking his head, he led the whimpering child towards the main building.

"Now you're for it," crowed one of the cronies but when Billy looked at him he hung his head and turned away.

If Billy expected to be greeted as the conquering hero he was mistaken. The rest of the children drifted off silently many glancing back at him just like they had done to the alien twin. When he caught Brooklyn Hopkins' eye her smile was half-hearted and she too looked away.

Billy understood why. They were scared, scared of him. He was scared too but he wasn't sure why. One thing he did know, he could do things other kids couldn't. Weird things. It didn't make him feel like a superhero. He felt frightened and very much alone. As he trudged back to the office children moved aside to let him pass.

CHAPTER 14

THE PIT OF SHADOWS

"What are you talking about?"

Mum was in the first stages of panic. Why had they let this mad woman into their house and why was Raymond acting so strangely? She looked at her husband but he lowered his eyes.

"Raymond," said Aunt Vera, "perhaps you had better show your wife the newspaper clippings."

Mum hated the way Aunt Vera called her 'your wife' but bit her lip. Raymond turned the pages of the album. When he was near to the last page a slip of paper, faded and discoloured with age, fell onto his lap. He picked it up and handed it to Mum. It felt dry and fragile like Nan's skin but the print was still clear and readable. She could see it had been cut from a very old newspaper with some care. Most likely by Great Grandmother Molly, she thought. The heading was in a large bold old-fashioned typeface. She tried to imagine how Molly must have felt as she cut it out. Were the light patches that pitted the surface tear stains? Was her grim task undertaken to the sound of the twins crying in their wooden cots? Mum began to read.

Disaster at Fernhill Colliery

Four Miners Perish: One Miraculous Escape

A massive explosion caused by escaping methane gas is believed to have been responsible for yesterday's explosion at Fernhill Colliery in South Wales that claimed the lives of four men from the same village. Philip Powell, Viv Warren, and brothers George and Raymond Thomas were added to the ever-increasing roll call of victims of these tragic accidents that bedevil the mining industry.

The mine owners have denied negligence and point out that every safety precaution available was in place and in full working order. They further state that even those miners in the habit of using canaries to warn of the presence of gas reported the birds appeared fit and healthy immediately before the blast. Witness reports describe a blinding white light unusual in such occurrences. One local compared the noise to cannon fire. Such was the force of the blast that the level at which the men were working was completely buried for hundreds of yards.

Despite strong denials from the owners Fernhill colliery has the worst safety record in the South Wales Coalfield and will now most certainly be the subject of an official investigation. Many locals who did not wish to

**be named said that there have been many
unreported deaths and 'disappearances' over
the last 18 months that have earned Fernhill
the unenviable nickname of 'The Pit of
Shadows'. Locals however were reluctant to
discuss further or in any more detail the
nature and frequency of these alleged
'disappearances'. It is also worth noting that
Fernhill is struggling to remain open due to an
inability to attract new workers. Grim times
indeed.**

**Under the circumstances the fact that one
miner miraculously survived the disaster is
even more remarkable. Glyn Jenkins emerged
from the chaos unscathed. He was unavailable
for comment yesterday but it is our
understanding that other miners have already
bestowed upon him the nickname 'Lazarus'.**

Molly set the scissors down and held the
clipping in her hand. He escaped once but now
the pit had claimed its own. She was thankful the
twins were sound asleep. This was a task she
wanted to finish without interruption. The album
lay open on the table ready for the photo and the
clippings. Her skin was clammy and her hand
trembled as she crossed to the table. Strange how
only the day before the hawker had knocked at
the door and sold her the album for a mere
farthing. The more she thought about it the more
it troubled her. She had never seen the man

before. He was not one of the usual door to door traders who regularly passed through the village plying his wares. Try as hard as she might she could not remember anything about him, what he looked like or what he wore. Molly had an eye for detail and a sharp memory but the image of him eluded her like a fish swimming among the shadows of a deep pool.

As she bent over to place the clipping inside the album a startled cry escaped her lips. She glanced across at the twins hoping she had not woken them. Her nerves were stretched tighter than the strings of a new bow. She could have sworn the page of the album was the skin of a living creature. She would need to get a grip of herself if she was going to go through with what she planned. The truth was although she tried to dismiss the stories the men had told her as nonsense born of superstitious talk and overheated imaginations they had badly frightened her. She knew they believed them to be true. Shadows and demons. Molly shook her head trying to clear her thoughts. This was no time to get cold feet.

She smiled as she remembered the first time she entered *The Black Diamond*. How quickly the hubbub had died, quieter than the chapel prayer meeting. Men at the bar stared at her making it clear she was not welcome. Even the card players stopped and turned their attention fully on Molly their winnings or losses forgotten. Some whispered that this was the widow of 'Lazarus' Jenkins and as word spread men turned away or dropped their gaze. Molly knew they were hiding something. Men always took the opportunity to look at her until their wives or sweethearts gave them a sharp elbow in the ribs.

"I'm afraid you'll have to leave Mrs. Jenkins. This is a men only pub see," said the landlord as he wiped a glass.

"Did anyone see what happened to my husband?"

Molly looked around the room but every head was turned the other way.

"Sorry for your loss but I must ask you to leave now," said the landlord making no attempt to move from behind the bar.

It was then Molly understood. They were not just unhappy a woman had dared enter, they were afraid. Molly was determined to find out why.

"Some of you men must know the truth. I will wait outside every day until one of you has the courage to speak to a poor widow."

She turned on her heels hoping her angry words would worry them like wasp stings. Outside she waited until closing time but when the men trooped out they drifted past without glancing at her. One crossed himself as he passed as though warding off an evil spirit. True to her word she returned every day until the number of men shuffling past grew less and less. Worried by this alarming drop in trade the landlord acted. One evening he approached her.

"Bad for business you are Mrs. Jenkins but seems like some of my regulars admire your determination. A few will speak with you."

He held up his hand before Molly could reply.

"They are waiting for you in the taproom."

Molly followed him around the back of the building. The landlord stopped outside a rough wooden door and yanked it open. She entered and found herself standing in a small paved hallway. Men's raised voices and the sound of laughter told Molly she was close to the bar. Opposite the door through which she had entered was another door. Through the frosted glass set in its upper half blurred shapes shifted in the candle light. It was as if she were part of some terrible secret plot, meeting her co-conspirators under threat of death should they be discovered. The landlord opened the door and Molly stepped inside.

The taproom was next to the main bar. Three men sat around a table lit by a single candle. They looked up as she entered the flame spilling a pale twitchy light on their faces. Each man wore a flat cap pulled low to cover his forehead while woollen scarves almost completely covered their mouths. One of the men stood and pulled out a chair for Molly. Molly sat with her arms folded and waited for one of them to speak. There was a long silence before one of them did.

"What is it you want Mrs. Jenkins?"

His voice low and muffled by the scarf.

"I want to know what happened to my husband," she replied, trying to keep the anger out of her voice. Why would no-one simply tell her the truth?

"What we want is not always good for us," said another.

"I will decide what is good for me thank you," said Molly.

"Did you know your husband was not the first?" said the third man.

Molly recognised his voice. He was one of the men who called at her home the night it happened. Did they think she was stupid? She knew how dangerous a life it was working underground. Never a month passed without some poor soul killed or injured. They must have guessed what she was thinking.

"There have been other disappearances."

Disappearances? What were they talking about? Her Glyn hadn't disappeared, he was dead. She recalled the newspaper report. It also spoke of unexplained disappearances.

"I don't understand."

"We never found Glyn's body. One minute he was there the next he was gone."

"There was no explosion like before and he was not trapped under a fall."

"A person can't just disappear," said Molly.

"Six men have gone missing in the last six months."

"Just like Glyn. One minute they were there the next they were gone."

Was this their idea of a joke, a very sick joke? No, these men were deadly serious. The very fact they had met in secret meant they were afraid. But of what? From the bar, she could hear the strains of Cwm Rhondda being sung with drunken gusto.

"*Pilgrims through this barren land.*"

Suddenly the world seemed a dark and threatening place. Her thoughts fled to the twins. Should she have left them alone with Mrs. Evans? She had no choice, she must know the truth.

"But that's not the worst of it."

The words chilled Molly to the bone.

"What do you mean?"

She couldn't imagine anything worse than what she had already heard.

"We found bodies," seeing the look on Molly's face the man quickly added, "Glyn was not among them mind."

"But most of the men who disappeared were," said another.

"What was left of them. We could only tell who they were from their clothes and things."

Molly gasped and covered her mouth with her hands. The room swirled and darkness threatened to swallow her. She gripped the table to steady herself and blinked hard.

"Mrs. Jenkins, are you alright! Here give her this."

The landlord leaned across the bar and passed one of the men a glass half full of some clear brownish liquid. The man took it and placed it in front of Molly.

"Morgan, what are you thinking man? Are you trying to frighten the woman to death?" said one of the men.

Molly pushed the drink away and stared at the three men.

"No, I'm alright. I came for the truth and have it I will."

She fixed the men with her eyes. They could see she would settle for nothing less.

"The level we worked in was the oldest. It stretched a long way under the earth but the earliest workings have long since been abandoned."

"No coal left see," said Morgan'

"There were places there carved into the coal and rock."

"What kind of places?" Molly asked.

"Mostly just small 'cubby holes' where men could sneak a few minutes' break but some were larger."

"There was one big chamber carved out by the old miners with the owner's permission."

"What for?" she asked.

"A chapel. Lots of men refused to work on Sunday's unless they were allowed time to worship."

"That's where we found the bodies."

Molly waited. Their story was proving harder to swallow than yesterday's left-overs.

"You found all the missing men in an old disused level. How is that possible?"

"Something carried them there."

The man leaned towards her and lowered his voice so Molly could barely hear him above the clamour from the bar.

"Some *thing*?" Molly repeated hoping she had misheard.

The man nodded, the silence hung heavy between them.

Molly forced herself to ask, "Were they murdered?"

"Slaughtered more like. Men murder, wild beasts kill for meat."

Molly was grateful she was sitting down. She leaned back in the chair and was tempted to take a sip of the amber liquid the landlord had supplied. Did they honestly believe an animal was responsible for the deaths of the men?

"They had been eaten?"

Molly realised she did not want to know the answer.

"We found gnawed bones among their remains. No dog that I know of could have left such marks."

"Rats!" Molly shuddered as she offered the most likely explanation. "It must have been rats."

"No Missus, not rats."

"Rats nor any other creature could have carried a man that far."

"Leastways, not one of God's creatures."

"What are you saying?"

Molly thought she knew but she wanted them to tell her plainly.

"Why do you think it left their remains in the chapel?" said one of the men.

"Unholy it is!" cut in Morgan before Molly could speak.

Molly clenched her fists.

"You think it was the Devil's work?"

Even as she spoke she hoped the men would laugh at the cruel joke they had played on her. No one did.

"Who else could it be?"

"There is evil down there Missus. All the men feel it."

"Then, there are the shadows."

"Shadows?" she tried to sound scornful, "I thought only children were frightened of shadows."

"We miners may be a superstitious breed but we are not afraid of the dark Missus."

One of his companions chuckled but it was without humour.

"Shadows of men that aren't their own."

"What do you mean, shadows that are not their own?" she asked, determined to get to the bottom of this dark mystery.

"We all cast shadows from our lamps but these are different. The shadows are tall and bent over with their arms held out like the talons of a great bird about to strike."

"And their heads," said another, "too large for their bodies."

"And always it is one particular man the shadow hovers over."

"And what becomes of that man?" Molly asked but already in her heart she knew.

"He is not long for this world."

Something one of the men said earlier nagged at her.

"You said you found most of the men who disappeared apart from Glyn. Was there anyone else?"

"One other besides your husband."

"Did the shadow hover over them too?" she pressed.

There was a pause as the men considered what to say.

"Not so much a shadow, more a dim light. . ."

He stopped, searching for the right word.

"Like moon glow," said another, "the same for both."

"And you are sure their bodies are not left down there like the others?"

Even as she spoke Molly realised the shocking truth, she believed these men.

"We searched everywhere Missus. We found all there was to find."

"I want you to take me down there and show me the last place you saw Glyn alive."

Not until now had Molly understood how desperate she was to discover the truth.

The man leaned back in his chair and gazed at Molly.

"Nothing on God's earth could drag me back down to that place."

He spoke slowly and with such feeling Molly knew she could not change his mind. She turned to the others. They lowered their heads.

"I have some money put away. . ."

"We don't want your money Missus."

"Go home. What else is there for you to do now you know the truth? The level will be sealed soon and whatever ungodly creature stalks that cursed place will be buried inside."

The men stood. There was nothing more to say but Molly had one last question.

"The men who disappeared, what kind of men were they?"

It seemed to catch them by surprise. They looked at each other before one of them spoke.

"Let's just say Missus, they will not be greatly missed by us or their families."

"You men had best be going I am calling time in ten minutes," said the Landlord.

They touched their caps and left. As the last of the men passed through the doorway he turned to Molly.

"God bless you Missus, you and your children."

With that he was gone. Shadows and demons. Could it be true?

"Tales to frighten children," uttered a voice.

Molly jumped, then she saw the figure sitting in the far corner. She was sure there had been no-one else in the room but all the time he had been listening to every word.

"Your husband was a good man. I will take you to the place."

Cloaked in shadows Molly could not see his face.

"When?"

It did not matter to Molly who he was, only that he would take her to the place Glyn was last seen alive.

"I have some arrangements to make first. Tomorrow evening. I will call after dark," he said. "It would not be good for the men to see I have gone against their wishes. Is it agreed?"

Molly nodded but could not bring herself to thank the man.

"Tomorrow after nightfall it is then."

The man stood and without another word followed the others out into the dimly lit streets.

"Time for you to leave Mrs. Jenkins. Five minutes to closing."

The landlord sounded as if he would be glad to see the back of Molly.

"Who was that man?" said Molly.

"What man?" he said.

CHAPTER 15

THE GATEWAY

Mum dropped the album into Dad's lap and smiled when the corner caught him flush in the tummy. He grunted. Aunt Vera lowered her brows.

"Well?" she said.

"Well what?" said Mum. "Great Grandfather Glyn was lucky enough to survive a disaster and the reporter tries to make a story out of it so they can sell more papers, what's new?"

"Back then newspapers only reported the facts," commented Aunt Vera.

"So, you're saying Great Grandfather Glyn came back from the dead like some zombie?" said Mum.

It was time to put this nonsense to bed.

"I'm saying great grandfather Glyn never came back at all," said Vera.

It would not be long now before Mrs. Evans came to mind the girls. She was a kind soul but could tease out secrets as easily as she did the deepest splinters. What would she think when a stranger came knocking the door after dark? Best tell her the truth or she was likely to invent stories that would be much more hurtful. But what was the truth? Was she really looking for her husband? The day of the explosion he had returned a different man. Since that day she no longer needed to hide from the neighbours until the bruises faded and the swelling around her eyes returned to normal.

The men in the tavern told her the miners they found in the abandoned chapel would not be missed. It made her ashamed to remember that when she first learnt of the tragedy she half hoped Glyn would be numbered among the dead. What had changed him so much that now his loss was a pain almost too great to bear?

Molly jumped at the sound of tapping on the door. Was it too late to change her mind? Mrs. Evans stood on the threshold in a state of fluster. Her large cheeks glistened like freshly picked apples. Beads of perspiration shone like dew on her forehead.

"Quick let me in for pity's sake," she wailed as she squeezed past Molly who stared out into the gathering dusk. "Something is following me, shut the door."

Molly slammed it shut. Her thoughts turned to the shadows the men had described. Shadows and demons.

"What was it like?" she asked her nails digging into the palms of her hands.

"Big and ginger," said Mrs. Evans fanning herself with the newspapers as she slumped into the nearest chair.

"Ginger?" Molly unclenched her fists. "Like a cat you mean?"

"Cat!" said Mrs. Evans, "If it was, it was the biggest God ever created."

Molly moved towards the door.

"What are you doing? Don't open the door it could be outside waiting to pounce."

Mrs. Evans was teetering on the edge of hysteria. Molly opened the door.

Sitting about ten feet away in the middle of the street was the largest cat Molly had ever seen. She could understand why Mrs. Evans had been so terrified but the creature looked friendly enough. However, she took a step back when it began to plod towards her.

"Come in and shut the door unless you want the twins to grow up orphans," pleaded Mrs. Evans.

Molly smiled. Her neighbour had always been a drama queen. Besides if she was afraid of a giant cat she would never be able to face what she planned to do tonight. The cat's head was level with her waist and for a woman she was considered tall. It rubbed itself against her purring like a traction engine. Molly could not resist ruffling its large head. She stepped inside still smiling to herself and the cat meekly followed. Mrs. Evans' eyes switched from Molly to the cat and back again her mouth forming a perfect circle. Molly stifled a giggle as the cat padded over to the terrified Mrs. Evans and rubbed against her legs. Mrs. Evans shut her eyes, joined her hands and began to recite The Lord's Prayer.

"If he was going to eat you he would have done it by now," said Molly when it became clear Mrs. Evans was not going to open her eyes without encouragement.

Giving up on Mrs. Evans the cat crossed the room and curled up in front of the fire.

"Well," said Molly, "you didn't take long to make yourself at home."

"You're not going to let it stay inside the house?"

Mrs. Evans could not believe Molly would be so reckless.

"He'll be fine. Look," said Molly as she leaned over and tickled its great ginger tummy, "he's probably just a kitten."

"Kitten, saints preserve us!" said Mrs. Evans. "If you come home tonight and find a heap of bones where I should have been sitting don't say I didn't warn you!"

Molly knew that it would take more than a very large cat to keep her neighbour from any tasty titbit of gossip that may be on offer. Molly would have smiled but at the mention of bones an image of an abandoned underground meeting place and its grisly contents flashed across her mind. Her mood darkened. Perhaps it was time to tell Mrs. Evans the truth but before Molly could speak there was another knock on the door.

Mrs. Evans raised her eyebrows awaiting an explanation of who might be calling at this late hour. Molly was about to speak when the cat suddenly stood with its back arched and hissed.

"Hush!" said Molly stroking its great head.

The cat stopped hissing and crouched down its eyes fixed on the door.

"That will be for me." She turned to her neighbour. "I have to go. I'll explain everything when I get back."

"Well!" said Mrs. Evans as Molly opened the door and slipped out into the night.

It took a few seconds for her eyes to adjust to the dim light shed by the gas lamp. The street appeared deserted.

"Did you hope I wasn't coming?"

A figure emerged from the shelter of one of the doorways. There was something familiar about his voice with its strange lilt that suggested he was not native to the valley.

"No!" she replied although doubts were beginning to crowd her mind. "I am ready whenever you are."

Her fingers closed around the handle of Glyn's old pen knife she had hidden in a pocket of her skirt. The blade opened in readiness. In readiness of what? Should she turn back and forget the whole thing? Why did she want to visit the place where her Glyn had disappeared anyway? It would not bring him back, nothing would.

"Second thoughts?" he said.

"Can we get on with it. I would like to get back before the twins' wake."

She hoped she sounded less afraid than she felt.

The man looked at her but she could not see his face. Shadows folded themselves about him like a shawl. He turned and strode down the empty street. Stars glittered against the blue-black sky and a full moon hung above the village like a giant pendulum marking the passing of the night. But it was not the moon that drew Molly's eyes. The stark silhouette of the pithead wheel, coffin black against the luminous silver orb, called her onwards. She bowed her head and followed but it was not his footsteps she was following.

Glyn had walked this way for the last time that cold November morning. The morning he had given her the photograph. She remembered standing at the door watching him walk down the street until he was lost in the jostling crowd of grumbling miners. Their frosted breath hung above them as though some great beast was passing into the primeval mist. He had not turned to wave or look back and she wondered why. She wrapped her shawl tightly around her to ward off the cold morning air but felt a deeper chill. She felt it now as the pithead loomed higher above her with every step.

Something else troubled her. Where was everyone? No lovers walked arm in arm under the cold moon. No children ran careless of time through the darkening streets. No old friends strolled down to the pub chatting of days and friends long past. No curtains twitched and no dogs barked. It was as if the whole world had been emptied of life except for the hollow echo of their feet down the narrow winding terraces. Where were the miners spilling out into the fading day after their shift hungry for home and a hot meal? She had not told Mrs. Evans where she was going or who she was going with. Something was not right. No, something was very wrong. Molly gripped the pen-knife tighter. Now she knew there was no turning back.

They passed through the silent and deserted engine house collecting two lamps before stopping outside the cage which took the miners down the shaft to the working levels.

"Behold," said the man," the gateway to another world."

As he spoke he stepped inside and beckoned Molly to follow. She hesitated. Glyn had told her the shaft was hundreds of feet deep. What if the cables snapped? A more worrying thought crossed her mind. What if the shaft went down to a place far more terrible than the coal face?

Molly stepped inside.

The cage door was little more than a large metal grid. It slid across with a clang. Molly shuddered as it dropped into a darkness lit only by light from their lamps. She did not know how long it would take to reach the bottom and the silence bore down upon her. She didn't want to speak to her companion but she had to break the suffocating stillness.

"Your name," she said her voice almost a whisper, "you have not told me your name."

"Anselm," he replied, "my name is Anselm."

CHAPTER 16

A VISIT FROM A VAMPIRE

"Now I think I understand."

Mum sat by Billy who was snoring gently, deep in sleep.

"Are you telling me Great Grandfather Glyn never survived the disaster and that the person who came back looking exactly like him was really somebody else?"

"Precisely!" said Aunt Vera sounding like a school teacher who has at last succeeded in getting through to a particularly dim pupil.

"But the person who came back wasn't human?" Mum continued.

"There you are Raymond," Aunt Vera sounded pleased, "I knew she would understand eventually."

"I most certainly do," said Mum.

Aunt Vera smiled. Dad looked alarmed.

"I understood you were an old witch. What I didn't know was you were an old witch with bats in her belfry."

Dad hung his head as Aunt Vera glanced across. She seemed at a loss for words. Dad got to his feet, placed an arm around Aunt Vera and led her gently to the armchair. Now it was Mum's turn to be speechless. Aunt Vera took a deep breath and looked up.

"My mother had a hard life with her husband," she began. "He liked to drink and when he was done drinking he would come home and beat her. She told me once that when she heard about the explosion her first thought was that perhaps he was among the dead. '*I almost dared to hope*' were her exact words. When she discovered he had by some miracle survived, she cried."

Aunt Vera paused as her voice began to break.

"When he came home things changed. He stopped drinking and stopped beating her. She told me, '*It was as if someone else had come back in his place, 'Someone good and kind'*. I think she fell in love for the first time."

Aunt Vera paused and dabbed at her eyes with a handkerchief. Mum scrabbled around in her pocket and produced a tissue. She blew her nose loudly. Mum was a sucker for a love story.

"A year after the disaster we were born. My mother told me it was the happiest time of her life. Then one day my father came home with a photo of himself. It was the only time my mother had been angry with him since the explosion. Money was scarce and with two children to bring up there was never anything to spare. It was only later she understood it had been a parting gift. It was the last time she saw him in this world. Later that day some men came to break the news that my father had gone. Disappeared without trace."

"Perhaps being so close to death is what changed your father. Made him seem a different man," said Mum.

It was noticeable how much softer Mum's voice had become.

"That's true," replied Aunt Vera, "if that was all the evidence she had."

"Evidence?" said Mum.

"She went after him," said Aunt Vera.

"She went after him," repeated Mum, "went after him where?"

Before Aunt Vera could reply Billy sat up and shouted.

Billy reminded himself this was only a dream. Even wimps could be brave in dreams. The squeaking stopped outside the door. Billy looked up. Someone was moving about around the bed opposite, he could see their shadow on the drawn curtains. Billy released the breath he did not realise he had been holding for so long behind clenched teeth. It was only a nurse. She had probably parked her squeaky wheelchair outside in the corridor or maybe it was an old nurse with creaky knees. Whatever, it was nothing to get worked up about. '*Too much cheese for supper*', Nan would say whenever Billy let his imagination get the better of him but when he felt a cold hand cover his own he nearly jumped out of his tracksuit.

Nan was looking up at him. The old Nan, his Nan. Her blue twinkling eyes full of life again but they were not smiling now. She was staring at him like she did when she knew he was telling a lie and her hand gripped his own with a firmness that surprised him.

"Billy love," she pleaded in hushed tones, "forgive me for not telling you. I thought I was doing the right thing."

"What are you talking about Nan, I don't know what you mean?"

"Don't let them take me. You must stop them."

Nan's gaze drifted towards the door and as he followed it her hand fell limp onto the bed. Billy turned to look at her but Nan had fled back to wherever she was hiding just like the pet tortoise he once had. Whenever it got frightened it hid in its shell and refused to come out even when Billy tried to tempt it with a sticky sweet. Nan's frail body was her shell and she had retreated inside where Billy could not reach her.

Something caught his eye. A light turned on in the opposite cubicle casting a sharp silhouette on the thin drapes. Billy did not like the look of it one little bit. It was the kind of shadow that made you dive under the blankets and reach for the mini-torch hidden under the pillow for just such emergencies. If the nurse was anything like the shadow all her patients were probably already dead of fright. Perhaps it was a doctor. Doctors could be weird like Frankenstein or Dr. Jekyll. In Billy's eyes doctors ranked just below headmasters, dentists and mad axe man in the category '*Least Wanted Next Door Neighbours*'.

The shadow was leaning forward as if it could not support the weight of its large head. Its arms were outstretched. Long fingers curled downwards like the talons of the velociraptors in *Jurassic Park*. Billy hoped it stayed behind the curtain until he woke. Then the squeaking started up again.

Matron entered the room pushing an empty wheelchair. One wheel squeaked exactly like Mr. Groucutt's trundle wheel. Just as well there was no one in it or they would probably have ended up on the floor with a broken leg. Billy knew this was not going to end well. Matron would not be happy to see him and would call his parents and Billy would be in for it dream or no dream. One look at Matron's face told him there was no danger she was about to phone his parents or anyone else's. Her blank eyes stared straight through him. They reminded Billy of the dead fish lying on the counter in the local supermarket that always freaked him out but this was even freakier. Dead fish don't talk.

"Come on Missus, time to go," said Matron doing her best impression of a Dalek.

Billy wondered if Matron was really a zombie and not a vampire after all. Were the zombie choir waiting in the corridor outside?

How did Matron expect Nan to answer anyway? Nan was ill. There was no way Billy was going to let Matron take her back to the nursing home. As Matron leaned forward to shake Nan's shoulders Billy stood up and shouted.

"Leave Nan alone, she's not going anywhere with you!"

Matron froze in the act of reaching out and turned towards Billy her eyes no longer dead and empty. They blazed with inhuman fury and were the colour of blood. Billy's worse fear was proved right. Matron was a vampire. He gazed in horror as Matron's lips parted in a snarl. She hissed, flicking a forked tongue between yellow fangs. Billy wondered if dream hospitals had visiting times. He hoped so because vampires didn't attack people in a crowd especially when they were carrying bunches of grapes, or was that garlic? Whatever, if Mum and Dad came through the door he wouldn't care what they were carrying. Even flowers would be ok.

Just as Billy thought he was about to be drained of blood by an overweight middle-aged vampire wearing surgical stockings Matron lost interest and turned back to Nan. The fingers of a plump pale white hand, its nails painted a livid red, curled around Nan's shoulder. Billy could stand it no longer.

"I said, leave her alone!"

As he spoke Billy got to his feet directly facing Matron. Nan lay unmoving on the bed between them. Matron hissed and drew her lips back over her fangs. Billy held out a hand to protect himself in case Matron lunged at him across the bed. Then something strange happened.

It was just like Ellis Kinsey and the conker. Billy didn't mean it to happen but it did anyway. His hand began to glow, not just his hand his whole arm. Although he could not see it, Billy's whole body began to glow and shimmer with a bright radiance that became more intense as his anger grew. All those times listening to Matron speaking to Nan like a little child welled up within him like a flood tide about to burst its banks. Matron's eyes widened and she took a step back from the bed. Billy didn't know vampires could get scared but Matron was. She almost stumbled over the wheel chair in her haste to move away from Billy. As she did she so she snarled but it was the snarl of a frightened animal, cornered and desperate. Why didn't she just leave if she was so scared.

"Go away!" yelled Billy. "I know what you are!"

Billy sensed she wanted to get away from him, he could almost taste her fear. He saw it in her wide startled eyes. Why didn't she just run? Billy would have if he'd been that scared. Matron glanced across to the cubicle opposite and back to Billy and suddenly Billy knew why she had not run away. Something was behind the drawn curtains. Something that frightened Matron even more than Billy.

CHAPTER 17

THE SHADOW IN THE PIT

"Billy are you alright love?" Mum placed a hand on Billy's forehead. It was wet and slippery but his eyes remained closed. "He's probably sickening for something," she said, "perhaps I should put him to bed."

"No, leave him," said Dad. "If we get a call from the hospital he'll need to be dressed ready."

Mum knew Dad was right. She felt a mingled pang of jealousy and guilt that Nan had become the most important person in her son's life. From now on things would be different she vowed. Aunt Vera was staring at Billy an expression on her face that Mum found unsettling.

"You were saying?" said Mum.

"I was?" replied Aunt Vera still gazing at Billy.

"About your mother," persisted Mum, "you said she went after Glyn."

Mum would never admit but she had become spellbound by Molly's story.

"Oh yes," said Aunt Vera turning to Mum, "so she did."

He did not speak again until the cage reached the bottom of the shaft. Molly wondered who was in the engine house operating the winding gear. How had Anselm managed to arrange a private visit? What had become of everyone? There was always the bustle of miners changing shifts but Molly had seen no-one. The men in *The Black Diamond* had told her the level Glyn had been working in was to be sealed. Perhaps it had been already, but was something still down there? She remembered the look they gave her when she asked them to show her the place where Glyn disappeared. Demons and shadows. In this dark underground place, they were not so easy to dismiss as old wife's tales. The cage jerked to a stop throwing Molly against her guide. Powerful arms gripped her by the shoulders.

"Careful my Queen, it would not be fitting to enter your realm on your knees."

Molly could not tell if he was mocking her or not. His speech was different, outlandish, not like that of the miners he worked with every day. Something else niggled, slipping her grasp, keeping just beyond the reach of her memory. She held up her lamp. They were in a wide space. Molly could not see the roof above her head. It was here men began the walk to their work stations. Many lay curled in cramped spaces for hours while they hacked away at the coal, burrowing ever deeper beneath the valley floor. Molly shuddered at the thought. They would have more room in their graves when they were dead.

"Follow me," said Anselm.

Molly could feel the heat of his breath on her cheek. She waited for him to take several steps then followed the swaying lantern he held aloft as it cut a path through the blackness. More than once she scolded herself for her folly. What did she expect to find anyway? The men said Glyn had disappeared but Molly knew that could not be true. She would not rest until she had done everything in her power to uncover the truth. But what power did she have? None! If the lamps went out she would be lost forever like Persephone in the Underworld with no Orpheus to fetch her back into the sunlit lands.

"We are almost there," he said slicing through her thoughts.

"Why did you agree to bring me here?"

It was a question she should have asked before.

It seemed a long time before he answered.

"He must have loved you very much," said Anselm ignoring Molly's question, "to have given up everything."

"What do you mean? We have nothing. What did he have to give up?" said Molly.

"A kingdom," said Anselm.

As he spoke the light from his lamp flickered and died. Molly held up her own but he must have stepped back into the darkness for he was nowhere to be seen. With her free hand Molly clutched at the shawl around her throat. She wanted to scream but who would hear her?

"Now I understand why," he whispered.

She had not heard him move but he was standing close behind her.

Molly fumbled in her pocket until she found the knife. She must keep him talking. It was only a matter of time before someone came down and found them.

"Why do you talk such nonsense about kingdoms and the like. My husband owned nothing. Even our house is not our own."

Molly forced herself to speak, to stay calm but each moment her heart beat faster until she feared it might burst.

"It is not your husband of whom I speak for it was not your husband who came back to you."

Anselm's whispered words crashed like storm waves inside Molly's head. She was trapped in some nightmarish fairy tale.

"Did you think any mortal creature could have survived that blast? Did you really think it was your Glyn you welcomed back to your home that day?"

Molly's head was spinning her legs suddenly weak and for a moment she thought she would faint. An image of the twins sleeping in their wooden cribs flashed before her mind's eye. She must stay strong for them.

"What nonsense is this? You have had your fun now take me back. Go and joke with your friends in *The Black Diamond* about the cruel trick you played on a poor widow."

She hoped to shame him or was it that she did not want to face the truth?

"Did you think it was lies the men told you?"

Anselm waited but Molly said nothing.

"The men who disappeared. Creatures that hunt and kill in the dark. Shadows and demons?" he said.

Molly recalled the meeting in *The Black Diamond*. The men had made her believe. Tough hard men who lived every day with death on their shoulder afraid of what lurked in the familiar darkness. They had refused her money and would not be shamed into returning. Then Anselm's sudden appearance. Had he been there all the time? She recalled the landlord's words.

"What man?"

"Who are you?" Molly could not disguise her terror.

Anselm stood silently enjoying Molly's fear. At last he spoke.

"Do you not mean, *what* are you?"

When Molly did not reply, Anselm answered for her.

"We are an ancient race, the Angelis, appointed Guardians of the Realms."

"Realms?"

Molly hoped Anselm was just some madman trapped in his own fantasy. Being cornered by a lunatic, however dangerous, was better than believing he spoke the truth.

"Did you think your world the only one? There are worlds and realms beyond number and not all exist within the boundaries of Space and Time."

"You're mad!"

Anselm ignored the insult.

"Aren't you curious to know his name?" he asked.

"Whose name?"

Molly tried to sound as if she did not understand or care. Anselm was not fooled.

"The one who came back in your husband's place. The one who is father to your children."

When Molly did not answer, he continued.

"In your tongue, it is 'Thorn'. He was guardian of the portals to your world."

Anselm waited but Molly either could not or would not reply.

"He committed a great sin"

"Sin?" said Molly.

"He fell in love," said Anselm as though the thought amused him.

"Is falling in love a sin?"

Molly hoped to keep him talking. Soon someone must come.

"It is a weakness. It was Thorn's weakness. It caused his downfall and placed your world in danger."

Anselm was smiling as if the idea gave him pleasure. Molly lifted the lamp higher so she could see his face.

"I know you!" Memory flooded back as though a dam had broken. "You sold me the album. You came to my house."

"You think you know me?"

Anselm snatched the lamp out of Molly's grasp and flung it to the floor. Molly gasped and waited for darkness to engulf her but the darkness was held at bay by another light. Anselm's body glowed, not white but a luminous green that reminded Molly of mould and decay. Anselm was no longer clothed in the drab garb of a miner but like pictures of knights Molly had once seen in a book. A long tunic partly covered what looked like chain mail. Upon the tunic was emblazoned an image that made Molly's blood run cold. The creature stood upright but stooped forward as though it could not hold the weight of its great head. Talon like arms reached out in the act of seizing its prey. Molly knew she was looking at the shadow the men in *The Black Diamond* had described. The shadows that brought death. Shadows and demons.

"Now you see me for what I am."

As Anselm spoke Molly gazed into dark eyes that burned fiercely. His pale face was framed by long black hair cascading over broad shoulders. A belt encircled his waist from which hung a sword. Behind him something emerged from the darkness. As it drew near to the lurid green radiance of Anselm's body Molly could trace the outline of its monstrous form. Horror and fascination fought for control of her emotions. There could be no doubting now that the men had told her the truth. Even stooping it was almost as tall as Anselm. Its pointed ears were flattened against its large head and its yellow eyes gazed at Molly with a cold intelligence that made her think it was nearer human than animal. Molly could smell its stinking breath. What she believed were talons were actually hands. Long powerful fingers continually flexing and unflexing as it stared at her. Molly could imagine what damage those curved nails might do to human flesh.

"You are safe with me," said Anselm.

"With you! I will never be with you." Molly spat the words.

"I am not like Thorn. I do not need to be loved or even liked. I take what I want and you are very beautiful Molly. Even Helen for whom men destroyed a great city would not compare with you. Come, leave this squalor behind, your subjects await you."

Anselm held out his hand and as he did so a bright light appeared behind Molly. She turned hoping above hope that someone was there but the light did not come from a miner's lamp. An oval of swirling golden brilliance, taller than a man, was set in the seam of anthracite. Even as she gazed into its depths she felt her feet drawn towards it.

"No!" she cried. "My babies."

"They will be taken care of," Anselm replied. He turned towards the creature standing at his shoulder and whispered, "Go, do with them as you will."

The shadow-being hissed and loped off into the dark. Molly screamed and lunged forward desperate to stop the creature even at the cost of her life but Anselm barred her way seizing her roughly by the wrists.

"Now there is nothing to keep you," he said. Molly struggled but Anselm was too strong. He released his grip and she fell sobbing to the floor.

"Come my queen, we must go."

Anselm bent over to lift Molly to her feet confident he was now master. The knife pierced his wrist with all the venom of a mother's anguish. He cried aloud and stepped backwards as Molly scrambled to her feet. He recovered quicker than expected and moved towards her eyes ablaze. Molly stepped back and heard him cry.

"Wait!"

But it was too late. She felt as if she was falling from a great height and suddenly her world was a swirling pool of light in which she sunk deeper and deeper.

The Pit of Shadows

CHAPTER 18

DEMON IN THE NIGHT

"She what?" said Mum.

Aunt Vera folded her hands and sighed. It seemed as if Mum's stubborn resistance had worn her down.

"It's a great story I'll give you that," Mum continued, "even if it is a bit too scary for bed time. But do you seriously expect me to believe your mother was kidnapped by an evil angel? Aliens maybe, angels are definitely old hat."

"She was not kidnapped," Aunt Vera spoke slowly placing great emphasis on each word, "she passed through a portal."

"A portal?" repeated Mum half questioning and half mocking.

"A doorway," said Aunt Vera, "a door to other worlds."

"And she just left you and Nan to the mercy of Mrs. Evans and the demon thingy while she boldy went where no great grandmother has ever gone before?"

"She had no choice," Aunt Vera said.

"You might as well tell me the rest I've got nothing better to do. Raymond go and make us another cup of tea."

Mum's use of the term *us* made Aunt Vera smile inwardly. Mum was softening whatever she might say. Raymond disappeared into the kitchen and Mum settled down to listen to the rest of Aunt Vera's story.

Mrs. Evans watched the door close behind Molly. She waited a few seconds before crossing the room and opening the door enough to get a clear view. She was careful to keep a wary eye on the monstrous cat that now lay sprawled in front of the fire like a ginger rug. Molly was already halfway down the dimly lit street struggling to keep pace with a tall figure Mrs. Evans guessed was Molly's man friend. Strange though, why weren't they walking side by side? There was not a man in the village who would not have been proud to be seen alongside Molly.

Now all she had to do was wait for Molly to return to discover his identity. She watched as they disappeared into the shadows. Tomorrow she would have a tasty piece of gossip to dangle before her neighbours. When the whispers began and the ugly rumours started who would Molly have to blame but herself?

A low guttural snarl scattered her thoughts like startled crows. The giant cat was staring at her it's green eyes the size of sliced melons. It was as if it read her mind and was not pleased. Why an earth had Molly let the beast into the house? Why had she let it stay when she had two little ones sleeping in the next room? Molly's actions were another example of her lack of common sense. She obviously didn't care what decent people thought and deserved any criticism that came her way. Mrs. Evans was sure the deacons of the local Baptist church would have something to say about Molly's reckless behavior.

She eyed the cat warily. It was staring at her through narrowed eyes in a manner that made her feel very uncomfortable. If she opened the door wide perhaps it would return to wherever it came from. If it did she imagined the local farmers would be missing a few sheep before very much longer. She waved her hands hoping the animal would get the message and leave.

"Shoo, go on you monstrous fat creature, be on your way, shoo!"

The cat simply stared at her with baleful eyes. Mrs. Evans decided to step outside where it was safer and rethink her plan. She felt a twinge guilty leaving the twins alone with a dangerous carnivore but she had been paid to baby-sit not tame wild animals. Besides it had been Molly who invited the beast into her home. If it ate her children she had no one to blame but herself. Having washed her conscience clean Mrs. Evans decided to seek help from Tom Wilkins. Tom was the ostler at the local colliery and well used to dealing with large stubborn animals. The fact he lived three streets away meant the creature would probably have enough time to eat at least one of the twins before they returned. Still that couldn't be helped and one baby was better than none.

She began to hurry as fast as her short chubby legs could carry her dumpy body down the empty street. Light from a gas lamp feebly attempted to hold back the night but she had only gone a few paces when it spluttered and died. Mrs. Evans stopped dead in her tracks. She hated the dark. Glancing over her shoulder an inviting patch of light from Molly's open doorway folded its way across the road like a welcoming carpet. As she hesitated between the dark and the savage beast something caught her eye. Someone was moving towards her through the shadows. She did not recognise him but this was any port in a storm time.

"Hello," she gasped, "help me please for pity's sake. There's a monstrous. . ." The words died on her lips as the moon slipped between ragged black clouds. In the eerie glow of the moonlight she could see that whatever was moving towards her would offer no help or protection against the creature she had left behind. The stitch that stabbed at her side was proof she was not caught in some horrible nightmare. She recalled a film she had once seen at the local cinema. It haunted her dreams but at least she knew it was only a fantasy conjured up by film makers in Hollywood. What faced her now was not a dream or some make believe monster but a living breathing horror.

The film had been called *Nosferatu*. The main character Count Orlok was a vampire. How anyone could have mistaken him for a human being even in in a film was beyond her. Yet Count Orlok was slightly more human than the *thing* that now loped towards her. This creature stooped forward. It's legs those of a powerful animal and it's yellow eyes more feral but in every other way it was a spit for the vampire Count. She could not outrun it and there was no one to call for help. Besides there was not a man in the village who would dare stand against such a nightmarish creature. She clasped her hands and tried to pray but her breath came in short sharp gasps and she choked on the words. Gripped by a terrible curiosity she watched it draw closer before falling to the ground in a dead faint.

Mrs. Evans opened her eyes slowly. At first, she could remember nothing. A grey fog of confusion swirled in her head. She sat up and looked about. To her horror she was sitting in the middle of the road. It was night. How had she got there? Then like a swollen river bursting its banks memory came flooding back. Unwelcome and unbidden the real horror of her situation returned. The creature had gone and she knew with an awful certainty where. Slowly turning her head, she looked back towards the house.

Framed by the light from the open doorway was a monstrous silhouette. She knew now that the creature had not come for her but for Molly's babies. Although she had run from the cat-thing she had never truly believed the twins were in danger. Now she understood the creature standing in the doorway was intent on causing them terrible harm. What could she do? She must do something before it entered the house and discovered the twins asleep in their cot. Summoning all her courage she cried out.

"Help, someone please help!"

Her words barely rose above a whisper but the thing in the doorway turned towards her and hissed.

"Their blood is mine."

The creature spoke and the shock was so great her legs turned to jelly. She slid to the floor and began to whimper. There was nothing she could do to save the little ones. Nothing anyone could do. Hunger burned in the thing's eyes and nothing would keep it from its kill. It turned back towards the house just as another shadow filled the doorway. Chaos erupted.

Mrs. Evans was used to being woken in the dead of night by tom-cats fighting for territory. What she now heard was a hundred times worse. The monstrous ginger cat launched itself at the creature. They rolled around on the floor in the darkness merging into one grotesque snarling shrieking mass. The shape repeatedly shifted and changed as they fought for mastery. After a fierce struggle, the Count Orlok look alike drew back and hissed angrily. Blood ran down the side of its face where a deep wound had been gouged by the cat's massive claws. It bared its own yellow fangs and in that instant Mrs. Evans knew she was in the presence of a living breathing vampire. The huge cat arched its back and growled a deep warning. The vampire flexed its long fingers and prepared to attack but suddenly the street flooded with light. Doors flew open as startled householders stepped into the street.

The creature turned its head and sniffed the air as a fox does when it scents hunters close by. A cry of rage that was almost human rent the night air. The vampire, if that indeed was what it was, loped away through the pooling shadows that lay just beyond the fingers of light reaching out from the open doorways. Neighbours huddled together in excited groups trying to make sense of what they had heard or thought they glimpsed disappearing into the darkness. Men ushered their wives indoors for many already guessed at what had passed so closely by. Dead bolts were slammed tight and curtains drawn as fear claimed the still deserted streets. Tomorrow the shaft would be sealed but was it already too late?

Mrs. Evans scurried back to the house her heart pounding with each step. The cat lay across the threshold it's great head resting heavily on its paws. It's body shook with heaving gasps of painful breath. It did not look up at her as she drew near. From one of its closed eyes a trickle of blood wound through thick fur before spattering the doorstep with giant red raindrops. Mrs. Evans knelt and stroked its head now matted with drying blood. The creature had come to her aid when no one else would. She shuddered to think what might have become of Molly's twins if it had not. Mrs. Evans slipped inside the house to find some milk and a clean cloth. The cat dragged its way in behind her and lay down in front of the flickering embers of the coal fire.

Kneeling beside the wounded beast she bathed it's eye as best she could. After she was finished it mercifully fell into a deep sleep. Mrs. Evans bolted the door and then entered the bedroom. The twins slept blissfully unaware of the nightmare that had threatened to cross the threshold of their innocent dreams. She gazed at them for a moment before moving to the small window that faced north. Above the village loomed the mountain. A watchful black sphinx against the star bright sky. But it was not the mountain she gazed at through fearful eyes. Set on its southern flank like a row of jagged teeth was *Crawsay's Castle*. It was what her old schoolteacher had described as a 'folly'.

Mrs. Evans had been surprised to learn that the castle was not a castle at all. It was built by the coal owner Rupert Crawsay to demonstrate his vast wealth and authority. What the Normans had failed to achieve with their mighty armies had been accomplished by the coal owners with wealth and the promise of work for hungry desperate souls. They wielded their power as ruthlessly as the Normans wielded the battle axe carving for themselves empires deep underground. *Crawsay's Castle* sat proudly on the mountain side a constant reminder to the people who lived in the valley below of who was their lord and master.

As children *Crawsay's Castle* had always seemed a dark forbidding place. Although it had been empty as far as anyone could remember no child ever dared venture inside through the narrow, cracked windows. Awful stories grew up around it like the ivy that crawled along its crumbling battlements. Countless were the tales of vampires, werewolves, ghouls and other nameless horrors glimpsed prowling in its shadows. Tales to frighten children but now it was not just children who turned their eyes towards its towering turrets and wondered what lurked within. The village was a small place. Dark rumours of unexplained deaths and a creature who hunted in the deep underground night swept through it like a plague. Tonight the rumours had given way to a terrible reality and she had looked into its dreadful eyes and lived. She just hoped Molly was safe wherever she was.

CHAPTER 19

BILLY: SUPER-HERO

"You should write horror stories, shouldn't she Raymond?" said Mum.

Mum's attempts at sarcasm were becoming feebler as the night wore on. Raymond said nothing.

Vera was not listening. Her attention back on Billy. The way Vera looked at Billy disturbed Mum even more than Vera's *Tall Stories From the Dark Side*. Perhaps there was insanity in the family. If that was the case and Vera was loopy then what about Raymond? It was just as well Billy was sound asleep and not having to listen to Vera's lurid tales, even if they were hugely entertaining. Perhaps it was best to humour the old dragon for the time being. Besides whatever else she might be she could certainly spin a good yarn. Like it or not Mum was hooked.

"That cat in the story," said Mum, "the one that saved you from the vampire thingy. It does sound a bit familiar?"

"Does it?" replied Aunt Vera absently.

Billy suddenly twitched in his sleep. Aunt Vera sprang to her feet and stood over him like a mother hen. Mum edged closer to Billy.

"Nothing to worry about," she said, "he always does that when he's dreaming."

Billy watched Matron cower before him. From behind the drawn curtains in the cubicle opposite something hissed. It was an unpleasant sound that belonged in a jungle not a hospital ward. Matron shuddered and took one hesitant step towards Nan's bed. Billy stepped forward to meet her. He was no longer afraid of Matron. He was no longer afraid of anything. Sometimes in the summer after a sudden storm the rainwater would cascade down the secret quarry they called 'The Roller' like a waterfall. Billy and his friends would take off their clothes and run naked under the tumbling icy water. He felt something like that now only this time the water flowed through him with irresistible force sweeping everything before it. Matron whimpered and glanced behind her. She stepped backwards trying to avoid Billy's eyes.

"I said leave Nan alone," Billy repeated firmly, "go away."

Matron whimpered again and sunk slowly to the floor. Behind her the curtains in the cubicle drew slowly apart and something stepped out looming over Matron like a hideous shadow. Its large bald head tilted forward as it peered at Billy with dead hungry eyes. The corneas were not milky white but deep red pools in which burned livid yellow rings of Beltane fire. Set inside their burnished circles black pupils glittered like cursed gemstones. Its skin was paler than even poor little Spencer Coombs. When Spencer took his shirt off in the schoolyard last summer all the girls screamed and ran away. Mr. Groucutt got cross and told Spencer to put his shirt back on because he looked like a dead slug. Spencer's Mum even came up the school to complain.

"Your blood is mine!" hissed the creature.

Billy should have been terrified but he wasn't, not a bit. He had never been a super-hero before, not even in a dream, and he liked the way it made him feel. The creature raised its hands. Its fingers were long and thin with hooked nails that tapered like talons. For a moment Billy expected it to claw at his face but instead it raised them as if trying to fend off a blow. Billy said nothing. The surge of energy flooded through him and he was swept along by its power. In one swift movement, the creature swooped and flung the terrified Vampire-Matron over its shoulder before loping out through the doors. Billy listened to its angry hissing until he could hear it no more.

"You look tired out love."

It was Nan, the old Nan, sitting up in bed smiling at him. Billy flung his arms around her and sobbed with joy while she gently stroked his hair. After a while he pulled himself free and gazed at her. Although she was still smiling there were tears in her misty blue eyes.

"I'm so proud of you cariad."

"Nan, I thought you'd never come back," he didn't mean to but Billy couldn't disguise the hurt in his voice.

"Billy, I have to leave you again," said Nan looking at him the way she did when she knew something had upset him.

"Leave? Where too?"

"Where you can't come, at least for now," she said placing her hands over his.

"Why must you go?"

"It's my time Billy."

"But I need you."

Nan gazed at Billy and he felt like the sun had appeared from behind the dark clouds of a long winter. Soon it would disappear again and the cold night would return.

"Billy, you are stronger than you know. Like a great tree. Soon others will find shelter under your branches. You felt a little of that strength tonight didn't you?"

Billy recalled the great flood tide of power that surged through his body. He nodded.

"But this is just a dream. Anything can happen in dreams."

"You are special Billy and so are your dreams. Remember that." Nan was serious now so Billy knew this was important. "Someone else needs you Billy, someone I love. You must help him."

"Who do you mean Nan? How can I help him?" He was about to say, "I'm only a boy," but he knew that wasn't true anymore.

"He will take my place. You mustn't leave him alone. Do you promise me cariad?"

Billy nodded. He could never refuse Nan anything.

"Now give me a hug."

Billy didn't need a second invitation. Nan smelt of lavender and Spring.

"What's the time now love?"

Billy released hold of Nan and turned to look at the clock on the wall.

"It's twenty to four," he said but Nan was lying back on the pillow her eyes shut tight. She looked so peaceful that Billy did not have the heart to wake her. He lay down beside her on the hard bed. The last thing he remembered thinking was, "Can you fall asleep in a dream?"

"I see what you're doing." said Mum.

"You do?" replied Aunt Vera.

"The cat in the story, that's Buster, isn't it? And *Crawsay's Castle* that's, well that's *Crawsay's Castle*. The boys were always telling spooky stories about that place. Trying to frighten us wimpy girls."

Mum smiled at the memory of carefree bygone days.

"Did they succeed?" asked Aunt Vera who seemed to be taking the whole thing far too seriously for Mum's liking.

"There was no chance we'd have gone near the place anyway. Besides, neither would the boys. They were more scared than us. Especially after what happened to the old tramp."

Mum stopped smiling now.

"Old tramp? What old tramp?" said Vera.

"Some old wino. Lived in the top terrace. He was always drunk. Used to stand outside the school gates and sing to the kids in the yard until the teachers moved him on. He was harmless enough. People mostly felt sorry for him. Had a bad time in the war apparently. He'd often wander off up the mountain or into the woods on his own to get drunk."

"What happened to him?"

Aunt Vera was staring at Mum her eyes sharp and restless.

"Must have had a heart attack or something. It was a while before anyone knew he was missing. A group of Venture Scouts came across one of his shoes in the wood near the Castle and the police began a search. He was found eventually, or what was left of him. Foxes got there first."

"Foxes?" Aunt Vera raised her eyebrows.

"What else could it have been?"

Aunt Vera stared at Mum without saying a word.

"Oh, for goodness sake you're not trying to tell me it was that demon thingy again?"

Secretly Mum had thoroughly enjoyed Aunt Vera's stories but now they were getting a little too close to home.

"Look Raymond and I appreciate you coming around but it's very late . . ."

"You're right!" said Aunt Vera stopping Mum dead. "It is very late and getting ever later. There is no time to waste. Raymond fetch Buster."

"Raymond!"

There was a warning in Mum's voice that her husband never normally ignored. This was not a normal night. Turning his back on his wife Dad disappeared into the kitchen. He returned with Buster trudging behind him. Aunt Vera turned to the great cat.

"You know who I am don't you?" she said.

"Why is she talking to the cat? Raymond, enough's enough!" said Mum.

"It's time to reveal yourself," said Aunt Vera.

Mum was about to speak when something extraordinary happened.

CHAPTER 20

METAMORPHISIS

A few weeks back Billy came home with some Science homework. His class were studying the life cycle of a butterfly. Billy had been amazed to learn something that started life looking like a fat green worm stuck on a leaf in somebody's back garden ended up as a beautiful creature that could fly wherever it wanted to go. Miss Lewis showed them a film in which the whole process had been speeded up. It was called metamorphosis. Billy caught some caterpillars afterwards and put them in a glass jar. He waited twenty minutes, longer than the film, but nothing happened so he let them go. Billy thought they were probably shy and wouldn't do their thing while people were watching.

What Mum now witnessed was another sort of metamorphosis and it took a lot less than twenty minutes. One moment Buster was crouched on four huge paws and the next he was standing upright like a man. His face changed even as Mum gaped unable to believe her eyes. Buster was now almost human in a feline kind of way. A long mane ran down the length of his back like a silky dark ginger Mohican haircut. He folded powerful arms, narrowed his one good eye and stared at Aunt Vera.

"Buster?" said Mum totally flabbergasted and almost speechless.

It was when Buster opened his mouth and spoke that Mum's jaw dropped open like a Venus Fly-trap. The voice that rumbled upwards from the creature's deep furry chest sounded a bit like a bass baritone with bronchitis.

"It is you?" said Buster.

"Yes, it's me," replied Aunt Vera her voice thick with emotion.

"What of the other?"

Before Aunt Vera could answer the phone rang like the bells of *Notre Dame*.

Dad was on it before the third peal. Silence clothed the room like a shroud as he answered.

"Hello. Yes, it is. I see."

Dad replaced the phone.

"What is it Raymond?" asked Aunt Vera.

Dad turned to Aunt Vera his face ashen.

"It's Nan. We have to get there as soon as we can."

"What about Billy? Shall I stay here with him until you get back?" said Mum.

"No, wake him. He'll never forgive us if we leave him behind," Dad was already reaching for his coat.

"But what about . . ."

Mum never finished her sentence. She turned to face the creature that had emerged from Buster's chrysalis but it was gone. Instead the great ginger cat stared back at her as though he had never gone away. Mum blinked.

"Are you going to wake Billy?" said Dad. "We don't have much time."

Mum shook Billy gently by the shoulders. He stirred, opened his eyes, stretched and looked about him.

"Is it time to get up for school?" he asked rubbing his eyes.

"No love," answered Mum, "we have to go to the hospital to see Nan."

"I've just been there."

"Pardon?" said Mum struggling to get Billy into his coat.

"Must have been dreaming," he said then stopped as he caught sight of Aunt Vera.

"This is Aunt Vera," explained Mum, "Nan's twin sister. Remember I showed you her photo in the album earlier?"

Billy stared at Aunt Vera but said nothing.

"Hello Billy, we meet at last."

Aunt Vera smiled for the first time and Mum was suddenly struck by how like Nan she was.

"Come on," Dad said, "we have to go."

Billy was bundled outside. The icy wind stung his face making him blink.

"Why don't we take my car?" said Aunt Vera.

Parked behind Dad's 'rust bucket' was a large grey shiny 4 x 4. Dad didn't object so Aunt Vera opened the doors and they all clambered aboard. There was a smell inside Aunt Vera's car that Billy could not place. Real leather was a new sensory experience. He snuggled back into the plush upholstery and gazed out of the window. The engine roared into life at the first attempt. Billy wondered if all cars were supposed to start first time like Aunt Vera's. She didn't have to swear at it once. Mum put her arm around Billy's shoulders as the car moved away into the still night.

"We'll have a car like this soon love," Mum whispered.

Billy couldn't care less. They sped past rows of silent terraced houses with their dark watchful eyes. Only the rustle of discarded take away cartons blown along the pavements by the restless wind disturbed the stillness. The car slowed and turned left as they reached the junction at the end of the street. The road led from the bypass down the steep hill that skirted the village shopping centre. This route also took them past the 'back lane' that led to Valleys Primary School. Billy looked out of the window ready to catch a glimpse and wondered if what Mavis Trott had said about the teachers was true.

Mavis Trott was a tall ungainly girl with a large Adams Apple that moved up and down when she spoke. It always fascinated Billy who never listened to everything she was saying because he was too busy watching to see where it stopped. Just like Brooklyn Hopkins she always seemed to be wherever Billy was but Billy didn't mind too much because Mavis had one very special gift. She could tell a good story. Billy was never sure if they were true or not but they were worth hearing. There was always an open-mouthed audience gathered around her. Billy had his suspicions that some of her stories were borrowed from the local library. Mavis always had her head buried in a book.

One time an argument broke out about what teachers did during Summer holidays. Mavis waited until there was a lull before dropping her bombshell.

"I know what they do."

"Bet you don't!" said Brooklyn Hopkins. "You think you know everything but my Mam says you make most of it up."

Brooklyn and Mavis never seemed to agree on anything. Billy couldn't understand why.

"Don't!" said Mavis.

"Do too!" insisted Brooklyn.

This would have gone on until one of the girls lost their temper and the pushing, kicking, hair pulling and name-calling would start. But it didn't because wimpy Spencer Coombs stuck his sticky beak in.

"How do you know then Mavis?"

"Because I've seen them," said Mavis.

It was the way she said it that shut Brooklyn up and drew the rest around her like moths to a flame. There was something dark and sinister in her voice and narrowed eyes that commanded attention.

"My cousin Pheobe and me were playing in the school yard last summer. My Mum said to watch the time but we must have forgot. Pheobe accidentally threw my Frisbee on top of the roof. I had to climb up to get it."

"Now I know you're lying. You can't climb to save your life."

Brooklyn's comment was met by a chorus of disapproval from Mavis' captive audience. Brooklyn stomped off somewhere to sulk leaving Mavis to continue her story unchallenged.

"It was getting dark but I wasn't going to leave my new Frisbee behind. My Mam would kill me."

This was met with knowing nods and mutterings.

"I managed to get as far up the drainpipe so I could see through the window."

Mavis paused for effect. The cries and shouts of the boys playing football faded into the background.

"What did you see?" asked a little Year Oner unable to stand the suspense any longer.

"The teachers. They were hanging from the ceiling."

Mavis paused and studied the faces of her listeners. No one dared say a word. Mavis held the little group in the palm of her hand except for the little Year Oner who was beginning to show signs of panic.

"Were they all dead?" he squeaked.

"Worse than dead, they were hanging upside down like bats. Like those chrysalis thingies that Miss Price told us about."

"We haven't done that in our class yet," Spencer said.

"Ever seen a fly caught in a spider's web?" continued Mavis. Everyone nodded. Some of the girls shuddered at the thought. "They were like those flies, all wrapped up tight. Just hanging there."

"How do you know it was the teachers and not giant flies then?"

Spencer was nobody's fool.

Mavis narrowed her eyes until they were just dark slits in her pasty face.

"Because one of them turned his head and looked straight at me."

Spencer winced.

"Which one?" he persisted.

"Come on you lot didn't you hear the bell?" said Mr. Groucutt who had crept up unnoticed. One of the girls screamed. The children fled from the yard like a shoal of fish chased by a hungry seal.

Mr. Groucutt shook his head, emptied the slops of his mug onto the yard and trudged after them.

Billy looked out of the window as Aunt Vera's 4 x 4 approached the entrance to the 'back lane'. The 'back lane' was less than one hundred yards long. It was more of a gulley than a lane formed by the back gardens of two parallel streets whose gardens faced each other 'back to back'. There were lots of hiding places thanks to a variety of sheds and garages that had been built at the bottom of the gardens. At the end of the lane was the side gate to the school. Billy would be able to see right down the lane even if only for a moment. The moon had torn itself free of the black ragged clouds and Billy would get a clear sight of the school. Were the teachers inside hanging from the ceiling like bats? It was hard to imagine Mr. Meredith hanging from the ceiling. Everyone knew he suffered from blood pressure especially when he shouted. Billy knew how red your face got if you stood on your head for more than a minute. Mr. Meredith would probably have exploded by now.

He leaned forward to get a better view. It was only a glimpse but it was enough to set Billy's heart racing as he pressed back as far as he could into the back seat.

"You alright love?" asked Mum.

Billy did not reply he was far away. Mum must have realised how stupid the question was given the circumstances and left Billy in peace.

The 'back lane' had been bathed in moonlight forcing the shadows to retreat into the nooks and crannies where they lurked in deep dark pools of inky blackness. Billy had been straining to catch sight of the school. Maybe the caretaker had left a light on in one of the empty classrooms. One of the teachers might be dangling from the ceiling at this very moment about to emerge from his chrysalis into, what? Most probably not a butterfly of any kind thought Billy and then he saw it. A shadow, even blacker than the others, moved out into the moonlit lane. Its large head was turned towards him. Eyes that reflected the pale moonlight gazed straight at the car as it flexed its long talon like fingers. Only an instance then the car sped past and it was gone.

"Did you notice anything strange about the cat tonight Raymond?"

Mum broke through Billy's dark thoughts. Dad mumbled something nobody could understand. Dad always did that when he didn't want to give Mum a proper answer. Mum usually kept on until Dad cracked but tonight she just fell silent. Everyone was left alone with their thoughts. No one spoke until the car reached the entrance to the hospital.

"Here we are," said Aunt Vera as the car turned into the visitor's car park.

CHAPTER 21

A PROMISE OF GHOSTS

The chill night air greeted them as they stepped out of the car. Billy glanced around. Except for a scattering of cars it was completely deserted. He couldn't help wondering if something was hiding behind one, watching their every move with dark intent. What he had glimpsed in the 'back lane' made him realise his dream had not been a proper dream at all. The thought frightened and excited him at the same time. He looked across at the squat outline of the hospital. Some of its windows were lit but most were not. Billy wondered behind which one Nan now lay.

"Come on love," said Mum, "best not hang about. You'll most like catch your death."

Embarrassed by her thoughtless turn of phrase Mum threw an arm around Billy's shoulders and shepherded him towards the hospital. Dad and Aunt Vera were already striding ahead. With each step, the hospital loomed nearer and Billy felt Mum's arm tighten on his shoulder. They passed through the entrance into the large brightly lit foyer. Dad took the door to the right and everyone followed in silence. Their hollow footsteps echoed down the long corridor. Occasionally they passed a porter or little groups of nurses chatting and laughing but nobody even glanced at them.

"This is it," said Billy stopping outside the doors to one of the wards.

Everyone looked at him.

"How do you know?" asked Mum staring at Billy.

"I just do," he replied.

"He's right," said Dad and buzzed the intercom. "It's Mr. Jenkins. You sent for us."

The doors clicked and Dad pushed them open. A nurse in a dark blue uniform just like the one Matron wore was waiting for them. Something was wrong. Billy could tell by the look on the nurse's face. She had shifty eyes that avoided everyone. She took Dad to one side and began speaking in hushed tones. They looked just like Dad's when he had forgotten to do something he had promised Mum. As they spoke Billy glanced down the corridor. It was not as impossibly long as the one in the dream and there was no sign of a lift. Through a half open door he saw a worktop on which stood an electric kettle. Facing him at the end of the corridor a bored male nurse sat sipping from a mug behind a large desk. He glanced up at Billy then looked away. The nurse finished speaking. She stepped past Billy and they all trooped after her like visitors being shown around a stately home. Billy knew because he had visited one once.

Billy would never forget that school trip. It was another unwelcome reminder that he was not like everyone else. Mr. Groucutt told them the day before that it was an educational visit not a school trip. It was no use. Everybody knew if there was a bus it was a trip.

"No sweets, pop or crisps," Mr. Groucutt warned as he scowled at them, "and don't bring any money because there isn't a shop."

All this did was remind everyone to bring sweets, pop and crisps. Tomorrow morning, they would huddle together in the yard and compare how much money they had to spend. Billy would keep well out of the way then.

"Can we bring a bucket and spade sir?" said Spencer Coombs.

"What did I just say?"

The pencil Mr. Groucutt had been fiddling with suddenly snapped in his hand.

"No sweets, crisps and pop?" replied Spencer smiling that stupid smile of his. "You didn't say nothing about buckets and spades sir."

Mr. Groucutt seemed to be struggling for breath. His eyes bulged, reminding Billy of the bullfrog he had caught near the pond, as his face slowly drained of colour.

"No," he said at last, "and I didn't say anything about deckchairs, candy floss or inflatable crocodiles either!"

"You can get them in the shop by the beach sir," replied an enthusiastic Spencer. Spencer was a stranger to sarcasm and common sense.

"Coombs! We are going on an educational visit to a stately home. The nearest beach is at least thirty miles away. Is that clear?"

Mr. Groucutt sank back in his chair like a boxer who cannot get up for another round.

"I can't go there," panic spread across Spencer's face, "my Mam won't let me."

"What are you talking about now boy?"

Mr. Groucutt was aging by the second.

"*Crawsay Castle*," a murmur rippled through the class like a cold wind in an empty house, "it's haunted."

"That's right that is sir," said Ross Tudor, "I seen it."

"We are not going to *Crawsay Castle*. Don't you listen to anything I say?"

Mr. Groucutt realised what a stupid question it was even as the words escaped his lips. Then the bell rang but Mr. Groucutt had already thrown in the towel.

"No eating on the bus!" yelled the driver as Billy and his classmates boarded like pirates taking an enemy vessel.

"It's alright," said Mr. Groucutt, "they've been told no pop, crisps or sweets."

"Hmmph!" came the curt reply as the driver shook his head, sighed and placed both chubby hands firmly on the wheel. "They do know they're not going to Barry Island?" he asked as he peered out of the window.

Considering the baggage they were carrying, Spencer Coombs and his Mum were making fair headway down the street. Spencer lugged a large plastic carrier bag bulging with crisps, sweets and pop. His mother struggled to avoid hitting parked cars with the large inflatable dolphin she carried under one arm.

"Yoo-hoo!" she cried waving her free arm wildly at the bus. "Wait for us."

"You can't bring that thing on here," said the driver gruffly as Spencer and his mother stood panting at the foot of the steps. "Health and safety see," he explained before either of them had a chance to ask why.

"Never mind love," said Spencer's Mum giving the driver a hard stare, "I've given you enough money to buy a new one."

She leant over and gave Spencer a big smacker on the lips to a chorus of hoots and giggles from inside the bus.

"Can you put some of this on him?" said Mrs. Combs as she half climbed the steps and handed Mr. Groucutt a tub of sun cream. "He's got very sensitive skin."

Mr. Groucutt stared at the cream as if he had just been handed a live grenade with a faulty pin. Spencer pushed past him and sat down on a seat next to the window where he began to blow kisses at his mother who stood outside still cradling the plastic dolphin under her arm.

"Can we go now?" said the driver.

As the bus pulled off the kids at the back began to sing '*Ten Green Bottles*'.

"Shut up!" yelled Mr. Groucutt.

It turned out Billy's partner Emlyn Gregory had been to Miskin Manor with his parents during the holidays. Emlyn was the class bore. Thirty minutes in his company and even bugs snugly tucked up in comfy rugs lost the will to live. Billy gritted his teeth and stared out of the window trying to ignore Emlyn's droning prattle. Then something peculiar happened. Billy began to find Emlyn interesting. It turned out Miskin Manor was the oldest house in the district. In fact, it was more like a small castle than a house, enclosed by a large stone wall to keep out robbers and stuff. During the Civil War when the King got his head chopped off its owner had chosen the wrong side. He was executed for his trouble or died in a battle or something. Emlyn couldn't quite remember. Anyway, his wife had been so upset she climbed to the top of one of the battlements and threw herself off. Billy tried to imagine Mum doing the same thing if something terrible ever happened to Dad. She'd probably make do with kicking the cat.

"The man who showed us round said her ghost still haunts the place," said Emlyn.

"Her ghost?" Emlyn had Billy's complete attention now. "Did you see it?"

"No," said Emlyn sounding disappointed.

"Bet Ross Tudor will," said Billy.

They both laughed.

"The people who show you round dress up in old clothes and talk funny," said Emlyn.

"What, like Daleks?" said Billy.

"No, like they did in the old days. You'll see," said Emlyn before changing the subject without pausing for breath.

He babbled on but his words flowed over Billy like the rushing water of a restless brook. Billy's thoughts were firmly fixed on battles, headless kings and unhappy ghosts.

"Right! Stay in your seats until the bus stops," said Mr. Groucutt as it turned into the car park of Miskin Manor.

Cue general mayhem as children grabbed rucksacks and shoulder bags and fought to be first into the aisle.

"Hang on!" shouted the driver attempting to make himself heard above the uproar. "This is Parry's Coaches not the flipping Titanic."

"Sit!" yelled Mr. Groucutt. "Wait till the bus stops."

This order was met by a tidal wave of protest but for once Mr. Groucutt stood firm. A few minutes later the whole party stood in the car park in mutinous mood.

"Look," shouted Brooklyn Hopkins, "there is a shop."

"You'll have time to visit the shop on the way out," promised Mr. Groucutt hoping that this would be enough to quell the growing grumblings of rebellion.

"This way," he said but children were already rushing past leaving him floundering in their wake.

It just so happened the entrance to the shop was also the entrance to the grounds of Miskin Manor. Mr. Groucutt broke into a sprint and chased after his wayward class like a cowboy in an old Western trying to head off the 'baddies' before they reached the pass. It would be a close-run thing.

Billy was left alone in the car park. He wasn't interested in the shop. Not just because he had no money to spend but because something else took his attention. On the other side of the car park rising above a high stone wall like a whale breaking surface was a house. It was bigger than *Crawsay Castle.* A huge mountain of stone dotted here and there with small irregular shaped windows. Who could possibly live in such a place Billy wondered.

"Big innit," said the driver loudly enough to startle Billy who forgot he was there.

The driver laughed as Billy almost jumped out of his skin.

"Better not go inside if you frighten that easy sonny," he said, a rather unpleasant smile breaking across his pudgy face.

"Jenkins what are you doing? Get in here!" shouted Mr. Groucutt's head as it poked around the doors to the shop.

"Full of ghosts see. Lost three children on a visit last month. Went in and never came out again." The driver was enjoying himself now. "Make sure you don't get left behind in there mind."

"Hurry up Jenkins! We haven't got all day."

Mr. Groucutt's stressed tones echoed across the car park.

There were gardens in front of the house with low hedges cut like a maze.

"Must be a maze for midgets," said Rhys Rowlands who fancied himself as the class clown.

Billy usually laughed at Rhys' nonsense but not today. The gravel path on which they stood between the 'midget mazes' led straight to the entrance of *Miskin Manor*. A large wooden door set back in the wall gaped open-mouthed at Billy. Set directly above it one large square window looked down at him like the dark empty eye of a blind cyclops.

"Right, find your partner and make a straight line," barked Mr. Groucutt.

Everyone shuffled into their places with hardly a murmur. *Miskin Manor* stared at them in a very unwelcoming way. Melanie Pritchard began to snivel.

"Sir, Melanie's crying," said her partner Mavis Trott.

"What is it now Melanie?" inquired an impatient Mr. Groucutt.

Melanie Pritchard was always snivelling.

"Ross Tudor said it's haunted. I don't like ghosts. I want to go home."

Mr. Groucutt took a deep breath.

"If there are any ghosts, which I very much doubt, they will probably be more worried about us than we are about them."

Melanie stopped snivelling while she tried to work out what Mr. Groucutt meant.

Spencer Coombs raised his hand.

"Yes Spencer! What is it now?"

"Are we still going to the beach after dinner?"

CHAPTER 22

MISKIN MANOR

"Good day young maisters and mistresses. I bid ye welcome to *Miskin Manor*. Pray thee, step inside."

The door opened seemingly by magic as soon as Mr. Groucutt set foot on the stone flagged porch. Out stepped a large man with a big belly wearing what looked like a stetson. His shirt was white with large turned down collars. He wore baggy trousers bunched just below the knees where they met a long pair of thick stockings that disappeared into clumpy black boots.

"We thank ye most kindly, kind sir," replied a flustered Mr. Groucutt.

"Are they talking Welsh?" whispered Melanie Pritchard.

"Dunno," replied Mavis Trott, "I can't understand what they're saying anyway."

"Excuse me," interrupted Spencer in a loud voice, "are you a cowboy?"

Mr. Groucutt glared at Spencer who for once took the hint and fell silent.

"I, young maister, be Selwyn Pollock, Colonel Roderick's Land Agent. Tis my business to tend the master's estates while he be away at the wars. Now, come maisters and mistresses there is much for thee to see and time marches on." With that the large man in the cowboy hat disappeared inside.

"Sir," wailed Melanie Pritchard, "what if he's a ghost?"

"Just get inside!" hissed Mr. Groucutt.

As they passed through the large oak doorway a lady in mop cap and dowdy old-fashioned clothes waited to greet them.

"This be Mistress Selby," said Selwyn, "very proud to own the title of 'Maid of all Work'."

"That I am most truly," replied Mistress Selby. "Come hither children there is much work to be done."

At the mention of work a ripple of alarm spread through the group. Selwyn smiled.

"Methinks they be not of a workish mind," he said.

"Methinks they be not also," said Mr. Groucutt struggling with the strange language.

"Are you ghosts?" blurted out Melanie Pritchard without warning.

Selwyn and Mistress Selby smiled.

"My hope is I and Mistress Selby have yet many goodly years young Mistress. But there be some who speak of strange ungodly apparitions they have sighted in this house."

Melanie had no idea what Selwyn was talking about but the way in which he said it made her bottom lip quiver. Mr. Groucutt and Mistress Selby spotted the warning signs.

"Don't be affrighting the young maistress with thy loose tongue and fanciful tales Selwyn."

As she spoke Mistress Selby placed a comforting arm around Melanie's shoulders and led her gently into the adjoining room.

"Come young maistress let us be about our tasks. I need thy help in the kitchen."

Melanie smiled, flattered to be the centre of attention for once.

"The only apparitions Selwyn hath been witness to hath been when he is in his cups."

The class dutifully followed Melanie and Mistress Selby except for Billy.

"Jenkins," said Mr. Groucutt, "I've left the worksheets on the bench outside."

He paused. Selwyn was looking at him with a puzzled expression on his face.

"Get thee hence and bring them, um, hence. Forthwith!"

Billy didn't move. What was Mr. Groucutt on about?

"Go and get the worksheets boy."

Selwyn shook his head and Mr. Groucutt smiled sheepishly. Billy ran off to get the worksheets.

Thankfully they were still where Mr. Groucutt had left them on the bench at the end of the path. The top sheet had one word written across it in bold capital letters –

ITINERARY.

 Billy sat on the bench and began to read.

1. See how servants prepared food.
2. Find out about medicines and cures.
3. Find out what gruesome punishments were in store for criminals.
4. Listen to tales of battles and see the weapons of warfare.
5. Try on replica armour.
6. Make candles.
7. Shop – time permitting.

Billy didn't much mind missing number one but the rest of the activities sounded cool, especially the gruesome punishments bit. He tucked the worksheets under his arm. They were much lighter than the newspapers he was used to carrying. As he walked down the path listening to his feet crunch on the gravel something caught his eye. The window above the doorway was no longer dark and empty. A pale light glimmered and Billy thought he knew what it was. Once, when there had been a power cut, Dad lit candles and stuck them around the house. Billy loved the way the light constantly shifted and changed throwing twisted shadows across the walls. Dad held a candle under his face and crept up on Mum. He looked scary so Billy wasn't surprised when she screamed but Dad was when Mum kicked him hard in the shins.

Somebody had entered the room and lit a candle. Whoever it was maybe they were watching him now. The thought made him uneasy and he hurried up the path to the house. As he passed over the threshold into the entrance hall he paused and looked up the great wooden staircase that led to the balcony on the first floor. He was tempted to sneak up the stairs and find the room with the lit candle but he remembered what Selwyn had said about apparitions and decided against it.

Mr. Groucutt and the rest of the class were watching Mistress Selby prepare a meal. She seemed to be doing something unspeakable to a large bird with a long neck that still had some feathers stuck to it.

"Gross!" cried a voice that sounded like Spencer Coombs.

Billy was about to join them when a sudden noise startled him and he dropped the worksheets on the floor. It had been the creaking of the stairs. Billy knelt and as he retrieved the worksheets he glanced up. A woman was standing at the top of the staircase looking down at him as though she was just as shocked to see Billy as he was at seeing her. For a moment, they stared at each other neither speaking. From the way she was dressed, Billy guessed she was not supposed to be one of the servants.

Long auburn ringlets rested on the large white collar of her red silk dress which reached to the floor. Her eyes were deep blue and she looked as if she had been crying. She was very pretty and although Billy wanted to say something his tongue was tied in tight knots. The lady in red put a finger to her lips and beckoned Billy to follow her. Billy was undecided what to do. She was very beautiful but so was Snow White's stepmother and look how that turned out. Taking a deep breath Billy placed his foot on the first step.

"Where have you been Jenkins, back to school?"

Billy's heart almost leapt through his jumper. For a moment, he had forgotten everything except the beautiful lady in the red dress.

"I hope you haven't been to the shop. Why are you standing on the bottom of the staircase?"

At that precise moment Selwyn appeared.

"Get thee hence into the kitchen with thy classmates," continued Mr. Groucutt with one eye on Selwyn.

Selwyn smiled. Neither Selwyn or Mr. Groucutt even glanced in the lady's direction and when Billy turned to look back she was gone.

The visit was a surprising success. Billy learnt lots of cool stuff. Many children didn't live long in those days. Colonel and Lady Roderick lost their three children while they were very young and the poorer people got off even worse. Selwyn explained that this was due in part to another outbreak of the *Black Death* and the *Civil War* didn't help either. That was the war where Colonel Roderick chose the wrong side. The

Black Death was a terrible plague that killed whole villages. No one knew how to cure it. Some people tried to move away but the *Black Death* followed them. Some people tried burning spices and others even drank their own urine which made all the girls shudder and the boys giggle.

Selwyn and Mistress Selby told them how people were punished if they did wrong. It sounded much more fun than the boring punishments around today. People could be put in something called *stocks* and everyone threw disgusting things at them. You could be whipped for stealing a loaf of bread which seemed to worry Ross Tudor.

"Could you get whipped for nicking chocolate?" he asked.

Mistress Selby smiled but Mr. Groucutt gave him a hard stare.

"Just wondered," he said, looking innocent.

Women who talked too much were made to wear something called the *Gossips Bridle*. It was a kind of cage made of iron that fitted over a woman's head. A sharp piece of iron covered with spikes slotted into her mouth so if she tried to speak her tongue was ripped to shreds. Mavis Trott nearly fainted.

"Did it hurt?"

You could always expect a stupid question from Spencer. He never let you down.

"Well young maister," replied Selwyn, "tis a question Mistress Selby could answer better than I."

"Pay him no heed," said Mistress Selby in a cross voice. "Inquire of him how he came by the *Drunkard's Cloak*."

"Twere the anniversary of my birth and I partook of one too many cups," replied Selwyn.

Billy quickly worked out that what Selwyn called 'cups' his father called 'pints'.

"What was a *Drunkard's Cloak*?" he asked.

It was a large wooden barrel with holes cut out for the head and arms. Anyone who got drunk in public was made to wear one so people could make fun of them. Billy imagined half the male population of Fernhill would be wearing one most Monday mornings. It would make getting to school dangerous with a real chance of being crushed to death by a crowd of walking beer barrels.

Rich people were treated differently when it came to serious crimes like murder. You could be boiled alive for trying to murder someone.

"Bet that hurt," blurted Brooklyn Hopkins. "My sister fell asleep on a tanning couch once and her bum was sore for weeks."

Poor people were hung while women could be burnt at the stake. Rich people were luckier. They had their heads chopped off which, according to Mistress Selby, was a much nicer way to die. Traitors had their head stuck on a spike in London somewhere.

"Isn't that what happened to Colonel Roderick," said Mavis Trott showing off. She smiled a smug sort of smile and waited to be told how clever she was. It never happened. Instead Selwyn and Mistress Selby exchanged dark looks. Mavis' smile faded.

"What?" she bleated.

"Who told thee such evil tidings?" said Selwyn.

Melanie Pritchard stepped away from Mavis and moved as close as she could to Mr. Groucutt.

"I, I just know," stuttered Mavis, then brightened, "Emlyn told me."

She pointed a finger at Emlyn Gregory.

Emlyn shuffled his feet and stared at his shoes.

"Never," he mumbled red faced.

"The Master is away fighting for our Sovereign King, God Bless Him. We have had no word that any such evil fate has befallen him," said Mistress Selby in a stern voice.

"Careful young maistress," Mavis began to chew her nails as Selwyn spoke, "we have no truck with witches."

"Witches? I'm not a witch," whimpered Mavis Trott turning to Mr. Groucutt for support, "tell them sir!"

Mistress Selby and Selwyn stared at Mr. Groucutt who was still struggling with the language barrier.

"She doth have her moments," he chuckled. Nobody smiled.

"Doth she now?" said Mistress Selby who seemed strangely excited by Mr. Groucutt's comment. "Be there times when she doth speak of things that are yet to pass?"

"She most certainly doth not," replied Mr. Groucutt who felt the whole thing was getting out of hand.

"Then we will spare her the *Ducking Stool*," laughed Selwyn as he ruffled Mavis' hair.

Mavis sighed and the tension was released like air from a spent balloon. Everybody laughed except for Emlyn who could only manage a weak smile. It was just as well Mavis wasn't a witch or she would never have survived the *Ducking Stool*. If you floated to the surface they burnt you at the stake for being a witch. If you didn't you were pronounced innocent. Not that it made much difference thought Billy as you were drowned anyway.

"I know who's a witch," announced Selwyn Coombs, "she's been a witch for a long time."

Everyone fell silent especially Mr. Groucutt who struggled to push his way to where Spencer was standing.

"Then tis thy solemn duty to reveal her name," said Selwyn suddenly all serious again.

"Miss Perry, our Deputy Head," said Spencer as Mr. Groucutt groaned out loud. "My Dad said she was a right old witch when he was in school and she's still a bloody old witch now."

There was an eruption of laughter that seemed to confuse Spencer. Mistress Selby stepped in quickly to shield Spencer from Mr. Groucutt who was edging closer.

"Methinks tis time the young maisters and maistresses were afforded a tour of *Miskin Manor*. Selwyn hasten thee about thy business."

As she spoke Mistress Selby ushered Spencer into the care of Selwyn who took the hint and placed a protective arm around Spencer's shoulders.

"Best come with me young maister. It would not do for thee to get lost," he warned.

Billy took one look at Mr. Groucutt's face and realised getting lost was the least of Spencer's worries. Selwyn led them back out into the entrance hall.

"Tis wise thy keep close to me," said Selwyn as he stood at the foot of the great wooden staircase.

Melanie began to snivel again.

"Melanie Pritchard shut up!" said Mr. Groucutt.

"Methinks we had best begin," said Selwyn.

He turned and began to ascend the wooden staircase. The children followed close behind and the old wood groaned and creaked in protest as they climbed.

The tour of *Miskin Manor* had begun.

CHAPTER 23

THE RED LADY

As they climbed the stairs Billy hung back. He had decided to keep an eye out for the beautiful lady in the red dress. Why had she wanted him to follow her? Perhaps this was part of the trip and that's why Mr. Groucutt had sent him back to get the worksheets. No, that couldn't be it. Mr. Groucutt had stopped him following the lady. There must be another reason but whatever it was Billy had most likely missed his chance of ever finding out.

The house was big but the rooms were dimly lit with wood panelled walls stained dark with age. They reminded Billy of the wood in Uncle Arthur's coffin. Arthur wasn't Billy's real Uncle. He was a resident of The Hollies and Nan's best friend. After he died Nan wasn't quite the same for a long time. The windows in every room were narrow and let in very little light so people used candles even in the daytime. Selwyn told them wood was plentiful from the surrounding forests which made Billy think he didn't get out much. Selwyn also explained that fire was their greatest fear because so much wood had been used in building the manor. The house smelt musty and unwanted. Nan had begun to smell like that. Like she didn't care anymore. The last time he visited her she told him he was the only light left in her life. Billy hadn't understood but now, in this gloomy room, he thought he knew what she meant.

"This smell's making me feel sick," moaned Brooklyn.

"Why is it so dark?" piped in Kayleigh Williams.

Kayleigh was afraid of the dark. Kayleigh was afraid of everything.

"Dark, maistress?" Selwyn sounded surprised. "The Manor hath many windows though glass be a great expense."

"My house has got triple glazing," said Emlyn Gregory, "and we're having solar panels in the roof."

"I know not what marvellous doings ye speak of?" said Selwyn scratching his head. "Come hither, I will show ye something wondrous."

Selwyn was as good as his word. The next room he took them to contained the largest bed Billy had ever seen. There were four wooden pillars on each corner supporting a wooden roof. Curtains were hung around the bed and when they were closed it made a pretty cool tent.

"Why are there curtains around the bed?" inquired a nervous Melanie Pritchard.

Before Selwyn could answer Rhys Rowlands beat him too it.

"So they can hide from all the ghosts and vampires and stuff," he said fixing Melanie with wide bug eyes.

"Sir, can we go to the shop now," blurted Kayleigh Williams near to panic.

"Do not fear young maistresses. No evil creature would dare enter the Manor. We be all God fearing Baptist folk."

Melanie and Kayleigh did not look convinced. They soon cheered up when they entered the next room. All thoughts of ghosts and vampires faded as they gazed upon the array of clothes spread out on trestles before them. The boys' eyes lit up at the sight of armour and weapons. Mr. Groucutt was quick to restrain the more enthusiastic among them.

"Wait a minute! Form an. . . " he paused his face a mask of strained concentration. "Get thee into an orderly, um, queue forthwith."

Billy stood by the door. Much as he wanted to try on the armour he wanted even more to catch another glimpse of the Red Lady. He watched as Spencer Coombs was fitted with a huge breast plate that touched his knees. There were giggles as he staggered under its weight and when Selwyn placed the helmet on Spencer's head even Mr. Groucutt broke into a laugh.

"I can't see nothing," shouted Spencer.

He sounded as if he were down the bottom of a deep well.

"Stop it Spence," pleaded Ross Tudor, "I'm going to pee myself!"

Selwyn showed no mercy to either boy as he handed Spencer a huge pike. Its long shaft was made of wood and its iron head was a sort of spear and axe welded together. It proved the straw that broke Spencer's back. Without warning Spencer toppled forward dropping the pike in the process. The children scattered screaming as they attempted to avoid being impaled by the falling weapon. Billy was forced to step back onto the landing and that was when he saw the Red Lady again.

At least Billy assumed it was her. The landing extended a long way on either side of the balcony. So far in fact that the ends were as murky as a pond disturbed by careless feet. Near the far end of the landing they had yet to visit Billy thought he caught sight of a red silk dress disappearing into one of the rooms. What should he do? The Red Lady had called to him before so she must want him for something. No one would miss him. They were too busy digging Spencer out of his armour. Half expecting Mr. Groucutt to roar at him any minute he dodged the shadows and crept down the landing.

The last door on the right was slightly ajar. Light peeped through the gap. Someone was inside. He tapped on the door lightly.

"Enter!" came a woman's voice. Billy knew it must be her.

Taking a deep breath, he entered.

She was standing beneath a large portrait with her back to him. The portrait was of a family. Billy guessed the man in the picture must be Colonel Roderick. He stood next to a young woman who was seated. Billy guessed she must be Lady Roderick. Two girls of about three and seven stood directly in front of the Colonel. In a wooden crib by Lady Roderick's feet a baby lay fast asleep. Billy felt sad as he looked at the faces of the children they had lost. Colonel Roderick had long dark hair and a beard. His clothes were silk but not brightly coloured except for the sleeves and collars of his jacket. The collars were large and white while his sleeves seemed to be slashed to allow white silk to peek through. His trousers were of the same material and colour as his jacket bunched at the knees like Selwyn's. Billy could not help thinking he had seen him somewhere before.

"Was he not a comely man?" said the Red Lady as she turned to face Billy.

For a moment Billy, could not speak. She was very beautiful; her dark blue eyes the colour of the violets Nan loved so much. Auburn hair hung in ringlets about her bare white shoulders. But it was not her beauty alone that struck Billy dumb. Although the lady in the portrait wore a blue dress there was no hiding the fact that she and the woman who now stood before him could have been twins.

"I hast not seen thee before, what is thy name?" she asked.

"Billy," was all he could manage.

"Ye are newly appointed to this household? Pray tell, what are thy duties?"

As she spoke Billy noticed that the rims of her eyelids were red and sore. He did not know what she meant by 'duties' but he supposed it didn't really matter as she was only an actress. Emlyn had explained it all to him on the bus. It was clever though how they picked one that looked just like the real Lady Roderick. Still it was only polite to answer.

"I've got a paper round," he explained.

The lady looked puzzled. She was as good as those actresses on the tele.

"Thy tongue and thy garments are strange to me. No matter. Can I trust thee child?"

She drew closer and knelt before him placing two hands on his shoulders. Billy blushed and nodded.

"This day evil tidings hath come to this house."

She paused and bowed her head. Her shoulders shook and Billy knew she was pretending to cry again. He had to admit she was good but maybe she was overdoing it a bit. After what seemed like ages she raised her head. Her face was streaked with tears. It was clever how she did that. Perhaps she had a raw onion tucked up her sleeve like magicians did with handkerchiefs. She stood and Billy could see that she did have something in her hand only it wasn't an onion but a large envelope.

"Take this I pray thee and give it to my Land Agent. Hast thou met him yet?" Her eyes bore into Billy.

"Selwyn, you mean?" said Billy wanting to make sure he got it right so Mr. Groucutt wouldn't yell at him.

"Selwyn? I know not any Selwyn," she sounded annoyed like Mum whenever Billy brought the wrong thing back from the shop. "I speak of Robert Courtney. He is one I trusted, to my cost," she sighed. "Twas after his coming the shadow fell upon us."

Billy was about to protest that he hadn't met anyone called Robert but this was just acting after all so it didn't really matter. Besides he didn't like it when the Red Lady got cross even if it was only pretend.

"Make haste child," said the Red Lady.

He held out his hand and took the envelope. It was heavy. The paper was thick and felt rough to the touch unlike the smooth paper in the school exercise books. In the centre of the envelope a great blob of red wax had been pressed down with something. It made a picture but Billy couldn't quite make out what it was. It smelt of candle wax.

"Conceal it on thy person," commanded the Red Lady.

Billy wasn't sure he liked this part of the trip. He slipped out of his rucksack and hid the letter inside while the Red Lady watched his every move through red rimmed eyes.

"Now child, get thee hence. I would be alone."

The Red Lady's eyes wandered to the far corner of the room and Billy noticed for the first time a staircase that must lead up to somewhere near the roof.

Billy closed the solid oak door behind him. He could still hear her sobs echoing down the passageway. She's brilliant at her job he thought as he hurried back up the landing. As bad luck would have it, Mr. Groucutt appeared from the room with the armour before Billy had got even half way back. Mr. Groucutt's eyes narrowed as he spied Billy. Billy stopped dead in his tracks. Mr. Groucutt was having a bad day and Billy had stepped right into the line of fire. Billy smiled but it probably came out a stupid grin because Mr. Groucutt clenched his teeth. If Mr. Groucutt had been taller with more hair, better looking and a lot younger he would have been the spit of that cowboy, Clint something.

"Billy Jenkins! Where have you been this time boy?"

Maybe it was Billy's imagination but Mr. Groucutt even sounded like the cowboy.

"The lady wanted me sir."

"What lady?" Mr. Groucutt's eyes were mere slits.

"The Red Lady."

It was the truth it just didn't sound it.

"The Red Lady," repeated Mr. Groucutt, "and where is this Red Lady?"

Billy pointed back down to the far end of the landing. He didn't take his eyes off Mr. Groucutt in case he had to move quickly before Mr. Groucutt grabbed his ear and give it a sharp tweak. The look on Mr. Groucutt's face made Billy worry that his ears weren't the only part of him under serious threat.

"Perhaps you had better introduce me to this Red Lady of yours."

Although Mr. Groucutt smiled his eyes remained threatening black slits. Billy heaved a sigh of relief. Mr. Groucutt must be acting too. This was all a part of the trip even if it hadn't been on the itinerary. Taking Mr. Groucutt at his word Billy began to make his way back down the corridor. He could hear the heavy tread of footsteps and the creaking of floorboards as Mr. Groucutt followed close behind.

"Where goest thou?" Selwyn's voice echoed off the timber panelled walls.

Billy felt Mr. Groucutt's hand on his shoulder. Mr. Groucutt took a deep breath and exhaled slowly, always a warning sign.

Selwyn was standing in the corridor with a small group of curious children huddled together behind him. From the room, could be heard the clanging of metal and the excited voices of his classmates. Billy noticed that the girl next to

Selwyn was wearing a dress like one of the
children in the portrait. It was Kayleigh Williams.
She would have a fit if she knew who it belonged
to.

"We goest to see the Red Lady," replied Mr.
Groucutt.

Billy could hear Mr. Groucutt's teeth
grinding together.

"Red Lady? If it be Mistress Roderick you
seek you will not find her yonder."

Mr. Groucutt gripped Billy's shoulder so
tightly his knuckles turned white.

"Why doth that not surprise me?" he said.

Billy wrenched himself free.

"She's down there in the last room. She's
been crying. She gave me a letter. Honest!"

More children were spilling onto the landing
to see what the fuss was about.

"Come I will show thee," said Selwyn.

Selwyn stepped forward followed by Billy
and Mr. Groucutt with the rest of the class in hot
pursuit.

"Billy's seen a ghost," whispered Ross
Tudor.

A girl whimpered. Selwyn stopped outside
the room where the Red Lady was. She didn't
seem to be crying any more. He produced a large
iron key from somewhere and unlocked the door.
Mr. Groucutt stepped inside. Billy held his
breath.

"Jenkins, get in here boy."

Billy knew he was in deep trouble. Mr. Groucutt had given up on the strange language. Billy stepped inside. There was no portrait hanging from the wall and no sign of the Red Lady. No sign of anyone. The room was completely bare.

"But she was in here. She spoke to me. Maybe she's gone up those stairs." The words stumbled off Billy's tongue. His heart sank as he realised that even if the Red Lady had climbed the staircase she could hardly have taken the portrait and the furniture with her. Had he imagined it all? No, he had proof. There was the letter.

"The stairs have been sealed young maister. The Mistress be with her sister whilst the Colonel is away at the wars. Twas once the nursery in happier times. After the cursed *Black Death* took the children Colonel Roderick commanded the room henceforth be emptied and shut."

Selwyn's words confused Billy even more. What was going on? How had they managed to clear the room so quickly?

"Billy really have seen a ghost," blurted Ross Tudor and immediately Kayleigh Williams and Melanie Pritchard started to wail.

"When are we going home sir," blubbed Kayleigh between sobs.

Billy was saved by the appearance of Mistress Selby at the head of the stairs.

"Selwyn," she cried, "fetch these good folk to me and be quick about it. We have yet to make candles and the day is shortening."

Selwyn squeezed his way passed the tight ranks of excited children.

"Come, it be not wise to keep Mistress Selby waiting," he warned.

Satisfied there was nothing else to see the children followed Selwyn.

"I'll deal with you when we get back Jenkins!" snarled Mr. Groucutt as they made their way back down the corridor towards the stairs.

Above his classmate's restless chatter Billy was sure he could hear the faint sounds of sobbing in the distance.

Normally Billy would have enjoyed the candle making session but the circumstances he found himself in were nowhere near normal. Now and again he glanced up from his task only for other children to look away quickly. Billy knew they had been staring and were afraid of being found out. What if he was like that boy in the film who kept seeing dead people everywhere? Perhaps he was going mad.

"You alright Billy?" asked Brooklyn Hopkins, her big blue eyes wide with concern. Billy nodded.

"Perhaps you did see a ghost, a real one, I have."

Billy knew Brooklyn was only trying to make him feel better. She was the one real friend he had. The only one willing to sit next to him. He wasn't going to get her into trouble.

"Nah, I was joking," he said. "I just wanted to make Ross jealous."

"Oh!" said Brooklyn in a small voice. He could tell she was disappointed but couldn't decide whether it was because there was no ghost or because he had lied. They finished making the candles in silence.

"I trust that ye have enjoyed thyselves young maisters and maistreses?" said Selwyn. "Hast thy any questions before thee depart?"

"Is the shop still open?" asked Mavis clutching her rucksack.

"Sensible questions!"

Mr. Groucutt fixed his eyes on Spencer Coombs whose mouth flapped shut like a dead fish.

Billy raised his hand. A hush fell on the room as every eye turned on him.

"Does Robert Courtney live here?"

Mr. Groucutt was about to shout at Billy but something in the way Selwyn and Mistress Selby exchanged startled glances stopped him dead.

"There be no one here by such a name. Where didst thou hear it?" asked Mistress Selby who, Billy thought, was staring at him very strangely.

He was tempted to explain it was the Red Lady but thought better of it. In fact, he had already decided never to speak of her again no matter how much Ross Tudor nagged him.

"Must have been on the tele," he lied.

It was becoming a habit that Nan would never approve of.

"May I have a word with thee Master?" inquired Selwyn as he guided Mr. Groucutt into the entrance hall.

"Thou had best tuck thy candles in thy rucksacks," said Mistress Selby to the children.

Billy loosened the straps and pushed his candle inside. As he did so his hand brushed against what felt like sand paper. The envelope! The Red Lady had been real no matter what anyone said. Ghosts didn't hand people real letters, did they? He looked up determined to attract Mr. Groucutt's attention. Mr. Groucutt and Selwyn were deep in conversation. Selwyn must have asked Mr. Groucutt a question because Mr. Groucutt shook his head. Both men turned to look in Billy's direction. Billy quickly turned away. They were talking about him. He fastened his rucksack and decided not to say anything more about the Red Lady or the envelope.

Children shuffled quickly into their lines anxious not to miss the visit to the shop. Billy was left on his own. Even Brooklyn found an excuse not to stand next to him. Mr. Groucutt thanked Mistress Selby and Selwyn and it was time to leave. As they trooped out through the great oak doors Billy sensed Selwyn and Mistress

Selby's eyes fixed on him. Then the doors slammed shut as if *Miskin Manor* had spit them out of its mouth. Billy glanced up at the window but there was no sign of light only a blind darkness stared back at him.

The orderly march soon became a mad dash for the shop that sent gravel flying in all directions.

"Ten minutes and then straight back on the bus!" yelled Mr. Groucutt attempting to convince startled visitors he had some sort of control over his class.

Billy did not run. There was little point. He had no money anyway. He pushed his way through the crowded shop. Mr. Groucutt and the shop assistant were surrounded by marauding children determined to empty the store of its contents. It was how Billy imagined General Custer looked when he made his last stand. There was no danger of Mr. Groucutt being scalped, his hair had done a runner long ago. Billy was as visible as a shadow in a dark room and that was when it happened.

CHAPTER 24

A REALLY 'BAD EGG'

Billy's foot struck something solid and he stumbled forward. It was a book. It must have been knocked off the shelf in the melee surrounding him. The shop assistant valiantly struggled to get children into an orderly queue while Mr. Groucutt yelled on the top of his voice adding to the general confusion. Billy stooped down to pick the book up. It had fallen open. There were no pictures to arouse his interest and the writing was small and cramped. He was just about to put the book back on the shelf when he saw it. Two words. They leapt out from the page as if they had been scribed in letters of flame.

'*Robert Courtney*'.

Billy had never stolen anything in his life but he did not even think twice about thrusting the book into his rucksack. He looked around. Had anyone had seen him? They were all busy jostling and elbowing each other for the best place in the queue. Hoping no-one noticed his red face Billy made his way to the door. It was only several feet away but it was the longest walk Billy had ever taken in his life. His sweaty hands gripped the door handle.

"Jenkins!" bawled Mr. Groucutt and Billy knew his worst fear was realised.

What would Mum and Dad say? What would Nan think?

"Tell the driver we'll be there in ten minutes."

"Yes sir," he said letting out a huge sigh of relief.

The shop door closed behind him and Billy knew there was no turning back. He had crossed a line. He was a thief. Selwyn told them thieves were whipped and branded so everyone would know what they were. The book was a heavy weight in his rucksack. If this was what guilt felt like he wondered why anybody ever bothered to steal anything.

The bus was parked with the doors open. The driver slumped back in the seat reading a newspaper.

"Sir says he'll be ten minutes," said Billy.

"And the rest!" muttered the driver lowering the newspaper as he answered. "What's the matter with you?" he demanded looking at Billy far more closely than Billy was comfortable with.

Even the driver could tell he'd done something bad. Billy could stand it no longer. He was about to blurt a confession when the driver interrupted him.

"Look like you've seen a ghost," he said chuckling at his own joke.

Billy climbed onto the bus and sat down. He was shaking. Beads of perspiration trickled down his spine and his hands trembled as he rummaged in his rucksack for the book. The cover was cream with no picture except for a copy of Colonel Roderick's coat of arms in the centre. Above it in old fashioned black type was written:

'The Definitive History of 'Miskin Manor House'

Below was the author's name, 'Professor J. Gangley-Jones.' Billy flicked through the pages until he found what he was looking for. The name Robert Courtney appeared several times in one part of the book so Billy turned the pages back until he found the chapter heading. It read:

"1648 – 49 A Dark Period."

Billy was a good reader, the best in the class. Time spent with Nan was never wasted. She had given him the greatest gift it was within her power to give, a love of reading. Books became portals to other worlds where Billy could escape without need of a passport. When other kids went to Majorca Billy fled to Narnia. On sunny days, he would wander up the mountain track to his Secret Place. There he would lie on his back and read against the shifting pattern of clouds and the blue endless skies. But this book was different. Somehow Billy felt it had come looking for him. How stupid was that? How could a book possibly look for someone? It had been knocked off the shelf and he had tripped over it. Simple as that! Why then didn't he put it back? Why had he hidden it in his rucksack? Why had he stolen it?

"Being poor is no excuse for being dishonest," Nan once told him.

Yet as Billy held the book in his hands he knew he had done the right thing but he could not say why. Whatever, the deed was done. Billy began to read.

"1648 was a year shadowed by dark tidings for Colonel Roderick and his family. The Civil War still raged but in the Spring of 1648 Colonel Roderick returned home to Miskin Manor and was joyfully received by his wife and servants. Accompanying him was a certain Robert Courtney.

Courtney found favour with the Colonel after the Battle of Shrewsbury where it is rumoured he saved the Colonel's life. The Colonel was soon recalled to the wars leaving Courtney, who had received a superficial wound in the battle, behind as his Steward.

Shortly after the Colonel's departure the household was devastated by a series of tragic events. The first involved one of the servants.

Accusations of witchery were levelled at Jemimah Penfield whose position within the household was that of Maid of All Work. The accusations appear to have been initiated by Robert Courtney. It is unusual for a woman of such good standing to have been accused of witchcraft. It was usually the old, poor or infirm who were subjected to such treatment.

Nothing is recorded as to her fate but her name does not appear again in any records. We can only assume that either justice such as it was prevailed or, fearing for her life, she fled.

Billy didn't blame Jemimah Penfield for running away. He would have done the same. Drowning or burning didn't seem like much of a choice. Bit like school dinners really.

"Shortly afterwards the household suffered the loss of Colonel and Lady Roderick's two daughters and infant son. Although the most commonly held explanation is that they succumbed to the pestilence known universally as The Black Death historians have since questioned the validity of this theory."

Billy struggled with some of the words like, '*rumoured*', '*succumbed*', '*pestilence*', '*universally*' and '*validity*' but he understood enough to grasp the meaning. He read on.

"Many argue that if the Black Death were indeed the cause of the tragic demise of the infants why was no one else afflicted? Such was the virulence of the disease that it undoubtedly could not be confined to just three persons. It is

almost certain that many, if not all the household would also have fallen victim to this dread plague. Contemporary records suggest there were those within the Colonel's household of the same opinion."

Selwyn had told them about *The Black Death*. If that hadn't killed those little kids what had? Billy looked out of the window. Still no sign of Mr. Groucutt and the rest. He read on.

"Blame was laid at the door of the 'witch' Jemimah Penfield."

Thing is, everyone knows witches are not real. So how did the children die? Billy was beginning to think that Robert Courtney was '*a really bad egg*' as Nan would say. What had the Red Lady said?

"Twas after his coming the shadow fell upon us."

Billy read on.

"Distraught by the loss of his children, the Colonel ignored his wife's plea to come home. Robert Courtney remained in the position of Steward until his eventual return. Unfortunately, Colonel Roderick never returned. He was mortally wounded in the Battle of St Fagan's and carried from the field. He died later that very day. The death of her

husband following the grievous loss of her children was a burden too great to bear. Lady Roderick threw herself from a battlement. The fall proved fatal and for a time Miskin Manor fell under the sole Stewardship of Robert Courtney."

"What you reading?"

Billy jumped while his heart changed gear into overdrive. Emlyn Gregory stood over him clutching his rucksack and a large brown paper bag bearing the Miskin Manor Coat of Arms. The bag had been crammed almost to breaking point but it was not the contents that drew Billy's attention. There was something about the coat of arms that caught his eye. Before he had a chance to look properly Emlyn stuffed it on the wrack above along with his rucksack.

"Looks boring," said Emlyn as he sat down next to Billy. The seat groaned. "No pictures or nothing and look how small that writing is. Bought it for your Dad, did you?"

Billy nodded although he knew there was no chance of Dad ever reading anything unless there was a picture of someone getting murdered on the cover. He shut it quickly as if the contents held a secret he did not want to share. There it was again, the Roderick Coat of Arms. It was sort of engraved on the front cover so at first glance it was almost invisible. A shield split into quarters. The top left and bottom right quarters contained the letters *E* and *R*. Billy guessed the *R* stood for *Roderick* and the *E* stood for the Colonel's first name. In the bottom left was a drawing of a house that looked a lot like *Miskin Manor* but it was the picture in the top right that made Billy stare. It was not a lion or a unicorn or one of those birds that came out of the fire but something Billy had never seen before.

The strange creature was bent over as if its bald head was much too heavy for its thin body. Its ears were strangely pointed and the artist had given it a large eye in a long boney face. At first Billy thought it was carrying knives in its outstretched arms. Looking closer he could see that they were in fact nails or talons on the end of skinny fingers. If Billy had chosen a Coat of Arms he would certainly not have chosen something as gross as that thing. Billy loved reading books about knights and stuff but this design was a new one on him.

"Whoooooo! Watch out Billy boy!" shouted Rhys Rowlands as the rest of the class announced their arrival. "Seen any more ghosts?"

"I did!" said Ross Tudor quickly. Hoots and jeers from the others. "Honest! He had his head under his arm because someone chopped it off."

"If you don't sit down Tudor I'll be the one doing the chopping!"

Mr. Groucutt sounded close to breaking point. There followed a mad scramble for seats. Billy shoved the book into his rucksack.

"Did you really see a ghost?" inquired Emlyn looking at Billy with puppy dog eyes.

Billy glanced at the house just in time to catch sight of something falling, something red. It plummeted too quickly to be a leaf but Billy already knew what it was. In his mind's eye he saw violet-blue eyes open wide in anguish as red lips formed a perfect '*O*'. Auburn ringlets streamed behind her pale face and her red silk dress flapped like ragged raven's wings. Then she was lost behind the grim stone wall.

"Nah," said Billy as the bus pulled out of the car park, "I was having you on."

CHAPTER 25

SOMEONE I LOVE

"Would you mind waiting in here while I take Mr. Jenkins through?"

The nurse opened the door of a small side room next to the ward Billy recognised from the dream. It was where Nan had said goodbye. He sat on one of the hard plastic chairs and gazed at the floor. Mum sat next to him and placed an arm around his shoulders. Aunt Vera sat opposite. No one spoke. In the distance they heard footsteps, the sound of someone coughing and the slow tick of the clock on the wall. After what seemed an age Dad and the nurse returned. Dad was crying. Not like Kayleigh Williams whenever she scraped her knees. Silent tears ran down his cheeks as he looked at their upturned faces. He shook his head slowly.

"I'm so sorry," said the nurse, "Mrs. Jenkins passed away five minutes before you got here."

Mum stood and threw her arms around Dad.

"Would you like to see your sister?" said the nurse to Aunt Vera.

Aunt Vera nodded and turned to Billy.

"Come with me Billy?" she said holding out her hand.

Billy took it and they followed the nurse into the ward. It was just as Billy remembered in the dream except for one thing. The bed where Nan had been was empty. The nurse drew back the curtains where the creature had hidden. Nan lay on the bed just as she had in the dream, looking just as peaceful. Aunt Vera leant forward and kissed Nan on the cheek. She whispered something Billy could not hear then stood and turned to him.

"Come and say goodbye to your Nan Billy."

Billy did not move. He could not speak but it did not matter. He and Nan had already said their goodbyes. Mum entered and threw her arms around Billy. She gave Aunt Vera what Nan would have called an 'old fashioned' look.

"What time was it when. . ."

Mum struggled to complete the sentence.

"Twenty to four," said the nurse but Billy already knew.

The male nurse was still sipping from his mug of coffee and did not look up as they passed the desk on the way out. The hospital was coming to life. The morning shift was arriving and Billy wondered how life could go on as if nothing had happened. It was as though nobody noticed the most important person in the whole world had just left it. Dad carried a plastic bag full of Nan's things. Billy could see Nan's purple shawl poking out of the top. It didn't seem much for a lifetime of hard work.

A faint glimmer of pale sunlight lit the horizon as the automatic doors slid apart and they stepped outside. They walked towards the car park their breath forming silver halos over their heads. Billy shivered as the cold morning air seeped through his clothes and onto his skin. There were lots more cars in the parking lot now. Lots more places to hide behind thought Billy. He was suddenly angry with Nan. Why had she left him when he needed her most? What was it she had said? Something about him being like a tree, something about him having special powers and there was something else. Billy tried to think as they hurried across the car park. Yes, that was it, he had to help somebody special, somebody Nan said she loved. Why hadn't Nan said who?

The sudden shriek of a car alarm startled them. They looked around. There didn't seem to be anyone else about but something must have set it off. Billy thought he knew what it was and quickened his step.

"Come on let's get inside out of the cold," said Aunt Vera as the car beeped a welcome.

Billy did not need a second invitation, glad to feel the security of glass and steel surround him. He scanned the car park and thought he saw a movement to his left. Was that a shadow slipping its way towards them or just the early morning light playing tricks with his imagination? He yawned and immediately felt ashamed. It did not seem right just to carry on as normal now Nan was gone. A sudden sense of loss overwhelmed him and he buried his face in his hands the tears falling freely his body shaken by strong tremors.

Dad placed a hand on his knee and gave it a gentle squeeze but no one spoke as they drove home through the grey empty streets.

Aunt Vera parked the car in the nearest space to the house and they all trooped inside. Billy made straight for his room. No one tried to stop him. He heard Mum ask Dad and Aunt Vera if they wanted a cup of tea then he closed the bedroom door. He sat on the edge of the bed and stared down at his scuffed trainers. Nan had bought them for him with what money was left over from her pension. Matron gave her a monthly allowance and Nan had saved for ages to make sure Billy was no different from the other kids. Mum said they would never have to worry about money again. It didn't matter what Mum or Dad bought him nothing would ever be as precious as those old scuffed trainers.

He could hear muffled voices downstairs and was glad they had left him alone. What would he do without Nan?

"Someone else needs you Billy. Someone I love. You must help him. He will take my place. You mustn't leave him alone. Do you promise me cariad?"

He recalled the Dream-Nan's words like the echoes of distant thunder. Who had she been talking about? No one could possibly take her place.

The Gaffer sat on the edge of his bed and looked out of the window. It was early morning and in the garden outside birds should have been cheerily greeting a new dawn. Yet the garden was lifeless and empty as if every living creature had moved silently away. No birds sang since the Shadow appeared. The house was different too. No one laughed any more. The other day he overheard his son and daughter-in-law speaking in hushed tones unaware he was just outside the door. When he entered, they stopped and pretended they had been reading but neither of them would look him in the eye. He supposed that business with the postman had been the last straw. He had overheard the angry postman describe the incident to his embarrassed son.

"Listen Mate, I may be used to being attacked by savage dogs but I draw the line at homicidal geriatrics! He wants locking up he does. Came rushing out of the bushes with a sharp stick and a hammer. I only just made it to the van in time."

The Gaffer tried to explain that he had mistaken the postman for the Shadow but his son only shook his head and turned away. His son would not listen and refused to let him finish. He was angry and not for the first time.

"No more Dad! When is it all going to end? First chickens then gnomes and I don't even want to think about the golf balls and now, vampires!

Vampires sneaking around in our garden. Please!"

The Gaffer watched his son strut back to the house. It was true, there was a vampire in the garden. It watched the house from the undergrowth of thick shrubbery and trees that surrounded their immense lawn. Or was there? Perhaps his son was right and he had begun to lose his marbles. No, he had seen it several times prowling around in the evening shadows. The night before last it had brazenly walked across the lawn towards the house. They had stared at each other as he stood by the French doors and watched it approach. His son and daughter-in-law had their backs to the window watching some boring soap on TV. He tried to warn them but by the time they managed to part company with the sofa the creature had slipped back into the tangle of undergrowth.

"I can't believe I'm actually standing here looking in my garden for a vampire. When will I ever learn? That's it, I'm off to bed. Tomorrow we need to talk Dad."

It sounded serious and that's when the Gaffer decided to take the war to the enemy. He pretended to go to bed and waited until he heard snoring. Then he tip-toed down stairs. An hour later he was armed with a hammer, a sharp stake fashioned from one of Mrs. Gardner-Allen's wooden spoons, and a string of onions. It should have been garlic but onions were all they had.

The Gaffer reasoned it was better than nothing and hung them around his neck.

Wrapped in a thick blanket he opened the French doors as quietly as he could and slunk across the lawn like a midnight fox. He carefully selected his spot. The base of a massive elm tree would provide him with comfort and cover. He snuggled down between its spreading roots and waited.

His mind drifted back to his days in the desert far behind enemy lines. He remembered the scorching heat by day and the biting cold by night. They hunkered down between undulating dunes hidden from sight by tatty old camouflage nets. Fear tasted bitter in their mouths but it also bound them together with bonds time could not sever. Young men facing the enemy in a strange land. How he longed for those heady days when danger was a wine drunk together. Now he was old and alone hunting an enemy that had stepped out of a nightmare.

Nearby the bushes rustled and the Gaffer gripped the wooden stake and hammer tightly. He knew what must be done. A hedgehog poked its snout into the air, caught the Gaffer's scent and shuffled back into the night. Overhead an owl hooted a grim warning. The Gaffer closed his eyes and leant back against the solid trunk of the tree. An old soldier knew not to waste his energy until it was time to face the enemy. He closed his eyes and drew the blanket tight about him. He would not sleep but remain in a state of relaxed awareness. When the time came, he would be ready.

He was woken by a bout of cramp. The Gaffer yelped, struggled to his feet and began to furiously massage the back of his calf. As the pain eased he was surprised to find himself in the shrubbery at the bottom of the garden. A pale sun shone through watery grey clouds and memory came flooding back. He scrabbled on the grass until he found the hammer and stake angry with himself for having fallen asleep on watch. He may be old but he helped defeat Rommel in the desert and was not going to be beaten by some ugly vampire with a big head. Then he heard the noise. The slap of feet on the gravel path. Experience taught that a surprise attack was the best course of action. He half limped half charged out of the bushes wielding the hammer and stake above his head, a wild Viking warrior thirsty for blood.

"Geronimo!" he cried.

The startled postman dropped his letters on the path and fled back to his van. He refused to come out until Mr. Gardner-Allen had assured him his father was safely locked away in his bedroom. That was why the Gaffer now sat on the edge of his bed staring down at the hold all packed with clothes and campaign medals. Later that morning they would drive him to the nursing home. He recalled the last occasion. He had been saved then by the little boy who turned up like a fairy godmother to rescue him from the Matron with the facial tic. There was something about that child. This time there would be no rescue. This time he had crossed the line. This time he would not resist. To be a burden was bad enough to be an embarrassment was more than he could bear.

Billy just couldn't think of who Nan might have meant. Then it struck him. It could only be Aunt Vera. She was Nan's twin and she was old. The idea pierced his gloomy thoughts like a shaft of sunlight but then the dark clouds returned. It could not be Aunt Vera. She didn't seem like the type of person who would need help from anybody let alone a little kid. But he knew beyond doubt that he was no ordinary kid. He could no longer hide from the truth. Yet, Nan said "help *him*". It could only be Dad. But Dad was Dad, how could he take Nan's place?

Tired of the puzzle Billy flopped back on the bed, his mind a faulty DVD player rewinding and reliving the events of the night. Something nagged at him like an aching tooth. As they walked down the hospital corridor Billy had thought about the school trip. The trip he still had nightmares about. The trip where he had begun to understand just how different he was.

Billy sat up. He leaned over and pushed his arm down between the bed and the wall. Beneath his bed was a treasure trove he had hoarded like a squirrel. They were perfectly safe and secret there. Mum never cleaned under the bed. His fingers brushed over some old Star Wars figures, a tub full of Lego and a WWW Wrestling Ring before they closed on the thing he had been searching for.

It lay flat against the bedroom floor as he had left it. He could feel its rough surface lick his fingers like a cat's tongue. He pulled it free. The great wax seal looked just as fresh as the day the Red Lady had given it to him. Slipping his fingers under the flap of the envelope Billy broke the seal. A large chunk of wax fell onto the bed. The image of the creature with the large head stared up at him. Billy opened the envelope. The Red Lady told him to give it to Robert Courtney but he had failed her. He unfolded the thick parchment. Would it be a betrayal to read it or leave it unread? He heard Mum and Dad's bedroom door shut and made his decision.

CHAPTER 26

WARLOCKS AND ORLOKS

"Do you think I should go upstairs and see if Billy's alright?" said Mum.

"It might be an idea to give him time on his own," said Aunt Vera.

Dad came in carrying two cups of tea. He set them down on the coffee table.

"Aren't you having one?" said Mum. Dad shook his head and left. They listened until they heard the bedroom door close behind him.

"They both need a bit of space. Men like to be on their own at times like this."

Aunt Vera leaned over and placed her hand on Mum's as she spoke. Mum nodded and suddenly tears welled up. Aunt Vera handed her a tissue. Mum wiped her eyes and blew her nose. Alerted by the noise Buster plodded into the room. Mum looked at him warily.

"Did that really happen earlier?" asked Mum clinging to the hope that the events of the night had somehow caused her to experience a vivid hallucination.

"Did what happen?" said Aunt Vera calmly sipping her tea.

Mum wondered whether she should drop the subject altogether. Stress can do strange things to the mind. What if she had imagined it? Aunt

Vera would think she was a nut case. No, she had to know.

"That business with Buster," said Mum keeping her eyes firmly fixed on the great ginger tom cat, "the way he. . . changed."

Aunt Vera took another sip of tea then placed the cup on the table. She folded her arms and looked Mum in the eye.

"Well," she said, "on the one hand you could say yes, on the other hand you could say no."

"Either he did or he didn't!"

Mum was beginning to get annoyed with Aunt Vera. Why did the woman insist on speaking in riddles?

"He is what he has always been."

Aunt Vera's smug smile reminded Mum of the *Mona Lisa*. That woman got on Mum's nerves too.

"You mean he's always been a big ugly ginger tom with one eye?"

That was the good news. The bad news was that Mum had begun seeing things.

"Ugly?"

Mum turned towards the sound of the deep rasping voice. Buster stood there arms folded glaring at Mum through his one good eye.

"Among my own I am much admired."

"You always had an opinion of yourself," said Aunt Vera before turning to Mum. "You see only what he allows you to see. This is his true form."

Mum watched helpless as the cat creature took one pace towards her. She pushed her way as far back against the sofa as she could. It lowered its head and spoke,

"I am Bws-Ta. It is an honour to serve the House of Jen-Kins."

"What's . . .it. . .talking. . . about?"

Mum was beginning to hyperventilate.

"You remember I told you about my mother, Molly?"

Aunt Vera leaned towards Mum and spoke in a quiet calm voice. It seemed to work. Mum dragged her eyes from Buster and looked at Aunt Vera like a child seeking help solving a difficult problem.

"Yes," replied Mum but even that was an effort.

"How she passed through a portal, a door to other worlds?"

This time Mum simply nodded.

"We were left alone and in great danger. Buster was sent to protect us."

"Protect you? From what?"

Mum recalled the words Aunt Vera had spoken earlier that night? It seemed a lifetime away now. She had said Billy was in grave danger.

"Tell me," she demanded.

There was fire in Mum's belly and anyone or anything that threatened her son had better watch out.

Aunt Vera and Buster exchanged glances before the creature spoke.

"He is here. Close. His scent is strong."

Mum looked anxiously from one to the other. "Who's here?"

Mum was ready to burst with frustration.

"The thing that was sent to kill Nan and me," replied Aunt Vera.

"Shadow filth!" growled Buster.

"You mean that shadow demon vampire thingy?"

It was the best description Mum could come up with.

"The one the cat fought the night your mother left? The cat that lost its eye." Mum looked up at Buster

"They are beings of the dark night whose shadow brings sickness and despair. You are right in calling them vampires. They feed on the pain and misery of others."

Aunt Vera stared past Mum into a distant past.

"If they are threatening my Billy I need you to tell me everything."

Aunt Vera turned to Buster.

"Tell Billy's mother all you know," she said, "about the shadow creatures and what happened to Molly."

Buster squatted down cross legged on the floor and bowed his head. For a moment Mum thought he would ignore Aunt Vera. Suddenly a deep growl broke the silence. Buster began his story.

"They have a name, orloks. I first heard the Shaman speak of them when I was but a cubling. One night in our Winter lodges as the shadows from the fire danced on the aya skins above his head he spoke of them and my blood turned to ice. . ."

Billy was about to read the first line of the Red Lady's letter when he heard a voice deep and gruff. It came from downstairs. He paused for a second. A scent drifted up from the parchment. He recognised the perfume the Red Lady had worn. He saw again the sadness in her eyes. Now he shared her pain. Billy began to read.

"Master Robert Courtney,
If that truly be thy name. I know what thou art. The dark spell you cast upon my husband. The curse you brought upon this house. With you came the SHADOW that haunted our nights and the dread sickness that took away my babies.
Do not think for a moment I believed your foul accusations against my trusted servant and true friend Jemimah Penfield. You sought only to remove the one soul who stood by me. The only soul besides myself who perceives your true nature, WARLOCK."

Warlock? Billy's eyes widened. Nan had told him a story once about witches. He had asked if men could be witches. Nan explained that a male witch was called a warlock. Was Robert Courtney a warlock? Even if the Red Lady believed Robert Courtney to be a warlock in those days lots of people were accused of being witches. Maybe it was just coincidence. His gaze fell upon the big chunk of wax that fell off the envelope when he broke the seal. The creature that Billy had seen lurking in the shadows earlier stared up at him. Was this the same shadow the Red Lady spoke of in the letter? Billy shuddered. He stood and looked out of his bedroom window searching the dawn silvered streets for the thing that once stalked the corridors of Miskin Manor. Lights were coming on as people got ready for work. A new day was beginning. His first without Nan. Billy sat back on the bed and picked up the letter.

"Now this day the greatest misfortune has overtaken me. My beloved Edward is lost, fallen in battle. You are now master of Miskin Manor in all but name. You and the Nameless Horror that dogs your footsteps. Think not that I shall yield to your base demands. I have seen how your eyes watch over me. I go to the only place where your evil cannot follow. I go to be with those I love.

May God deal with you as you deserve."

For a while Billy stared at the letter remembering her pale sad face. He had been the last person to see her alive. How was that possible? Yet he knew it was, because he was different from other children. Very different. For a moment, the thought filled him with dread until the grief of his own loss pushed him down on the bed where he cried himself to sleep.

CHAPTER 27

THE PLEDGE OF INGAS

Red tongues of fire licked the Shaman's pale-yellow eyes as he stared beyond them into a darkness deeper than the surrounding night. Outside the wind brushed against the half-moon lodges tugging at the awning ropes still visible above the drifting snow. There would be no hunting tonight. No tender aya meat to feast upon. Instead of filling their bellies the Shaman would fill their minds with the ancient lore of the Gingas. The Shaman raised his hand and the howling wild pack wind slunk past until all Buster could hear was the pounding of his racing heart. He sneaked a sly look sideways and saw awe and wonder written on the fire fanned faces of the other cubs. Then the Shaman spoke. A low rumbling that began deep in his throat growing louder with each heartbeat to fill the lodge like smoke from the blazing fire.

"In the sun days, in the green time, in the long ago of our years, Ingas led the Old Ones in the paths of Peace and Plenty. Ska, gateway to worlds, was yet young, fresh made by the hand of Moa, Maker of All."

Outside the wind shrieked in its blind rage and Buster found it hard to imagine such a time of peace and plenty.

"Where is the gateway?"

The words slipped carelessly from his lips. The shocked cubs turned to the one who had dared interrupt the Shaman and ask the question that burned in their hearts. Buster felt the fur bristle down his spine and wished he could claw them back out of the smoky air. The Shaman smiled a slow smile and closed his eyes.

"Tonight, I will show you, but there is one who has already crossed its threshold."

The Shaman opened his eyes and his yellow gaze fell upon Buster like the first rays of a new dawn. Buster shifted on his haunches knowing every eye in the lodge rested upon him. The Shaman continued.

"It was in the heat of a Long Day while Ingas sat in the shade outside his lodge that three strangers approached. As they drew near Ingas could see they were not of the Gingas. Light clothed their bodies. Ingas ordered the Elders to fetch food and drink. Then he stood and waited. As they drew near Ingas fell to his knees and bowed his head so it touched the dry earth. A voice spoke as gentle and powerful as the wind that blows through the prairie grass.

'Rise Ingas, First of the Gingas, we are but Messengers of Moa and have been sent to deliver His Words.'

So, spoke Rowan, Great Chief among the Angelis and Warrior-Guardian of Realms.

'These are my companions and brothers, Anselm and Thorn,' he said and fearless Ingas trembled before them. 'Mark them well for from this day forth your fates may entwine forever.'

'What is it you want Lord?' said Ingas knowing the destiny of his people lay in the answer Rowan would give.'

'That you serve Thorn and Anselm in their appointed tasks as Guardians to the Realm of Men.'

Ingas was troubled. He had heard of the Realm of Men. Word was that Man had been created in the likeness of Moa Himself, that Man held a special place in His purposes. It would be a heavy burden his people would bear until the End of Days when all Realms became One.

'If the Gingas are unequal to the task there are others who will gladly bow the knee at our bidding,' said Anselm.

His words struck at Ingas' pride. Hastily he replied and the fate of the Gingas was sealed.

'We accept Lord. I and mine are yours until all realms become one.''

Thorn stepped forward and placed a hand on Ingas' shoulder.

'Know this noble Ingas, once you pledge to stand alongside us our enemies become your enemies.'

'Thorn speaks truly. It is not an easy thing we ask of you this day. Do not bow the knee in haste or because of wounded pride.'

Rowan turned to Anselm as he spoke. Anselm held Rowan's fierce gaze for a heartbeat before turning his dark eyes towards the earth.

'I pledge the loyalty and service of the Gingas to the Guardians of the Realm of Men until the End of Days.'

Ingas bent his knee and it was done.

'There are gifts I bear from Moa Himself. I would speak with you alone.'

Then Ingas of the Gingas led Rowan, great Lord of the Angelis, into the cool of his lodge while Thorn, Anselm and the Elders waited outside in the heat of the day.'

The Shaman fell silent studying the upturned faces of the wide-eyed cubs.

'This night is your Time of Awakening. This night the gifts Moa bestowed upon the Gingas are yours by birthright. Do you choose to accept them?'

Buster was about to stand when the Shaman held up a paw, talons glinting in the firelight.

'Be warned, there is no turning back once the gifts have been freely received. Your fate will forever be linked to the fate of Men. Their enemies will be your enemies, the Orlok, chief among them. For thus began the bitter enmity between the Gingas and the Orlok, dark entities of the night.'

Orlok! Until now they had thought the creature but a mother's tale to frighten cublings.

Fear, that most unwelcome guest, took its place beside each cub as they watched shadows dance wildly on the aya skins.

'Behold!'

The Shaman bent forward and plunged his arm into a large urn that stood near his feet. In one swift movement, he held aloft an object. The cubs snarled and shrank back unable to look away from the grisly horror that dangled from the Shamans paw. An Orloks head stared at them in the firelight. It swung gently in the Shaman's grip as flames from the fire flickered across its face. The orlok's black eyes burned with hate and Buster growled deep in his throat as they seemed to turn upon him. The Shaman smiled.

'Behold your enemy, cublings of the Gingas, do you still desire your birthright?'

'Aieeeeeee!' they cried as one not wanting to show fear in the midst of the Elders.

Beyond the firelight in the shadows the Elders watched and remembered the day they had felt the same fear lay its icy paw upon their necks.

The Shaman returned the head back to the urn. He let his gaze fall upon each cubling in turn until all eyes were fixed upon him.

'It is time to reveal the Gateway to the Realm of Men. The first of the gifts Moa bestowed upon the Gingas through Rowan of the Angelis.'

The crackling of the logs echoed like thunder-claps as the Shaman suddenly scooped from his pouch a handful of dust and flung it onto the fire. Instead of thick smouldering smoke a dense mist arose enfolding Buster in a soft grey blanket. It was like the mist that rose from the Great River at the dawn of the day but it did not smell of fresh grass and flowers. Slowly it began to clear and strange, alien shapes formed in the semi darkness. Buster crouched down on his four paws ready to fight or flee and looked about him.

He recognised this place. He had been here before. Now he understood. The Gateway to the Realm of Men was through the Dream-Time. A cold sun shivered in a dark grey sky above his head. He was in a place full of lodges but unlike the lodges of the Gingas. These lodges stretched away on either side. At first Buster thought them to be one great lodge built not of aya skins but of stone. He looked for the lodge flaps but could see only rigid rectangles set in the walls like standing stones. Yet they were not made of skin or stone but wood. The Realm of Men must be rich in forests as was Ska. As he stood wondering one of the wooden flaps opened, then another and out into the grudging daylight stepped men.

Buster had never seen a man but it was said they were in form like the Angelis. The Shaman had spoken earlier of a light that radiated from within Rowan and his companions. These men were not clothed with light. Their grim faces were marked with blue scars from some tribal ritual or mementoes of old battles. More wooden flaps opened and more men spilled out onto the streets. Buster watched as they marched down the stone trail between the two lines of lodges. Where were they going? Then he saw it looming above the encampment and the hackles on his back rose.

It was round like the sun with black spokes radiating from the centre. It hung on black poles of iron that disappeared behind a cluster of large lodges. Buster guessed it was the sacred totem of the tribe. A high-pitched wail forced him to cover his ears and as he watched the men quicken their step he understood it was a call they were honour bound to obey. Around the totem the air was thick and dark. Buster sensed evil hung over the place like the shadow of a monstrous kark.

He was standing on one of the smooth stone trails that ran alongside the lodges. The wooden flaps were set back in the lodge walls and he flattened himself against one as he heard footsteps approaching rough and hard. Two men passed without glancing his way. He let out a deep breath relieved they had not seen him when the wooden flap behind him opened without warning.

Too late Buster stepped back onto the smooth stones. A man stood on the threshold. A man with fierce dark eyes, hooked nose and black mournful whiskers. His piercing eyes widened in surprise and in that moment Buster knew he had been discovered. Should he turn and flee or stay? Was this meeting his appointed destiny? Buster stood at a crossroads but whichever way he looked he could see only darkness. The man was looking at him and in that moment Buster knew he had come face to face with his fate.

A female voice sounded from within the lodge. The man nodded a silent greeting before stepping onto the stone trail following the path the other men had taken towards the looming totem. Buster watched him disappear and did not notice the woman. She stood on the threshold gazing after the man until he was lost among the throng crowding the narrow trail.

'Goodbye cariad,' she whispered.

There was a sadness in her voice that touched Buster's heart. He had never seen a fairer creature and could not imagine among the Angelis there was a female lovelier than the one who stood before him. Buster was so bewitched by her beauty he could only stand and stare. He heard the Shaman's voice echo inside his head.

'. . . there is one who has already crossed its threshold.'

The Dream Time! He had been here before in the Dream Time. Only then it was as though he peered through a swirling mist catching only fleeting glimpses. A man cubling with dark hair alone at night on the stone trail except for a large ginger creature that walked alongside him. A towering lodge made of wood and stone with dark winding pathways where evil shadows lurked unseen. A sense of danger, of orloks! An old man shivering in the cold night, crouching like a hunter waiting for his prey. Newborns nestling in wooden cradles. Twins. Confusing fragments of another world. Now Buster stood on the hard ground among the stone lodges and knew this was different from the Dream Time, this was real.

It was too late to run now she had seen him.

To Buster's surprise the woman turned back into the lodge. She could not have seen him. How was that possible? Perhaps he had not yet fully entered the Realm of Men and was not yet visible to them. Then why had the man acknowledged him but said nothing? The door was open. Buster stepped inside.

A single candle on a wooden trestle lit the room. Fire burned in a hearth set against the lodge wall. Something lay on the wooden trestle. A small slip of parchment with an image engraved upon it. Buster was startled by how the artist captured the likeness. Fierce dark eyes stared up at him as they had done only moments before and in them Buster saw a deep sadness. The cries of a newborn cubling drew him away from the trestle to an opening in the inner lodge wall. The woman was standing over the two wooden cradles he had seen in the Dream Time. She bent over and lifted a squealing cubling from its nest. It stopped crying and fixed its eyes upon Buster.

'What can you see cariad?' she cooed gently rubbing her face against the cubling, 'Dada's gone.'

She rocked the cubling to and fro singing softly. Its gaze never wavered. Its eyes were the deep violet that mingles with the blood red of a Ska sunset. After a while its eyes closed and the woman gently lowered it back into its nest.

'Sleep little one. When you wake Dada will be home.'

Her voice broke and she covered her face with her hands. Buster slipped out quietly. He was sure the child had seen him. The wooden flap was still open and Buster stepped onto the stone trail. A thick mist cloaked the settlement so he could not see his way. Confused he turned back towards the house but instead of solid ground beneath his feet he plunged into a darkness deeper than the night.

Myriad stars lit the spiralling whirlpool into which Buster plunged. He opened his mouth but no sound came. Instead of falling his body drifted like gossamer seed in an endless expanse of space. An overwhelming feeling of peace and well-being engulfed him. He closed his eyes surrendering himself completely to its comforting embrace. Voices as distant as the stars spoke his name. He opened his eyes and watched orange flecks of light float past his vision. The voices grew louder becoming one voice. His limbs grew heavy and he stumbled forward into the arms of the Shaman who was speaking his name.

Embers flew upwards from the blazing fire then died and fell as ashes to the ground. Firm hands gripped him by the shoulders. Slowly his spirit returned. Once again Buster stood in the Lodge of Elders gazing into the grave eyes of the Shaman. In the firelight, other eyes glittered in the semi darkness. The cubs gazed up at him their faces solemn as though they had witnessed an event of great meaning.

"Buster of the Gingas you have this night met your destiny. Your spirit crossed the threshold of the Realm of Men. It is time to receive fully the gifts of Moa for there is one here tonight who asks that you honour the pledge of Ingas."

The Shaman moved aside and a figure stepped forward from beyond the firelight. He was tall. A hooded cloak partly hid his face but from his bearing Buster knew he was a man. Yet Bws-ta was unprepared for the words the Shaman spoke.

"Welcome to our lodges Rowan, Great Lord of the Angelis."

CHAPTER 28

OLD SOLDIERS

Billy was in a garden. It was night. He stood in a tangle of bushes, trees and plants staring across a great stretch of lawn towards a big house. The house was framed by a harvest moon that spilled silver light over the rooftop. It was not the Red Lady's house. It was smaller and much more modern. 'Posh' was the word that sprung to mind. French windows faced out onto the garden. Light from a table lamp lit the room pushing the shadows back into dark corners. In its dim glow Billy could see someone moving around. Billy was overcome by an urgent need to discover who the shadowy figure was.

Avoiding the patch of pale light shed by the windows he crept towards the house. Billy knew he was not awake but he wasn't dreaming either. It was as if he had discovered a hidden place between dreams and the waking world. A place just as real but one in which he felt a strange power surge through him. A place where Nan had spoken to him and where monsters lived. He was not afraid for himself but for someone he knew was in great danger. He simply had to see who was in that room.

Flattening himself against the wall of the house Billy crept forward until he reached the window. He waited a moment listening for any sound from inside. Either the person had left the room or the triple glazing deadened any noise. He leaned sideways, making sure only his head and shoulders were visible, and peered through the window.

At first Billy thought the room was empty. Then he noticed the armchair. The high back of the chair was turned towards him. Someone sat in it. A bald head glistened in the lamplight like the helmet of a sentry patrolling the ramparts of a castle. What should he do? His first thought was to knock the window with his fist. He quickly decided it was a bad idea. This was not a game of *'knock ginger'*. Besides he promised Mum he would never play that game again after the incident with grumpy old Mr. Stevens. How was Billy to know he had a weak heart?

Before Billy could decide what to do the figure in the chair stood up. Billy recognised him straight away. He no longer had a large lump on his head but there was no mistaking it was the same man Billy had met outside *The Hollies*. Billy remembered the old man he saved from being dumped there. They had taken an instant shine to one another. Matron went ballistic and chased him through the rhododendron bushes. The man took his father and left. Billy waved at the black limo as it passed and from inside the old man waved back.

The Gaffer's son moved towards the window. Billy ducked and slipped back into the shadows.

He flattened himself on the grass and watched
Mr. Gardner-Allen place two hands on the glass
and lean forward. Billy was sure he was scanning
the garden searching for something, but what? He
was certain he had not been seen. There was a
strange glint in Mr. Gardner-Allen's eyes. Billy
tried to think what it reminded him of. Then it
struck him, he looked just like Mum when she
walks in her sleep. It had given Billy the fright of
his life the first time she wandered into his
bedroom in her flannel nightie and hair full of
curlers.

Mr. Gardner-Allen wasn't wearing curlers
because there was nothing left to curl but there
was no mistaking those empty eyes. Billy turned
his head in the direction Mr. Gardner-Allen was
staring and that was when he saw it. The
rectangle of light from the window became a
blank canvas framing a strange shadow. Billy
spun around to see if the thing was lurking in the
undergrowth watching him. There could be no
doubt. It was the same creature emblazoned on
the Roderick Coat of Arms, the one he glimpsed
in the 'back lane, the one that carried off Matron
in the dream hospital.

Something was not right. The shadow did not
come from the undergrowth it came from the
house. The light from the standard lamp cast the
shadow onto the lawn. It should have been Mr.
Gardner-Allen's. There was no way it was.
Puzzled, Billy edged back towards the shelter of

the trees and shrubbery. His dream was revealing something important. He just could not think what it was.

He was now close to the safety of the undergrowth. Moving backwards on his hands and knees he kept his eyes fixed on Mr. Gardner-Allen, if that's who it was standing at the window. The next moment the ground fell away beneath him.

He tumbled headlong down a steep slope. Soft earth shifted beneath his weight and as he fell head over heels he caught fractured glimpses of an azure blue sky in which a fierce sun dazzled his eyes. Billy sat up and looked around. He was no longer in the garden but lying at the bottom of an enormous sand dune. He listened for the sound of waves breaking on the shore but instead a harsh screaming filled the air. A plane hurtled down from the clear skies like an angry hornet. Billy watched fascinated. It could be a scene from the old war movies his father loved to watch whenever Mum was in a good mood. As it drew closer Billy could see a swastika emblazoned on its wings.

"Blimey mate, do you want to get us all killed?"

Strong arms gripped Billy by the shoulders and he was half wrestled half dragged to the floor. The next moment what Billy took to be a large blanket was thrown over him.

"Bloody stukas!" said another voice. "Jerry must have sniffed us out."

The ground beneath him shook in the wake of a tremendous explosion. Billy covered his ears but too late to stop his head ringing like the inside of a church belfry. Several more explosions followed each more distant than the last until a wary silence descended.

The tarpaulin was thrown back and Billy understood why he had not seen the men hiding at the bottom of the dune. It was almost impossible to make out the canvas from the surrounding desert and made them invisible to enemy planes flying overhead. Three men staggered from under its cover. They wore khaki shirts, shorts and steel helmets so Billy knew they were soldiers. Two of the men began to examine a large crater carved out of the sand by the enemy plane. One took off his helmet and scratched his head.

"I can't believe we're still in one piece," he said in bewilderment as he stared at the hole that could have become their grave.

"Someone must be watching over us," replied his companion.

The third soldier stood over Billy studying him through narrowed eyes. Billy looked up but the soldier's face was masked in sunlight.

"What unit you from?" said the soldier.

"99 Amelia Terrace," said Billy not sure if that was the right answer.

"Is that some sort of code?"

The soldier sounded suspicious.

"It's my house," answered Billy.

"You trying to be funny son?"

"Go easy on him Vic, he's only a kid."

The other two soldiers had wandered over and now flanked their companion.

"Exactly Sarge! What's a kid doing out here in the desert so far behind enemy lines?" persisted Vic. "You know how cunning Jerry is. He could be a spy."

"I'm not Jerry's spy," said an indignant Billy, "I don't even know Jerry."

One of the soldiers laughed. Vic didn't. He continued to stare down at Billy in a way that made him feel like he did when Ellis Kinsey and his gang surrounded him in the playground.

"Vic, go up top for a recce just in case Jerry is creeping around out there."

"Ok Sarge, but keep an eye on him. There could be more where he came from."

Vic stared at Billy for a few more seconds before clambering up the side of the dune.

"Walter, check the gear. Let me know the damage."

The soldier named Walter crawled across to the far end of the dune. The Sarge sat down next to Billy, took off his helmet and wiped the sweat off his brow. There was something very familiar about him.

"Well this is a rum do. Like Vic said, what's a kid doing out here in the desert behind enemy lines?"

Billy made no reply because he had no idea what the answer was himself.

"And if I'm not mistaken," the Sarge continued, "a kid with a valleys' accent like mine."

Billy blinked but said nothing.

"What's your name?"

"Billy."

"Where you from Billy?"

"Fernhill."

"Fernhill?"

The Sarge sounded shocked. His eyes narrowed just as Vic's had done.

"That's where I'm from. Quite a coincidence wouldn't you say Billy?"

Billy nodded. He was not sure what 'coincidence' meant but under the circumstances it seemed best just to agree.

"Small place Fernhill," the Sarge was beginning to sound like Mr. Meredith whenever Billy appeared in his office. "I wouldn't be surprised if we didn't know the same people. What do you think Billy?"

Once again, based on bitter experience, Billy decided a nod was the best response.

"Let me show you something."

The Sarge fished around in one of the two large pockets on the breast of his shirt. Eventually he produced an object and held it in front of Billy's face. It was a photograph of a young man and a dark haired young woman. They were arm in arm gazing lovingly into each other's eyes.

"Ever seen her before?" asked the Sarge.

Billy stared at the photo and nodded. He knew both. The Sarge looked shocked. It was a long time before he broke the heavy silence.

"Do you know her name?" he said in a husky voice.

"It's Nan," said Billy, "my Nan."

When the Sarge next spoke his words had an icy edge.

"Her name's not Nan. You're lying boy. The question is why?"

"I'm not lying. She's my Nan. Her name is Emma. Emma Jenkins." Billy placed a finger on the young man in the photo. "And that's you, the Gaffer."

There was no doubt in Billy's mind that the young man in the photo was the Gaffer. It was the same photo Billy had seen in the family album.

The Sarge's mouth dropped open and he gaped at Billy wide eyed."

"How," he began but the words stuck on his parched tongue and the question never left his lips for at that moment Vic returned scrambling down the steep slope of the dune in a cloud of sand.

"Jerry!" shouted Vic. "Take cover."

Once more Billy found himself manhandled to the ground as the soldiers scrambled to cover themselves with the tarpaulin. He struggled to break free but strong arms held him tight and he was yanked into the covering darkness. Billy blinked. Overhead a sickly moon held sway in a starless night sky. Instead of warm sand brushing against his skin like a dog's rough tongue he felt cold, moist, dew damp grass lick his face and hands. Billy sat up. The soldiers were gone. The desert had vanished. He was back in the garden facing the large house and he knew he was not alone.

The house was in darkness so Billy could not tell whether someone or something was still staring out onto the garden. He strained his eyes to see if anything was lurking nearby or crawling between the silver pools of moonlight towards him. A grunting sound made him spin around sharply. He had been right, he was not alone. A few yards away an old man sat propped against the base of a large elm. The old man's knees were tucked under his chin and he clutched a blanket tightly to his chest. Around his neck dangled a string of onions. He was snoring loudly. On the ground by his side lay a large hammer and a wooden spoon that had been sharpened at one end.

Billy was gobsmacked. He didn't think old people went camping but then this was just a dream. No, not just a dream, Billy doubted he would ever have a normal dream again. He approached the old man wondering if he should wake him. Two paces away he stopped. What was it the young Gaffer said about coincidences? Billy thought he understood now. The old man under the tree may not have been dressed in khaki but there was no mistaking he was the same man who had shown Billy the photo of Nan just minutes before. Minutes? More like a lifetime thought Billy as he recalled the bright alert eyes of the young sergeant he'd met in the desert. Another thought slithered inside Billy's head, just how different was he?

A movement in the bushes on the opposite side of the elm from where he stood caught Billy's eye. The orlok stepped into the clearing hovering over the slumbering Gaffer like a grotesque bird of prey. The Red Lady's words echoed in Billy's head.

"... the Nameless Horror that dogs your footsteps."

He saw her fall like a dead Autumn leaf and a sudden anger bubbled up from deep within.

"Don't touch him!" he cried and his voice was strong and commanding.

Startled, the orlok turned to face Billy. A coldness in its eyes matched the fire in Billy's. Suddenly a bird broke into song and in an instant, a joyous dawn chorus filled the garden. The orlok sniffed the air, snarled then turned to Billy.

"Your blood is mine Angelis."

It held Billy's gaze for a moment before slipping back into the dappled darkness of the undergrowth. Billy watched it go. He supposed he should be afraid but all he could feel was anger and disgust. One thing for sure, he was not going to leave the Gaffer keep his lonely vigil on his own. He sat down beside the old man determined to watch over him until the dawn fully broke. The Gaffers' rhythmic snoring was strangely soothing. Billy closed his eyes confident that he would not fall asleep because he was already dreaming.

CHAPTER 29

A GREAT WARRIOR OF THE GINGAS

The stranger threw back his hood and light shone forth chasing the shadows outside into the waiting night.

"It as an honour to be guest in the lodge of the descendants of Ingas, Warrior-King and Healer of Tribes."

The Shaman bowed his head and Rowan let his gaze fall upon the upturned faces of the awestruck cublings.

"I see your hearts are strong and true. A good omen. Tonight, the Gifts of Moa are yours. Use them wisely in pursuit of what is right and good."

Although the cubs did not speak Buster knew they felt his confusion. He did not know quite what he had expected but not this simple speech. He did not feel any different and was disappointed there had not been any great display of power or magic befitting such an occasion. It was as though Rowan read his thoughts.

"It is the foolish and weak in spirit who desire the empty trappings of power. Is that not so Shaman?"

The Shaman nodded.

"No creature drinks until he thirsts. When the time is needful the gifts will reveal themselves."

It was not the answer Buster or the other cubs had hoped for. What were these gifts? How could they be sure they truly owned them? Why did the Shaman speak in riddles?

"Return now to your lodges. Not as cubs but as Gingas who follow the path laid down by Ingas himself. Be proud. Be worthy. Be Gingas."

Before the words of the Shaman Buster's disappointment shrivelled and died like last autumn's leaves. Pride blossomed in his heart.

"Aieeeeeee!" he cried.

His voice was one with the other cublings who this night had taken the first step on the pathway of a destiny that stretched before them. How far and to what end none could tell for the way ahead lay hidden.

Proud parents ushered their cublings out of the Great Lodge and Buster watched them go envy filling his heart. He waited for the last to file outside before following.

"Bws-ta of the Gingas. I would speak with you."

It was the voice of Rowan. Buster froze, his thoughts scattering like hunted aya.

"There is nothing to fear. Come sit with us."

Rowan sat down cross legged before the fire and the Shaman followed his lead. Buster stood open-mouthed as Rowan patted the ground next to him. Forcing his body to obey Buster sat beside the Great Lord of the Angelis. Silence roared in Buster's ears more deafening than the great waterfall of *Erenlas*. The Shaman's eyes were shut, his head bowed as though his spirit travelled a distant trail but Rowan's golden eyes remained fixed upon Buster.

"Why did you ask me to stay?"

Rowan smiled at Buster's question as though it amused him.

"Always you seek the truth," he said, "the Shaman chose wisely. Tell me of your parents?"

"They are no more."

Buster spoke quickly. It was not something he would talk about. Rowan's eyes were fierce forcing Buster to answer.

"They were killed when I was a cubling."

"By orloks?"

Buster nodded and stared at the ground.

"Tell me," commanded Rowan.

The day had been long and hot. Clouds of dry dust billowed across the vast plains as the ayas fled before the hunting steeds of the Gingas. It had been a successful hunt. A small group of ayas, separated from the main herd, fled into a narrow ravine in the cliffs that flanked the northern boundary of the plains. Buster and his parents gave chase.

The deeper they rode into the ravine the narrower it became until they were forced to ride in single file. Overhanging bushes grew between clefts in outcrops of boulders above them blotting out the sun. The air became cold and moist and the hooves of their steeds echoed like drumbeats off the steep rock sides. With hardly enough room to turn there was no going back and still no sight of the ayas. Slivers of shattered sunlight scattered the trail ahead and Buster's father slowed the steeds to walking pace. Suddenly they stopped. In the rapidly increasing gloom Buster could not see what made his father rein in his mount. Without warning, Buster's steed reared and snorted in panic almost throwing him to the ground.

The ravine opened out onto a large enclosed circle of land bounded by high cliffs. Buster had never seen the ruins of the great amphitheatres built by the Ancients but he had heard tales. As he looked about he wondered whether they had stumbled upon one of these forgotten places. His father and mother dismounted but Buster remained on his steed absently smoothing the rough tuft of hair between its curved horns. It tossed its head and grunted and nothing Buster could do would calm the beast. Perhaps it could see the shades of the dead who once walked this place in life. Buster shivered and not because the sun was sliding away below the crimson rimmed horizon. He wanted to leave this place. The steeds too were anxious to be gone.

Black circular holes scarred the sides of the cliffs and Buster guessed they must be caves. Yet they were set the same distance apart as though purposely carved out of the rock face. They stared down at him watchful and unblinking.

"Look!"

Buster strained to see what had caught his father's eye as the shadows of the dying day crept towards them. A group of ayas drank from a black pool of brackish water that trickled from a rugged outcrop of rock. They lifted their heads and Buster hoped they would scatter and flee. Instead, they huddled together forming a tight circle, massive heads lowered, horns turned outwards ready to protect their young or die.

Buster's father dismounted, strung his bow and crept forward.

"Bws-ta, stay with the steeds," said his mother as she made to follow his father.

She paused and turned towards her young cubling. Her eyes were large and in them he saw his fear haunted face stare back at him.

"I do not like this place. It smells of death. If anything should befall us, you must find your way back to the others."

He wanted to speak, to plead with her not to leave him but his throat was dry. The words refused to come. Placing a hand on his thigh she looked up at him.

"Be proud. Be worthy."

She spoke the words softly before slipping away across the darkening earth.

Buster watched his parents move stealthily over open ground. The ayas shifted nervously lowering their heads. It did not seem right. They were downwind and could not be scented at such a distance. Yet something had spooked the creatures.

Buster bowed his head.

"I can remember no more," he said.

"Some of our scouts found him clinging to the horns of his steed. He did not wake for two days. When he did he could remember nothing."

There was a rare softness in the Shaman's voice and as he spoke to Rowan he kept his gaze fixed upon Buster.

"We followed his tracks. They led towards a narrow ravine. Night was falling around us and our steeds refused to enter."

"You were one of them?" said Rowan.

The Shaman nodded and Buster lifted his head. Why had the Shaman not spoken of this before? Their eyes met but it was the Shaman who looked away.

"Continue," said Rowan.

The Shaman paused. It was a trail he did not want to tread a second time.

"We set out at dawn. Even then our mounts had to be coaxed to enter that accursed place. The ravine was narrow so we rode slowly in single file. We held our bows in readiness ever watchful of the shadows cast by overhanging bushes and outcrops of rock. The ravine opened onto a circle of bare ground. An ancient killing place from which there is no escape. As I gazed at the high cliffs and saw the dark pattern of caves I strung an arrow to my bow. I signalled the others to do the same. There was no need, every Ginga had strung an arrow in readiness.

Your parents did not die easily Bws-Ta. The bodies of many orloks lay pierced with shafts. We had to dismount because the steeds would not go near them."

"Is that where you found my parents?"

Buster's question arrowed its way towards the Shaman. The Shaman turned to Rowan hoping to deflect it elsewhere. The Great Lord of the Angelis offered him no place to hide.

"This night he has become Ginga. Does he not deserve the truth?"

The Shaman nodded and turned to Buster as though carrying a heavy burden upon his shoulders.

"We wrapped their remains in aya skins and strapped them to the steeds."

He waited while the meaning of his words struck home. For a moment tears clouded Buster's eyes but then anger gripped his chest and filled his heart and he brushed away his sorrow."

"Continue," he urged the Shaman.

"Although the sun was climbing the heavens a chill touched our bones and we were anxious to be gone. It was an evil place. The caves belonged to the orlok. I had seen their like before. They seek out and haunt dark places especially those within the heart and mind of living creatures.

A terrible anger filled me like the fire that now burns within you. I crossed to where one of the orloks lay still breathing, in my hand the blade I use to skin the ayas. I knelt beside the foul creature and was about to raise my hand to strike when its eyes opened and it gripped my wrist. I could not break free."

"Did it beg for its life?"

Buster's eyes shone as he imagined the creature's fear.

"It said, 'No mercy Shaman.' Your father had been my friend. I struck down savagely."

"I wish I could have looked into its eyes?" said Buster.

He did not notice or care that the Shaman spoke as one who feels shame.

"You did," replied the Shaman as he turned his gaze upon the urn.

The image of the head dangling from the Shaman's hand twisting in the firelight flashed before him. Buster reached for the urn but Rowan placed a hand on his head and a sudden shock surged through his body.

The creature looked up at him. In its eyes an unholy flame flickered like the embers of a hateful dying fire. Buster turned his head. Orloks littered the ground. Feathered shafts flowered from their bodies staining the ground black with their foul blood. Without warning the creature lunged at him. Buster winced as its bony fingers curled tightly around his wrist. He tried to pull away but the orlok's nails dug into his flesh.

"No mercy Shaman."

Buster saw no fear. Even now the creature taunted him. Buster lifted his head and a cry escaped his lips scattering the scavenging karks. They rose as one flapping black cloud their shrieking cries mocking his own. In his free hand, he felt the weight of the skinning blade. In his heart grief and rage. The orlok was smiling as Buster brought down the blade. There was triumph in its eyes.

The knife sunk into the hard earth beside the orlok's head. Its eyes widened in disbelief and with a cry as desolate as the barren place it gasped its last breath. Buster dropped the knife and rolled away. He knelt and pressed his forehead against the dry ground knowing he had failed to avenge the death of his parents, knowing he was a coward.

A hand rested upon his shoulder.

Buster looked up into the face of Rowan. Rowan was smiling at him. Outside the wind howled against the night.

"Mercy is the weapon of great warriors," said Rowan. "Bws-Ta of the Gingas, I salute you."

He turned towards the Shaman.

"You have taught well Shaman. He is ready for the task."

'Task?' What was Rowan talking about?

"Come with me Bws-Ta, Mighty Warrior of the Gingas, there is someone you must meet."

Rowan stood. The Shaman and Buster followed his lead. Without speaking he led them out of the lodge's warm embrace into the cold hard night.

CHAPTER 30

THE GAFFER'S LAST CAMPAIGN

"Dad are you coming down for breakfast?"

Mrs. Gardner-Allen shouted up the stairs for the third time. There was no reply. "You have a word with him Vernon, I expect he's a bit upset."

From the kitchen came the sound of a newspaper rustling.

"Sulking more like. He gets more cantankerous by the day."

Mrs. Gardner-Allen sighed. Something was wrong. She couldn't believe her husband was going to take the Gaffer to the nursing home run by that dreadful woman with the twitch. She decided things had gone far enough whatever the Gaffer had done this time. Goodness knows he could be difficult but the house would be empty without him. This nonsense must end. She strode into the kitchen.

"Vernon!"

Her husband remained hidden behind the paper. Annoyed at being ignored Mrs. Gardner-Allen raised her voice.

"Vernon, put that paper down I want to talk to you."

"What?"

Mr. Gardner-Allen ignored his wife's request.

Something was wrong. Her husband had been acting strangely lately. She couldn't put her finger on what had caused the change in his behaviour but change it had. Normally easy going and good tempered he had become moody and distant. It was as if his old self was fading away and in its place a new version was emerging from some dark cocoon.

Mrs. Gardner-Allen reached forward and yanked the newspaper from her husband's grasp.

"Will you please listen to me?"

Mr. Gardner-Allen did not reply but the look in his eyes made Mrs. Gardner-Allen take a step backwards. She refused to be bullied.

"You can't be serious about sending Dad away?" she said, surprised by the tremor in her voice.

For a few uncomfortable seconds her husband stared at her without speaking. *"Where's my Vernon gone?"* she thought as she looked back into the cold eyes of the man who was becoming a stranger.

"I could just about put up with his barmy behaviour but now he's completely out of control. Do you really want to share your home with a senile homicidal maniac?"

"Dad's not dangerous. That business with the postman was a misunderstanding," said Mrs. Gardner-Allen springing to the Gaffer's defence.

"Misunderstanding?" sneered Mr. Gardner-Allen.

"Dad didn't know it was the postman, he thought. . ." Mrs. Gardner-Allen stopped abruptly in mid-sentence as she realised what she was about to say.

"He thought it was a vampire? That's alright then, everybody knows we have real problems with vampires in Fernhill," smirked Mr Gardner-Allen.

"He's your father," said Mrs. Gardner-Allen as she searched her husband's face for a trace of kindness.

"Exactly and it's up to me to make sure he doesn't harm anybody. He needs around the clock supervision. He's a danger to himself and everyone around him."

Mr. Gardner-Allen picked up the newspaper. Once again Mrs. Gardner-Allen found herself staring at the back pages. Without thinking she glanced out into the garden. There may be no such things as vampires but Mrs. Gardner-Allen knew something had changed. The Gaffer sensed it too, only he let his imagination get the better of him.

Her mind drifted back to her schooldays. She was surprised how vivid the waking memory was. It was the day she and her friends decided to slip back into their classroom to escape the biting cold Winter playground. They were sure no one had noticed. Climbing on the desks at the back of the classroom they watched little groups of children huddle together for warmth like mountain sheep in a storm. Bubbling with bravado they banged on the window, laughing and giggling at their shivering classmates. Without warning the door burst open and Miss Smith stood there large and threatening.

The laughter died on their lips. No one spoke. The silence a living creature, coiled and ready to strike. Mrs. Gardner-Allen still had nightmares about that moment. The garden felt like that now. Silent and empty of birdsong as though all living creatures had fled. Is this what had upset the Gaffer? Her husband said it was probably cats. There had been a sighting of a large ginger tom in the neighbourhood but surely the birds would not leave the garden for the sake of one cat however oversized. There might not be vampires in Fernhill but something was wrong and Mrs. Gardner-Allen was beginning to think her husband was part of the problem.

"I'm going upstairs to see if Dad's alright," said Mrs. Gardner-Allen.

Her husband grunted from behind the paper. Mrs. Gardner-Allen turned and found herself face to face with the Gaffer. He stood in the doorway wearing the beret he had worn in the war. Across his chest glistened a row of medals. At his feet, a bulging kit bag seemed about to bust its seams.

"Dad? What are you doing?" said Mrs. Gardner-Allen a sinking feeling in her stomach.

Mr. Gardner-Allen lowered the paper and peered at his father through narrowed eyes.

"You ready then?" he said as though he were about to take his elderly father shopping not depositing him in a nursing home run by a scary Matron with a facial tic.

"Vernon, you can't be serious?" said Mrs. Gardner-Allen but she might as well have been invisible.

Mr. Gardner-Allen and the Gaffer stared at each other across the room. It was the Gaffer who broke the uncomfortable silence.

"No need," he said, "taxi's outside."

"Dad you can't leave like this," said Mrs. Gardner-Allen on the verge of tears.

Mr. Gardner-Allen disappeared back behind the newspaper.

A horn tooted. The Gaffer picked up his kit bag and without looking back struggled to the front door. Mrs. Gardner-Allen glanced back at her husband before following after the Gaffer.

"Dad please, wait."

The Gaffer ignored her plea. The determined set of his shoulders meant his mind was made up and nothing on earth would change it now.

The taxi driver was loading the Gaffer's kit bag into the boot as the Gaffer opened the passenger door.

"Dad!"

The Gaffer turned to Mrs. Gardner-Allen his face grim.

"Don't go into the garden after dark," he said before easing himself inside.

The taxi pulled off and Mrs. Gardner-Allen watched it disappear around the curve of the drive.

The Gaffer was gone. Taking the corner of her cashmere sweater she dabbed her eyes. She waited until she could no longer hear tyres grating on gravel. A thick silence closed about her and she glanced towards the tangled undergrowth at the edge of the lawn. She could see or hear nothing but felt she was being watched from within the shifting shadows. A sudden chill brushed her skin. Drawing the sweater tightly about her she hurried back inside.

Matron stood by the window and watched the taxi pull up outside. She smiled as the driver opened the passenger door and helped the old man out. The Gaffer stood on the pavement looking towards *'The Hollies'* and Matron knew what dark thoughts filled his head. No, more than that, she could see them clearly like swirling tendrils of thick mist clouding the path ahead and shrouding the way he had come. It was a sixth sense that grew stronger with each passing day. Where this strange gift came from she did not know but she was sure it was linked to the vivid dreams that came each night. Now she walked the corridors sensing the worries and fears of residents as a fox scents its prey.

The first time she used it was against that horrible child's grandmother. The memory of the scruffy child with the dark piercing eyes still raised her blood pressure to dangerous levels. How he had loved his precious Nan. Matron took great delight in tormenting them both once the old woman's fears had been revealed by the strange power she now possessed. More than anything the old woman dreaded becoming a burden and hated being treated like a child. From that moment at every opportunity Matron took secret pleasure in treating Billy's Nan like a spoilt little girl. It was especially satisfying when Billy was present. She felt his dark hateful eyes upon her and tasted his hidden rage like a strange exotic fruit on her tongue. Yet the boy still haunted her dreams.

The taxi driver lifted the bulging kit bag out of the boot and was about to carry it up the path when the old man wrestled it from his grasp. Shrugging his shoulders, the taxi driver clambered back into his cab and drove off leaving the Gaffer alone on the pavement. Matron watched the old man struggle to lift the kit bag before trudging, head bowed, up the gravel driveway. She recalled Mr. Gardner-Allen's words the day Billy appeared like a dark stain on her starched blouse.

"We've changed our minds. The Gaffer, Dad . . . Dad, uh is not going into any nursing home . . . no. Uh, we'd miss him too much. Dear me, no, unthinkable! Just thought we'd come and let you know in person, so to speak."

And now here he was tramping up the drive towards her waiting arms. This time they had not even bothered to accompany their beloved elderly relative. Matron understood completely. Some people lived too long, what else could they expect? She glanced around the garden but no scruffy child lurked among the bushes just a stray dog, a poodle she thought, making use of the horse chestnut tree as dogs do.

The dog trotted across to the old man who paused to ruffle its head and catch his breath before lugging his kit bag the last few steps. It was uncanny the way the dog seemed to sense the old man's distress as it nuzzled against his hand. Matron and the dog watched the Gaffer stagger the last painful paces, his unhappiness as strong in her nostrils as the aroma of fresh cut flowers. The dog whimpered and scampered away down the drive. She would need to do something about the disgusting creature eventually but that could wait. Time to greet her new guest.

The Gaffer stood to attention outside the main entrance of *The Hollies*, shoulders squared, chest thrust forward. An old soldier preparing for his last battle. Marching forward he pressed the bell and stepped smartly backwards. After a few seconds, the door opened and Matron appeared squinting in the sunlight. She looked beyond the Gaffer as if searching for someone before turning back to the pathetic old man. Where did he think he was, the parade ground? She smiled to herself.

He would soon discover who gave the orders now.

"On your own?" she said.

Often sympathy could break the spirit quicker than harsh words. The Gaffer said nothing. He looked straight ahead as though he had not heard.

"I expect they have more important things to do."

Matron watched to see if her words had found their mark but the old man continued to stare into the distance. He would be a tough nut to crack but Matron relished a challenge. The old woman proved difficult but that was because she had the boy. The old man was alone. Loneliness would be her accomplice.

"Welcome to your new home," she said as she stepped aside and gestured towards the open doors. "Follow me, I expect you could do with a nice cup of tea. Unfortunately, you've just missed breakfast."

Matron turned on her heels and disappeared inside. The Gaffer waited a moment before lifting the kit bag and following.

The Gaffer blinked, his eyes adjusting to the dimly lit entrance hall. Matron stood with her arms folded watching him as he took in his new surroundings. Freshly cut flowers in a vase on a table near the entrance could not disguise the overpowering stench of chlorine mingled with urine. Behind Matron a corridor stretched away as far as he could see. Doors were set on either side and the Gaffer guessed one of them led to his new 'home'. A lumbering figure appeared at the far end of the corridor. As it approached the Gaffer could see it wore a crumpled blue uniform, the kind worn by male nurses.

"This is Ryland," said Matron as the figure drew near. "He will be looking after you from now on."

Ryland smiled, his small piggy eyes almost disappearing in his round face. He took a step towards the Gaffer and reached for the kit bag. The Gaffer tried to resist but it proved useless. Ryland was too strong and easily plucked it from the old man's grasp.

"Now, now Grandad," said Ryland softly, "don't be difficult. It wouldn't do to start off on the wrong foot, would it?"

"I'm not your grandad," said the Gaffer.

The smile melted and Ryland's small beady eyes peered coldly at the Gaffer. After a few seconds, it became clear the Gaffer was not going to back down.

"Follow me," Ryland said as he turned away and lumbered back down the corridor leaving the Gaffer with no choice but to trail behind in his wake.

"I'll bring you tea in ten minutes," Matron called after them.

The room was larger than the Gaffer expected. The carpet was blue as was the door only a shade darker. A white wardrobe stood in one corner and a wing backed armchair in another. Along one wall under the window was a wash basin and laminated worktop complete with electric kettle. The bed, set against the far wall, was covered in a floral-patterned duvet that matched the pillowslips and curtains. The Gaffer hated floral patterns of any kind. The proper place for flowers was in a garden. Next to the bed was a cabinet on which sat a jug of water. A dead fly floated on the greasy surface. The Gaffer gazed out of the window as Ryland dropped the hold all by the side of the bed.

"I'll leave you to make yourself at home," said Ryland allowing '*home*' to linger on his tongue.

The Gaffer made no reply and continued to stare out of the window. Ryland waited a few moments then shrugged his shoulders before closing the door behind him. There was the sound of a key being turned in the lock and then the fading echo of footsteps. The Gaffer sat on the edge of the bed. He often wondered what it was like for his old comrades who had been captured by the enemy and spent the rest of the war rotting in some prison camp. Now he would find out for himself but for him this war would never end.

The Gaffer carefully unpinned his medals before folding them neatly in their ribbons. There would be none awarded for this campaign. Opening the top drawer of the bedside cabinet he was about to place them inside when they slipped from his grasp with a clatter. Ignoring them he reached inside with trembling hands and took out an old photograph that must have belonged to the last occupant of the room. He studied the faded black and white image of a lost yesterday in disbelief. Surely it could not be? A pretty young woman with dark hair and bright blue eyes was gazing lovingly up at a young man. They were arm in arm smiling into each other's eyes and dreaming of a future that never was. Had she been here, in this place? Was this her room, the bed she slept in? If so, where was she now? Thoughts swirled around his head like autumn leaves in a storm.

The sound of the key in the lock startled the Gaffer. He hurriedly returned the picture to the top draw and stared down at his feet. Ryland and Matron entered.

"I see you haven't started to unpack then?" she said. "Still, plenty of time for that later. I've brought you a nice cup of tea."

The Gaffer lifted his head. He had missed breakfast and not had a drink all morning. His throat felt parched and dry. He reached out and took the drink. It was in a blue chipped mug not a cup but he had drunk from worse. The tea was cold and he spat a mouthful onto the carpet. Matron's eyes narrowed. Ryland shook his head slowly as he plucked the mug from the Gaffer's hand.

"Well, that wasn't very polite, was it? Not a good start, not a good start at all. I can see we may have to teach you some manners."

As she spoke Matron reached in her pocket and took out a small phial. The Gaffer watched her empty two purple pills onto the palm of her chubby hand.

"Still, I expect you must be a little upset. It's never nice knowing your family don't want you any more."

Matron offered the pills to the Gaffer but he shook his head and folded his arms.

"Not ill," he said clamping his jaw shut.

Matron's smile slipped off her face but Ryland grinned.

"It's just to help you relax. You've had a stressful morning. Now be a good boy and pop these into your mouth."

Matron's voice was soft and menacing. The Gaffer simply lowered his head until his chin touched his chest and stared hard at the floor.

"Very well, if you insist on being a stubborn old goat. Ryland!"

Keeping his head lowered the Gaffer tried to see what Ryland was up to out of the corner of his eye. Ryland picked up the jug from the bedside cabinet and poured water into a grubby plastic cup making sure the dead fly was included. He handed the cup to Matron. Then, with surprising speed for such a big man he wrapped the Gaffer in a meaty headlock with his left arm. The Gaffer tried to prise himself free but Ryland was too strong and he gave up the struggle his arms flopping limply by his side.

"Now open your mouth like a good boy," said Matron hovering over him like an overweight vulture.

The Gaffer ground his teeth together. A hug paw of a hand suddenly covered his face and for one terrible moment he thought he was going to suffocate. Ryland squeezed the Gaffer's face as if he were extracting juice from a lemon. The Gaffer's lips popped apart like a fish gasping for air and Matron dropped two purple tablets into his open mouth. The Gaffer felt them lodge at the back of his throat but before he could choke the contents of the plastic glass splashed against his tonsils washing the pills down his esophagus. Ryland released his grip and the Gaffer knelt forward, hands on knees, gagging for air.

"There," said Matron whose smile had now returned, "that wasn't so bad, was it? You just lie down and have a nice little rest and we'll give you a call when lunch is ready."

The Gaffer did not hear the door close above his strangled gasps for breath. Fifty years ago, that fat bully would never have dared lay a hand on him. He slumped back on the bed breathing hard. Fifty years ago, there was a girl with sparkling blue eyes. He remembered the photo in the cabinet and tried to push himself upright but a strange drowsiness enveloped him like a web. His eyes closed and he fell back onto the bed.

"We should go and see if he's ok," suggested Mrs. Gardner-Allen.

Her husband shook the newspaper but said nothing.

"Vernon, did you hear what I just said? I feel terrible we let him go off on his own like that."

Mr. Gardner-Allen lowered the paper and studied his wife for a moment before speaking.

"He'll be fine. Best give him a week or so to settle in."

"A week!" said Mrs. Gardner-Allen but her husband was no longer listening.

CHAPTER 31

A LIGHT IN THE DARKNESS

Rowan did not seem to feel the cold but it snapped at Buster with the savagery of starved mountain wolves. The Shaman led the way through the blizzard. With every other step his bent form disappeared in the swirling flakes of snow. Thoughts raced through Buster's mind as though fleeing the storm that howled about him. What was the task Rowan spoke of? Who was waiting to meet him? His mouth was dry. He felt more nervous than when he stood before the Shaman in the Great Lodge of the Gingas. He did not feel like a mighty warrior and hoped he would be worthy of whatever task had been chosen for him. They stopped outside the Shaman's lodge as Buster somehow knew they would. The Shaman lifted the flap and waited for Rowan to enter but Rowan stood aside and a firm hand pushed Buster forward.

Smoke from the central fire stung Buster's eyes clouding his vision. Herbs hung from lodge poles their fragrance pungent and heavy in his nostrils. He narrowed his eyes trying to make sense of the flickering shadows. One detached itself from the others and took shape before him. She was clothed in a blanket of thick dark fur that framed her pale features. This time she did not look through him as she had done in the stone lodges of the humans. She was as beautiful as he remembered except her face was thinner. Her eyes held the haunted look of the hunted.

"Molly, this is Bws-ta a Great Warrior of the Gingas. He will watch over your children and your children's children. That is his task."

Buster wondered at Rowan's words but the woman called Molly spoke quickly and scattered his thoughts like leaves in a gale.

"How? I've been away a long time. That creature will have. . ." she struggled to finish.

Her body shook tears coursing down her cheeks. Rowan placed a hand on her shoulder.

"Be at peace Molly. Time is not as you understand it. Bws-ta has this night received the Gifts of Moa. Ska is not like other worlds it is the Gateway to Realms. This night Bws-ta will return to yours. When the creature approaches your door Bws-ta will be there to protect your children."

Molly searched Rowan's face and he held her gaze unflinching. The words Rowan spoke should have sounded to Molly like the ravings of a madman but so much she could not explain had happened in a short time she simply nodded, then turned to Buster.

"Please," she pleaded, "save my babies."

"You will return to your children but first there is evil you must help undo."

Rowan looked at Buster.

"You remember the stone lodges where you first saw this woman in the dream time?"

"I remember," said Buster.

"Go there now," commanded Rowan, "your task has begun."

Buster waited for the Shaman to cast a handful of dust from his pouch onto the fire but he remained seated his eyes fixed on the failing flames. Rowan smiled.

"You need no help Bws-ta, the gift is yours. Close your eyes and receive it."

Buster closed his eyes and Rowan's voice faded until it became a distant echo falling into nothingness. He opened them.

A full moon streaked the roofs of the stone lodges with slashes of silver. Most were in shadow. Here and there a square of light interrupted the darkness. Buster crouched as a figure moved down the street towards him. He was outside the door of the lodge he had entered in the dream time. Light seeped beneath the closed wooden entrance and from inside Buster heard a crooning voice whispering soft and low. Buster guessed it was the woman and her cublings.

A sound of heavy footfalls grew louder by the second. Buster turned towards them a low growl rumbling deep in his throat. He stepped off the stone path to confront a large squat creature moving towards him. This would be his first battle. He would not fail. He watched as the creature passed through a sliver of light his body poised to spring. Instead he sat back on his haunches as a large female approached puffing and blowing from the effort of moving her flabby limbs. It was too late to hide so he simply sat and waited.

"Oh, my saints!"

The woman stopped dead in her tracks her eyes widening.

"Nice puss," she twittered skirting around the biggest cat she had ever seen in her life. She moved slowly her eyes locked on Buster as though any sudden movement might provoke the beast to attack. Backing away she edged step by step towards the safety of the stone lodges. Her destination appeared to be the very lodge Buster had sworn to guard with his life. Slowly he followed her plodding footsteps keeping enough distance so she would not panic. As she neared the lodge she broke into a staggered trot before hammering on the wooden entrance flap with chubby fists. The door opened and in the entrance stood the woman he had moments ago left in the Shaman's lodge.

"Quick let me in for pity's sake," wailed the large female as she squeezed past Molly who stood motionless staring into the gathering dusk, "something is following me, shut the door."

The door slammed shut. Buster sat down on his haunches his mind racing. He knew Ska was not like other worlds. Always it had been called the Gateway to Realms and now Buster understood nothing was ever as it seemed. All he could do was remain true to his oath, honour his tribe and strive to make the shades of his parents proud of what he had become.

Moa had granted him power to pass between the Realms of Time and Space. He lay and rested his great head upon his paws. Now he understood the nature of the second gift. Buster had become a creature of this world. He had not even felt the change nor did he feel strange in any way. Did this mean whatever Realm he entered he would become one of its kind? But what kind of creature had he become, what name had it been given? As he pondered these things the door opened and the woman Rowan called 'Molly' stood on the threshold looking straight at him. Without thinking Buster plodded towards her and rubbed his great head against her legs. He felt her fingers ruffle his fur as she stood to one side and let him cross the threshold.

Molly watched the cat like being fade before her eyes.

"Do not fear Molly," said Rowan gently, "Bws-Ta of the Gingas will protect your little ones."

A low moan disturbed them. Fingers of firelight touched the edges of the pile of aya skins upon which something stirred. Molly knelt beside Thorn and placed a hand on his forehead.

"He has a fever," she said, "will he die?"

"No, the Shaman has been granted the power to heal."

The Shaman scattered dried herbs on the fire and a soothing fragrance filled the lodge. Thorn fell still.

"He will be safe here," said Rowan, "but you must leave."

"Leave?"

Rowan sighed.

"If you wish to help Thorn you must leave but you cannot yet return to your world. Anselm desires to rule over the Realm of Men with you by his side. He will not rest until he finds you."

"Where can I hide?" said Molly.

"You cannot hide," said Rowan his eyes grave, "your paths have become entwined."

"Then what can I do?" said Molly.

"There is another way but it is fraught with danger," said Rowan.

Molly looked down at Thorn and thought of their helpless babies, the babies Anselm had sent the creature to destroy.

"What?" said Molly.

Rowan crouched so he and Molly were face to face. She felt his eyes search her own. When he spoke, his voice was soft and low.

"Anselm was not always evil. It was I who chose him to stand as Warrior Guardian over the Realm of Men. The Enemy proved too strong and he was deceived and drawn into its darkness. My poor judgement set him on that path."

Rowan paused and Molly sensed he was struggling with a great sadness.

"Thorn was also deceived," he said.

Molly's eyes flashed.

"Thorn? He took Glyn's place because he loved me," said Molly.

"It was love deceived him," said Rowan gently, "his duty was to all mankind not one woman, however desirable."

"How can one," Molly hesitated, "*being* protect mankind?"

"He cannot," replied Rowan, "the fate of mankind has already been decided by another. Thorn and Anselm were appointed Guardians to the portals of what is, and what has been until the End of Days."

"You mean the past?" gasped Molly the universe shifting like sand beneath her feet.

"It is where you must go now."

This was not a request but a command. Molly folded her arms ready to defy Rowan Great Lord of the Angelis.

"I will not run away. I left my babies I won't leave Thorn."

"I do not ask that you flee from your enemy Molly, I ask that you face him."

Molly gasped. Was Rowan suggesting she should step into the past, if that was even possible, and confront the powerful being that ordered the slaughter of her babies?

"Why should I?"

"You were not the first he sought to make his queen. There was another. Like you she was alone with her little ones with no one to protect her."

"You want me to go back and help her?" said Molly.

"Be her light in the darkness," said Rowan, "and you will grow strong."

"Strong enough to face my enemy?" asked Molly.

"With help," smiled Rowan.

Molly was silent for a long while. Outside the wind howled. Was it just the wind or could she hear the cries of other creatures mingled with the storm? Rowan also raised his head as though something had warned him of danger.

"They are close Molly. They scent you on the wind. You must go before your lead them to Thorn.

Molly glanced down at the man she had thought her husband and knew she would do anything to keep him safe. She faced Rowan and nodded.

"Come," said Rowan.

He led Molly towards the entrance hidden beneath thick drapes of aya skins and lifted them. Outside the blizzard raged and Molly could see nothing in the swirling vortex of frantically spinning snowflakes. As her eyes adjusted she thought she could trace shifting shapes lurching towards them through the storm. Was it her imagination or was Rowan about to throw her to the wolves or worse? It was as if he read her thoughts.

"Do not fear Molly, step outside, nothing will harm you."

Molly thought of her babies and of Thorn.

"This is a path you must take if you want to see your little ones again."

Molly's eyes flashed at Rowan. He lifted the flap higher. Molly stepped out into the angry night. She shut her eyes and waited for the icy sting of hail and snow to strike her cheeks. She felt nothing except a warm gentle breeze brushing her face and ruffling her hair. She opened her eyes.

The Shaman's lodge was gone. Overhead a pale sun shone in a corn flower blue sky. Molly stood in the courtyard of a great house, as big as Crawsay Castle where the coal owner lived. Neat gardens separated by small hedgerows arranged in strange patterns lined a path that led to a great wooden door set deep in the thick stone wall. Molly counted more than ten odd shaped windows and four great chimneys. The house and courtyard were surrounded by a high stone wall. Someone very important must live here thought Molly and then she remembered what Rowan had said.

"There was one other alone with her little ones. . ."

Molly thought of her twins and prayed the strange creature Rowan had sent would be strong enough to save them from the horror that stood behind Anselm in the pit. The horror that slunk off into the night.

"Be her light in the darkness," Rowan said

"Whose light?" wondered Molly as she gazed at the house. "Does the woman work here as a servant?"

Molly guessed a house this big would need many servants. Lost in her thoughts she was startled by a voice in her ear.

"Where has thou been woman?"

Molly spun around. A large man wearing a wide brimmed hat stood over her. He stared at Molly as he waited for an answer. The man's sudden appearance and strange speech caught Molly off guard. She couldn't think of anything to say. The man mistook her silence.

"What, cat got thy tongue woman?"

Taking Molly roughly by the arm he led her down the path.

"Come," he said giving Molly no choice, "the mistress spied thee from the window and would speak with thee."

There was no point struggling, he was too strong. Besides, where would she go? She did not even know where she was but the man's speech and clothes left Molly in no doubt that she had somehow been sent back into the past. There was no choice but to follow.

The massive wooden door opened without the man having to knock. A woman moved aside as they passed through. They stood in a wide entrance hall from which a large wooden staircase led up to a balcony. Molly climbed the staircase. With each step, a feeling she had been here before grew stronger. A long narrow corridor led off the balcony and without thinking Molly took the lead surprised that her feet knew exactly where they were going. Towards the end of the corridor she stopped outside a wood panelled door.

"What be thee waiting for woman?" said the man as he reached over Molly and knocked on the door.

"Enter," said a voice.

The man opened the door and Molly stepped inside.

A woman sat on a wooden chair next to a crib in which a baby nestled fast asleep. Behind her was a great fireplace laid for kindling. Above the fireplace hung a large portrait of the lady and her husband with their children. To Molly's eyes it seemed freshly painted. In the picture, the lady wore a blue dress. The woman facing Molly was dressed in red yet there could be no doubting she was the figure in the portrait. The artist had captured her violet blue eyes and auburn hair perfectly. She looked up as Molly entered and smiled.

"Where hast thou been," she asked, "the children have missed thee?"

Molly had not noticed two small girls playing with wooden toys on a rug near the window. They rushed over and flung their arms around Molly who, without a second thought, gently ruffled their hair. The girls squealed with delight. The lady continued to gaze at Molly awaiting a reply.

"I. . ." Molly stammered struggling for breath.

"No matter," said the lady, "I have joyful tidings to share with thee."

Molly's smile was one of relief.

"Colonel Roderick has sent word. He will be home within the week."

The lady stood and spoke to the man who had escorted Molly so rudely.

"You may go about they duties Steffan."

"But my lady," began Steffan who did not appear happy leaving Molly alone with his mistress.

The lady raised her eyebrows. Steffan bowed low and left. The door closed behind him with a solid thud.

"Is this not wonderful news?"

It was not a question so Molly smiled and nodded. Suddenly the lady's expression became grave.

"There was a battle and my Edward would have been killed but for the bravery of a comrade in arms. This noble soul was wounded and now travels home with my Edward. We must prepare a feast in their honour."

Lady Roderick laid her hands-on Molly's shoulders and looked deep into her eyes.

"Who better to help with the preparations than my 'Maid of all Works' and truest friend, Jemimah Penfield."

CHAPTER 32

THE BRASS KNOCKER

Billy awoke the next morning the returning sense of loss settling on his chest. A weight that threatened to crush the life from his frail body. Slowly the memory of the strange dream returned. He swung his legs over the side of the bed and leant forward. His last memory was of standing opposite a great tree against which an old man slumped fast asleep. The old man was wrapped in a thick blanket to ward off the chill night air. A string of onions dangled around his neck and by his side lay a hammer and a wooden spoon sharpened to a fierce point. Billy had wondered what the old man was doing alone at night in the garden but then the creature appeared and Billy understood. The old man was keeping watch over the big house where the rich people lived.

In the dream Billy recalled standing on the lawn facing the big house. Someone was inside looking out of the French windows casting a shadow on the grass. There was no doubt in Billy's mind that the shadow belonged to the same creature he challenged when he stepped out to defend the old man. But the silhouette of the person in the window looked ordinary. Why then did it cast such a sinister shadow? The dream was telling him something, something important.

Billy knew it was not a normal dream. He wondered if he would ever have a normal dream again.

Yet Nan had come to him in a dream, the old Nan, his Nan. Perhaps she would come to him again. A bright shaft of hope pierced Billy's gloom.

"Someone else needs you Billy. Someone I love. You must help him. He will take my place. You mustn't leave him alone. Do you promise me cariad?"

Nan's words rang in his head like Sunday church bells and each peal chimed a name, 'Gaffer'. Of course, it was the Gaffer Nan had meant, how could he have been so stupid. Slideshow images flickered inside Billy's head. A young man in a photo arm in arm with Nan; the puzzled expression on the sergeant's face when Billy spoke Nan's name in the desert so far from home; an old man refusing to get out of the car as Matron hovered like a vulture; the same old man asleep under a great elm as the shadow drew near. The Gaffer, Nan's lost love.

Deep in thought Billy washed, brushed his teeth, dressed and rushed downstairs. His mother was making toast. His father sat at the table head resting on hands. Dark shadows spread like stains beneath his red rimmed eyes. He looked up startled as Billy burst into the kitchen.

"Morning 'sleepy-head', do you want something to eat," said Mum.

She wanted to rush over and give Billy a hug, something she knew he would hate.

"Where does the Gaffer live?" said Billy.

Mum set the kettle down on the worktop wrong footed by the question and Billy's enthusiasm. She had been expecting an unhappy little boy not this bundle of impatient energy. She glanced at Dad who raised his eyebrows.

"The Gaffer?" she repeated slowly.

"Yes, the Gaffer, Nan's boyfriend, the one in the photo," said Billy.

Mum gaped at Billy wondering where this was going. She turned to Dad for support but he shook his head and took another sip of coffee.

"I've no idea where he lives," she said as the smell of burning grew stronger. Billy watched Mum try to salvage something from the blackened remains of a slice of bread.

"Somewhere posh I expect," she said as she gave up the fight and dropped the smouldering toast into the bin.

"'Number 1, The Croft'."

"Bleeding Nora," cried Mum, "I forgot you were still here."

Aunt Vera stood in the doorway with Buster at her side. Mum eyed the cat warily.

"Come over here by me Billy," she whispered not taking her eyes off Buster.

Buster plodded over and rubbed his great head against Billy's trousers.

"Why do you want to know?" asked Vera studying Billy through narrowed eyes.

Mum was beginning to simmer at being ignored by her young son and that interfering old busybody. As usual Dad was worse than useless he just kept gazing into the tepid contents of his cup. Mum and volcanoes had a lot in common and the bubbling magma of her anger was welling to the surface when Billy spoke.

"Nan told me I have to help him?"

Mum's mouth dropped open releasing nothing more deadly than hot air. Dad looked up and Billy waited for him to start shouting but he never did. Instead a worried expression clouded his round face.

"Then we had better go visit him," said Aunt Vera as though Billy's remark was perfectly normal.

"How could Nan...? " began Dad but left the sentence unfinished, it was somewhere he did not want to go. "Haven't you forgotten Vera, we have some arrangements to make today," he said.

"Yes," blurted Mum, "the people from the lottery should be ringing us anytime."

Dad sighed and lowered his head.

"I didn't mean those arrangements."

Mum bit her lip.

"The Gaffer and Emma were close once," said Vera, "it's only right he should know."

"Are you sure he'll want to know from you?" said Mum unable to resist a dig.

"Can we go now?" said Billy. "Nan said I mustn't leave him alone?"

Mum was about to object but the glint in Dad's eye made her think better of it.

"Take Buster with you," said Dad, "I'm fed up tripping over that flea-bitten cat."

Billy and Buster followed Aunt Vera without looking back.

"Billy, make sure you wear your coat," shouted Mum beginning to feel events were passing her by, "and take care."

It was just as Billy remembered in the dream. Aunt Vera's 4x4 crunched to a halt outside the front entrance to the Gardener-Allen's palatial home.

"Well this is it," said Aunt Vera, "ready? Buster you had better stay in the car, if they catch sight of you they probably won't open the door."

Buster who had been gazing at the trees bordering the far edge of the lawn leapt out of the back seat his large paws scattering the gravel.

"You always were a disobedient creature," said Aunt Vera, "try and stay out of sight."

Buster loped off across the lawn. As he neared the trees he crouched down preparing to stalk some unfortunate animal hidden in the bushes. His big ginger rump slowly merged with the undergrowth. Billy watched him disappear his attention drawn to the large elm whose branches reached out towards Billy. There could be no doubting it was the same tree the Gaffer had slept under in the dream that was not a dream. Apart from a rustle of leaves and crackle of twigs marking Buster's whereabouts in the shrubbery an eerie silence held sway. Billy guessed it was not birds Buster was hunting among the tangle of undergrowth but something far bigger.

"Don't worry about Buster," said Aunt Vera, "he can take care of himself."

She gently pushed Billy towards the steps.

"Go on," she urged, "this was your idea."

Billy climbed four stone steps that led to the large front door. In the centre of the darkly polished wood was a shiny brass knocker. Billy stretched to reach the solid ring that circled a head carved in bronze. Instead of hammering the door his hand froze in midair. The cruel face of the creature that haunted his dreams stared down at him. He glanced back towards the line of trees bordering the lawn and hoped the living creature was not lying in wait for Buster.

"Go on," said Aunt Vera, "fortune favours the brave."

Billy lifted the heavy brass ring and knocked. The sound echoed inside the house followed by muffled footsteps approaching. The door creaked open and a woman smiled at him.

"Hello," she said, "are you collecting for the school jumble sale?"

"Is the Gaffer in please?" said Billy.

Mrs. Gardner-Allen looked confused.

"The Gaffer?" she repeated as the child stared at her unblinking.

She was interrupted by the appearance of a man who pushed her aside. The man folded his arms and studied Billy as though he were something unpleasant left on the doorstep.

"What do you want?" said Mr. Gardner-Allen in a voice that made it clear his only interest was getting rid of the scruffy child littering his porch steps.

Billy did not answer. There was something different about Mr. Gardner-Allen. There was no doubting he was the same person who'd tried to dump the Gaffer in the Hollies, the one with the sinister shadow in the dream, but something had changed. Suddenly it came to him. Mr. Gardner-Allen reminded Billy of the bronze face on the door knocker.

"Well?"

Mr. Gardner-Allen was growing impatient.

"Can I see the Gaffer please?"

"What could you possibly want with my father?" said Mr. Gardner-Allen.

"I want to tell him Nan is dead," said Billy.

Mr. Gardner-Allen raised his eyebrows.

"Why would my father be interested in your Nan?"

A suspicious tone crept into his voice.

"He used to be Nan's boyfriend."

Mr. Gardner-Allen snorted.

"When they were in Junior School I suppose, back in the Dark Ages."

"They were very close at one time," said Aunt Vera as though correcting a rude child. Mr. Gardner-Allen glared at her but she did not flinch and he turned back to Billy.

"Don't I know you?" he said.

It was more an accusation than a question

"I know you," said Billy.

Mr. Gardner-Allen began to feel uncomfortable.

"You were going to dump the Gaffer in the nursing home before I told you about Matron."

"What about Matron?" said Mr. Gardener-Allen.

He recalled the unpleasant encounter all too well.

"She's a vampire remember," Billy reminded him.

"What is it with snotty kids and dipsy old men? Do vampires come with the territory?"

As far as Mr. Gardner-Allen was concerned the conversation was over.

"I've got to see him?" said Billy. "I've got a message from Nan."

"Your Nan," Mr. Gardner-Allen turned sharply, "I thought you said she was dead?"

"She is," said Billy deciding not to tell Mr. Gardner-Allen about the dream. He didn't think Mr. Gardner-Allen would understand. Truth was he wasn't sure anybody would.

Mr. Gardner-Allen shook his head and entered the house without saying another word leaving his wife alone on the doorstep. Mrs. Gardner-Allen began to shut the door then paused her pale face just visible in the gap.

"He's in *The Hollies*," she whispered, "he left earlier this morning".

She shut the door. The bronze face leered down at Billy.

The Hollies!

"They've gone and dumped him with Matron," said a horrified Billy.

CHAPTER 33

JEMIMAH PENFIELD

The first time she saw her face Molly had to stifle a scream. She was polishing a dusty brass plate when the reflection stared up at her. The clatter the platter made as it struck the bare wooden floorboards rang through the house like church bells sounding an alarm. She glanced around hoping the noise would not attract the other servants. She had not yet got used to their strange way of speaking and so avoided them as much as possible. Instead she would hide in the shadows and listen to them talk trying to get used to their speech. Now many of the servants kept quiet if she was near as though she were a spy on some dark secret mission.

The face she guessed belonged to Jemimah Penfield as did the frumpish figure she wore like a faded old coat. It was as if she were a guest in someone else's body, someone who had left behind their memories for Molly to use as she saw fit. Molly wondered what had become of Jemimah but suspected Rowan knew and would keep her safe. Molly hoped she had not upset Jemimah by dropping the platter in shock at the sight of her plain features. She stooped and picked it up staring at the jolly wrinkled face with the twinkling brown eyes gazing back at her.

Molly smiled, she liked what she saw and hoped Jemimah felt the same wherever she was.

Her thoughts fled to the Shaman's lodge where Thorn lay wounded and helpless while the wind and worse prowled and howled outside in the freezing dark. But most of all she fretted over the babies she had left behind and shuddered as she recalled the creature Anselm loosed to destroy them. Rowan promised Bws-ta would protect them. He also promised she would see them again if she helped the woman Anselm wanted to be his queen. That woman must be Lady Roderick who was both beautiful and high born. Molly was to be her '*light in the darkness*'. Although Molly could see only light surrounding her new mistress storm clouds gathered overhead and soon a black rain would fall.

"The mistress wishes to speak with thee."

Startled, Molly put down the platter. Mary Jane Hopkins the Chamber Maid was standing over her a sour expression creased her pinched face. Molly knew Mary Jane and many of the servants were jealous of Jemimah because Lady Roderick favoured her above them. She smiled at Mary whose scowl deepened.

"I will be about my business," said Mary Jane, "the beds will not make themselves and more will be needed tonight."

Molly watched her stalk out of the room and wondered why more beds would be needed. She left the kitchen crossed the entrance hall and climbed the great wooden staircase. The corridor was dimly lit by a small window at the far end but Molly knew the way as surely as if she was Jemimah herself. Stopping outside a door at the far end she knocked lightly and waited until she heard Lady Roderick's voice.

"Enter."

Lady Roderick sat next to a wooden crib rocking it gently. Before she had chance to speak there was an explosion of satin as the two girls flung themselves at Molly squealing with delight. Molly hugged them back. She was still amazed by the deep affection she held for children she hardly knew. It was as if Jemimah were reaching out to them through her. Molly's heart was heavy as she thought of the babies she left behind and the shadow that hung over them all.

"Girls return to your playthings. I wish to speak with Jemimah alone."

The girls released their hold and returned to their toys. Every now and then they would glance up hopeful Molly would soon join them.

Lady Roderick stood and clasped Molly's hands breathless with excitement.

"Edward will be home before sunset. News has just reached me," she gasped. "Two companions travel with him. Do you recall I told you of the one who saved my husband's life? How he was wounded? We must make him welcome."

"What can I do my lady?" said Molly with the voice of Jemimah Penfield.

"You must show our guests to their rooms. They will most certainly want to wash the dust of their journey away before partaking of a meal."

"But should not one of the manservants undertake this task?" protested Molly.

"No," replied Lady Roderick, "you are my truest and dearest friend Jemimah. It is your duty."

"You honour me my lady," Molly replied but secretly she worried her fellow servants would be unhappy and trouble would follow.

"Come Jemimah, I have something to show thee."

Lady Roderick turned to the girls.

"Watch over you brother for a moment."

The girls left their toys and sat beside the crib where their little brother lay sleeping. Lady Roderick led Molly to a tapestry at the far end of the room. She lifted a corner of the heavy material to reveal a hidden door. She placed a large iron key in the lock. The door creaked open. A flight of wooden steps twisted up into the gloom.

"Come," said Lady Roderick as she ducked through the doorway.

Molly followed up the narrow stairway. After climbing a little way light filtered down and a warm breeze brushed her face. She stumbled onto a small stone parapet, blinking in the late afternoon sunshine. Lady Roderick took her arm.

"Take care dear friend. I fear the fall would prove fatal."

Molly leaned against the stone wall her breath coming in short gasps.

"The sun is beginning to set," said Lady Roderick, "we shall see them soon".

The Glamorgan uplands stretched out before them. Rolling hills dotted with dark patches of woodland led down to open pastures where sheep grazed beneath the setting sun. They watched and waited as shadows lengthened and the crimson orb settled slowly upon the highest hill. Loneliness touched Molly as she realised the valley she called home was still a place of beauty. No rows of terraced houses lined its scarred sides. No pits spat their black waste onto the green hills. In the streets below no children laughed as they played their carefree games beneath dust clouded skies. Her own children were not yet born.

"Look," cried Lady Roderick breaking through Molly's thoughts, "they come."

In the distance four riders travelled along a winding road that led through open fields to the manor house. A livid sunset streaked the evening sky bathing them in a red glow. Molly was reminded of a sermon she had heard as a child in the local chapel that haunted her dreams ever since. Wild eyed with flowing white hair to match the preacher warned in gory detail of the coming of the Four Horsemen. The preacher described with great relish the destruction and horror they would unleash upon the world. As they drew nearer Molly's eyes were drawn towards the last rider astride a light grey mare. In her heart, she knew his name. It was Death.

"Come," said Lady Roderick her eyes shining, "we must ready the household."

Before following her mistress, Molly turned and looked back across the fields just as one of the riders reined in his horse. He sat upright in the saddle staring at the manor and as she watched she felt his gaze rest upon her. A chill crawled down her spine and Molly shuddered.

"Jemimah, make haste," Lady Roderick's voice echoed up the stairs, "they approach the manor."

Molly tore herself away and hurried down the stairs but in her mind's eye the rider on the black horse watched her every move.

The dying sun cast long shadows as Lady Roderick and the household servants, waited impatiently in the courtyard for the return of her husband. The two girls clung nervously to Molly's skirts while Lady Roderick cradled her infant son in her arms. Only the cry of jackdaws flocking overhead broke the silence until at last they heard horses' hooves striking cobbled stones. Three riders cantered into the courtyard. Lady Roderick rushed forward to greet the leader.

A large bearded man dismounted and held out his arms to embrace her.

"Surely this cannot be young Matthew," he said as Lady Roderick gently passed their infant son into his arms. "Why, how he has grown. T'will not be long before he takes charge of the estate I'll warrant," he laughed and handed the child back.

"Do not say such things," said Lady Roderick a frown furrowing her brow, "you will be master of this estate for many years yet."

Colonel Roderick took his wife's hand and gazed into her eyes.

"If it were not for new my comrades in arms Matthew would already be master."

He turned to his companions who sat patiently astride their steeds.

"Come," he cried, "my wife and I welcome you to our home."

One rider dismounted and limped slowly to where Colonel and Lady Roderick stood.

"My dear, allow me to introduce my saviour, Robert Courtney."

Molly froze and her grip tightened on the girls who pressed even closer to her side. Lady Roderick held out her hand. The stranger reached out and took it in his own.

"You spoke truly Colonel when you told us of your wife's surpassing loveliness. Your servant madam, from this day forth."

Lady Roderick blushed and withdrew her hand. The stranger held Lady Roderick's eyes until she looked away. Molly searched for the scar on the hand she had pierced with the knife on the night she followed him searching for the man she thought was her husband. But there was no scar because that night had not yet been. Molly knew the man before her. His true name was Anselm.

"Jemimah, show Master Robert and his companion to their rooms," said Lady Roderick. "Clean water and fresh clothes await you sirs."

"I fear Malacai will not be accepting your hospitality my lady," replied Robert Courtney.

The rider on the black horse bowed his head slightly. Molly watched him with interest. She could see he was an uncommonly large man even hunched forward in the saddle. The hood of a monk's black cowl covered the upper half of his face which was further shadowed by a wide brimmed hat.

"Malacai has pressing business, God's work," Courtney explained.

"God's work," said Lady Roderick, "is he a priest?"

"In a manner of speaking my lady, Malacai is a Witchfinder."

The servants glanced in Malacai's direction. Some crossed themselves and whispered prayers of protection against the Devil and his works. The black horse snorted and wheeled as Malacai dug his heels into its flanks. With a clattering of hooves horse and rider disappeared through the manor gates and were soon lost in the gathering dusk of twilight.

"Come," ordered Colonel Roderick, "there is a chill in the air. Jemimah show Robert to his room." Turning to the cook he said, "Prepare a hearty meal Mistress Clatworthy for we have ridden far on short rations."

The servants scattered glad to be about their business. Colonel Roderick lifted the girls into his arms and together he and Lady Roderick walked towards the house. Molly and Robert Courtney followed. Molly's heart beat so loudly she feared the being she knew as Anselm was sure to hear. She kept her head bowed to avoid looking at him and they entered Miskin Manor in silence. Candles feebly lit their way.

"Follow me sir," Molly heard herself say as she climbed the staircase holding a candlestick before her. Shadows slunk along the walls and the wooden stairs creaked a protest like bones stretched on the torturer's rack. At the top of the staircase Molly paused. The corridor stretched before her. It reminded her of the shaft in Fernhill Colliery, dark and forbidding. This time Molly had no knife. Hidden though she was in Jemimah's body Molly wondered whether Anselm would recognise her. Had they even met? The world was not a settled thing as she had once imagined and Robert Courtney was not a man like other men. The universe was shifting beneath her feet. One thing she knew for sure, she would protect Lady Roderick and her children with her life if need be. Molly stopped outside the chamber prepared for Robert Courtney. A shepherd inviting the wolf into the fold.

"Here is your chamber sir," she said opening the door.

She turned anxious to be gone but he caught her arm.

"One moment Mistress Penfield," his voice low and commanding, "have we not met before?"

His eyes searched her face as she struggled for an answer.

"That would not be possible sir," she stammered.

Robert Courtney smiled while light from the candle twisted his features.

"All things are possible mistress," he spoke as though Molly understood the meaning behind his words.

"I have to go sir, there is another guest to attend."

"Another? Have I not told you mistress? Malacai is about God's work. If there are witches within twenty miles he will sniff them out and deal with them as they deserve."

"I speak not of Malacai sir," she replied trying to stay calm, "your other companion."

Robert Courtney moved closer so Molly could feel his stale breath hot upon her cheek.

"What other?" he demanded.

"The rider on the pale horse."

Robert Courtney did not reply instead he studied Molly carefully. She held his gaze determined not to look away. After what seemed an age an unpleasant smile curled his lips.

"A pale rider you say? You are mistaken Mistress Penfield unless there is more to thee then meets the eye. There were but three of us upon the road."

His grip tightened on Molly's arm.

"No doubt Malacai will find your words of great interest when he returns."

The door closed in Molly's face and Courtney's veiled threat lingered in the air like smoke. Caught in the sudden up draught the candle flame flickered and died and the dark rushed to enfold Molly.

CHAPTER 34

MORE FAMILY SECRETS

"Mam, you'll never guess what they've done to the Gaffer!"

Billy charged into the living room. His mother and father sat side by side on the sofa which struck Billy as odd. They both looked glum, nothing odd about that. Neither spoke.

"Is something wrong?" said Aunt Vera.

"We've just heard from the lottery people," said Mum.

"And?" said Aunt Vera.

"You lost the ticket?" said Billy looking hard at his father.

It would not be the first time Dad had lost something important. He remembered how mad Mum got when he'd lost his job.

"No," replied Dad, "it's behind the clock on the mantelpiece."

"You got the numbers wrong again?"

Billy had no confidence in Dad's maths ever since that one-time Dad had helped Billy with his homework.

"No, I did not get the numbers wrong," said Dad in a miffed tone.

"The first time your father gets anything right so does half the population," said Mum, "typical of our luck that is!"

"Didn't you win anything?" said Billy not sounding disappointed.

"Not even enough to cover the funeral expenses," said Mum.

Dad gave her a hard stare. A shamefaced Mum pulled Billy towards her.

"But we will be able to get you that new tracksuit," she said hugging him tight.

Billy pulled away and faced his parents.

"What are we going to do about the Gaffer?" he demanded.

"It's nice that you're concerned Billy, but he's not really our problem, is he?" said Mum.

"He was Nan's boyfriend!"

That was a long time ago son," said Dad, "he's not family like Nan."

"That's where you're wrong."

Everyone turned to look at Vera.

"What are you talking about?" said Mum who had had enough shocks in the last forty-eight hours to last a lifetime.

"The Gaffer is Raymond's father," said Vera.

"What!"

Mum's mouth dropped open.

Dad's lips moved but that was all.

"War had just broken out," said Vera, "when Emma discovered she was having the Gaffer's baby. He had already enlisted and was due to join his company in Africa within weeks. She swore me to secrecy and so the Gaffer left not knowing he was to become a father."

"The Gaffer is my father, but I thought. . ." said Dad finding his voice then losing it again.

"You thought your father left when you were a baby," Vera finished Dad's sentence for him.

Dad nodded.

Mum was not convinced. She peered at Vera through narrowed eyes.

"So, you didn't steal your sister's boyfriend?"

It was more an accusation than a question.

Vera sighed and sat down on the sofa. Everyone waited with baited breath.

"It was Emma's idea. She wanted to break with Kenneth without him knowing about his child."

Vera paused.

"Could I have a glass of water please?"

Mum rushed out to the kitchen and returned with a glass of water. No one spoke as Vera wet her lips.

"Emma was afraid that if she met Kenneth face to face she wouldn't be able to go through with it so we cooked up a plan. Emma took Raymond and stayed with cousins who lived in the country. She helped on the farm to pay for their upkeep. I told Kenneth that she had run off with someone she'd met while he was fighting Rommel in the desert. He was heartbroken."

Vera took another sip of water.

"We kept in touch for a while. I think Kenneth was hoping Emma would come home once she knew he was back from Africa for good. There was no chance of that happening so I told Kenneth about the baby. Kenneth took the news very badly. I never spoke to him again. He still doesn't know Raymond is his son."

"I don't get it," said Mum, "if Nan loved the Gaffer why didn't she just tell him Raymond was his child?"

"That's why she didn't tell him," said Vera, "she thought he'd been in enough danger already, she couldn't bear putting him in any more."

"Danger, what danger?"

Aunt Vera glanced at Billy then back to Mum. Mum got the message.

"You don't mean. . ."

"The vampire in the Gaffer's garden."

At the sound of Billy's voice, it was Mum's turn to lose the power of speech. She gawped at Billy in disbelief.

"I also sensed its presence, its scent is strong. Orlok, shadow filth," said Bws-Ta standing with his arms folded behind Billy.

Mum was hyperventilating. Here was her little boy standing next to the creature that had once been their cat talking about vampires in some posh person's garden.

"You know about this. . . creature?" she said staring at Buster.

Billy ignored his mother.

"What are you going to do about the Gaffer Dad?" he urged. "You can't let Matron do what she did to Nan."

Dad looked up sharply.

"What exactly is Matron supposed to have done Billy?"

Dad sounded hurt.

"If you'd visited her more often you'd know," said Billy cutting Dad to the quick.

There was an awkward silence.

"You must leave this house," said Vera, "it's not safe any longer."

"Leave," said Mum beginning to feel stranded by events, "and where are we supposed to go, our holiday home in the Bahamas?"

"You have to stay with me," said Vera.

"With you," said Mum, "in Hogwarts on the hill? You must be joking."

Nobody laughed.

"She is joking isn't she Raymond?"

Raymond looked directly at Vera.

"Not until after the funeral. Nan is coming home one last time," he said then got up and disappeared into the kitchen. Mum followed hot on his heels.

Billy stood stiffly clenching his fists.

"What about the Gaffer?"

Aunt Vera placed a hand on his shoulder.

"We need a plan," she said.

Billy sat next to her on the sofa while Bws-Ta stood watch over them.

"What kind of plan?" said Billy having to speak loudly to be heard above raised voices from the kitchen.

"A plan to rescue the Gaffer from that dreadful place and that dreadful woman," explained Vera.

Billy's face brightened, Aunt Vera was the first adult to share his feelings for Matron.

"How?" he asked.

"To quote the Gaffer, first we need to go on a '*recce*'," said Aunt Vera a steely glint in her dark blue eyes.

"What's a '*recce*'?"

Billy was confused.

"You are about to find out," replied Vera. "Raymond," she shouted, "I'm taking Billy out for a run in the car."

There was no answer only the familiar sounds of Mum and Dad verbally reaching for the hammer and tongs.

"I need to get something first," said Billy.

They closed the door quietly behind them.

Matron sipped her tea and smiled. Strange how the stars could suddenly align themselves in your favour. Only yesterday that troublesome old woman had been taken to hospital and died the same night. If that wasn't cause enough for celebration Mr. Gardner-Allen had rung later that evening requesting a place for his father. Matron thought it poetic justice to put the old man in the room where that horrid child had spent so much of his meddlesome time. He had thwarted her once. Now the old man he had snatched from her grasp was safely locked away in the room that had only yesterday been his grandmother's.

Matron checked her watch. It was time. She stood, opened the door and stepped into the corridor. Moments later she heard a sound that brought a smile to her face. Ryland turned the corner at the far end of the corridor. Like a mouse caught in a trap the wheelchair squealed in protest but Ryland did not seem to notice.

"Time for walkies," said Matron to the old man in the wheelchair.

The Gaffer did not reply. His head lolled to one side and spittle trickled from the corner of his half open mouth. Matron knelt and looked him in the face but the Gaffer's glazed eyes stared past her to a lost horizon.

"Not very chatty this morning, are we? Perhaps a brisk walk in the fresh air will liven you up a bit."

Leaning forward Matron tugged the blanket that covered the Gaffer and folded it over her arm. The Gaffer slumped forward. Ryland thrust him back into an upright position.

"There," she clucked, "now the fresh air can get at you properly. Don't rush back it's not often we get a sunny day this time of year. Make sure he gets some colour in his cheeks Ryland."

"Even if it's only blue," sniggered Ryland.

Matron watched them go. She was not worried the Gardner-Allen's would suddenly have another change of heart. The unexpected phone call from Mr. Gardner-Allen had put her mind to rest on that score.

"Hello, the Hollies, Matron speaking."

There was a heartbeat's pause on the other end.

"I don't suppose you remember me Matron? I almost admitted my father into your care some time back but changed my mind last minute."

Remember? Matron would never forget. She took a deep breath.

"Mr. Gardner-Allen?"

"Yes, what a good memory you have Matron. Well, the thing is we've had second thoughts and believe the best thing for Dad is professional care that only a well-run nursing home can provide."

"I see, may I ask why the change mind?"

There was a longer pause.

"I think I can be frank Matron, I believe we understand one another."

Mr. Gardner-Allen spoke in hushed tones as though about to share some deep dark secret. Matron did understand. She had changed, was still changing, and so was Mr. Gardner-Allen. She sensed it. Whatever strange power was at work they had both fallen under its spell.

"Yes, I believe we do," she said.

Something unspoken passed between them.

"My father is going batty. He's become a danger to himself and others. He will probably need to be kept calm or restrained in some way."

"Of course," said Matron, "it's not a problem. We have considerable experience dealing with difficult elderly residents. When would you like to admit him?"

"Tomorrow morning if possible," said Mr. Gardner-Allen.

"I shall expect you," replied Matron.

The line went dead.

Matron smiled. She and Mr. Gardner-Allen were fruit growing on a branch of the same twisted vine.

Outside the wind was bitter. The Gaffer slumped in the wheelchair under the bare branches of a horse-chestnut tree. A smiling Ryland stood watching his patient shiver. Matron appeared and stared at the Gaffer for a long while.

"It's getting a bit nippy," said Ryland stamping his feet and rubbing his hands.

"Yes, it is," agreed Matron, "come inside and have a cup of tea."

"What about him?"

"He looks as if he's enjoying himself. You can bring him in later," said Matron.

"You're all heart you are Matron," said Ryland as he followed Matron indoors.

As they disappeared inside a large 4x4 ground to a halt at the bottom of the drive.

CHAPTER 35

THE RESCUE

Billy stared out of the window unable to believe his eyes.

"What is it Billy," said Aunt Vera, "what can you see?"

Where the Hollies should have been, a dark tower thrust towards the heavens its grim grey walls pitted with narrow barred windows. Above the broken tooth battlements monstrous birds wheeled and circled their harsh cries filling the leaden skies. *The Hollies* was still visible as if, like Jack's beanstalk, the tower had sprouted overnight entangling the nursing home in gigantic roots of stone.

"Billy?"

Aunt Vera leaned across and placed a hand on Billy's arm. A sudden shock rippled through her whole body and the tower took shape before her.

"Orloks," she muttered as Buster growled deep in his throat, "they have established a stronghold. This is worse than I feared."

Vera's gaze was drawn towards the peak of the tower. A figure leaned over the ragged battlements its large head tilted forward as clawed fingers gripped the cold hard stone, a misshapen eagle poised to swoop from its dark eyrie. Vera knew its intended prey was the child sitting next to her. Before she could stop him, Billy flung open the car door and jumped out, Buster followed hot on his heels. He must have unbuckled his seatbelt while she gazed in horror at the orlok in the tower. Vera clambered out after them, the tower fading like early morning mist.

The orlok snarled. The cursed child could not see him concealed in his stronghold. Yet each day the boy grew in power. It watched the child jump out of the car followed by the old female, spawn of the Angelis Thorn. Alongside them strode Bws-Ta, mighty warrior of the Gingas and the orlok's mortal enemy. The orlok tensed its talons. It had not expected the old female. It hesitated.

The dog was meant to distract the cat creature. Lead him away from the dribbling bait in the wheel chair. It would have been easier then to climb down and take the boy. The boy who was its greatest threat. Better to destroy your enemy while it is young. What should it do? Matron and the other human creature were ready to do his will. The orlok's thoughts like snaking tendrils wrapped themselves around their minds as poison ivy smothers a rotten tree. Dare it wait any longer? The boy had already challenged him in the dream-time and thwarted his attempts to take the old female and the old man.

Even as the tower faded Aunt Vera glimpsed a sight that chilled her to the marrow. An orlok crawled head first over the stone surface of the tower its long bony fingers gripping every crack

and crevice as it crept downwards like a
monstrous bat. Then it and the tower vanished.
Vera blinked. Straight ahead of her Billy was
racing across the lawn with Buster matching
every stride. She was about to shout a warning
until she saw where they were heading. Instead
she hurried after them praying the orlok didn't
suddenly appear and attempt to block their way.

Under the horse chestnut tree an old man sat
slumped in a wheelchair. Even as Aunt Vera
hurried to catch up she could see he was
shivering. The cotton pajamas, woolen cardigan
and slippers offered little protection from the
biting wind. A small white poodle nuzzled it's
head into the old man's limp hand as though
trying to wake him. Billy and Buster stopped in
front of the wheelchair.

"Is he dead?" Billy's voice was unsteady.

Vera knelt and took the Gaffer's hand.

"No, but he will be if we don't get him inside
quickly," she said.

Vera gripped the back of the wheelchair and
began to push the Gaffer towards the gravel path.
The poodle trotted alongside

"Where do you think you're going?"

Matron stood in the doorway her voice sharp
as the winter wind. Behind her loomed a sneering
Ryland. Aunt Vera turned to face them.

"Home," she said.

"Home?" repeated Matron. "Mr. Gardner-
Allen would have rung me. "Ryland, phone the

police. Tell them some mad woman is attempting to kidnap one of our residents."

"Another hour in your tender care and the only person you would need to phone is the undertaker," said Aunt Vera eying Matron coldly.

"Ryland, take Mr. Gardner-Allen back inside before he catches his death of cold," said Matron.

Ryland pocketed his mobile.

"Buster," said Vera as Ryland moved towards her.

Buster plodded forward and planted himself in front of Vera and the Gaffer. Ryland froze.

"What's the matter?" said Matron. "Surely you're not afraid of that scruffy bag of fleas? Get on with it."

"I'm allergic to cats?" said Ryland.

"If you want something done," said Matron taking a step forward.

Buster growled a warning deep in his throat.

"Billy take the Gaffer to the car," said Vera her eyes not leaving Matron.

Billy gripped the wheelchair and began to push when a sudden howl pierced the air, Buster!

The orlok seized its opportunity. Leaping at its enemy it slashed the great cat's haunches with cruel talons. Slowed by the pain Buster turned to face his attacker. Although the foul stench of the orlok hung heavy in the air it was nowhere to be seen.

Hidden within the shadow of the stronghold the orlok paused to enjoy Buster's confusion. It could taste the creature's fear and pain. Bwst-Ta, Great Warrior of the Gingas, was helpless before him. He would watch it suffer before inflicting the fatal blow. Soon the child would be alone and helpless.

Startled by Buster's yelp Billy looked back.

The nightmare creature from the dream time stooped over Buster arms raised above its hideous head. Long curved nails glistened like cruel knives and a glint of triumph lit its yellow eyes. Billy knew it was ready to strike a terrible blow. Why didn't Buster move away or attack the creature before it hurt him even more? Buster seemed confused just like Spencer Coombs when Ellis Kinsey and his cronies covered his head with a scarf and spun him round until he fell over. They laughed as Spencer tried to struggle to his feet stumbling like a Saturday night drunk.

"Buster no!"

The orlok heard the cry and turned its large head towards Billy. It would enjoy the pain in the child's eyes as he watched helpless while the cat-creature was killed in front of him.

Matron sensed this was her moment. A voice she could not refuse whispered dark thoughts.

"Get the old man!" she cried as she flew at Aunt Vera.

Ryland blinked. The giant cat no longer threatened. Its back was turned towards him and blood streaked its haunches. He ambled forward towards the old man in the wheelchair. The snotty boy would be much easier to deal with than his mutant moggy. Ryland hoped the brat he had come to loathe would resist and give him an excuse to inflict some pain. Ryland smiled.

It was not possible; the child was staring straight at him. Within the boundaries of their strongholds the orlok roam unseen, yet the child saw him. But this was not all. A bright light surrounded the child. It dazzled the orlok forcing it back towards the safety of the tower. The cat-creature growled and the orlok understood the boy had somehow lifted the darkness that cloaked it. Then all was blinding light and a fury of snarling fur. Claws raked the orlok. Fear, rage and confusion snapped its heels as it turned away from the hateful brightness.

Aunt Vera stepped nimbly aside and Matron sailed past like a ship driven to the rocks by a mighty storm. The impact with the frozen earth drove the wind out of Matron's sails. She struggled to her knees gasping for air. The voice no longer whispered inside her head. Matron blinked and looked around like a shipwrecked mariner trying to recover his senses after surging waves had tossed him onto a windswept shore. Her eyes focused on Ryland.

Ryland couldn't understand why the freak of a cat was fighting with itself. The brat was yelling at it but the cat was taking no notice. Stupid creatures cats. Meanwhile the old man was alone. Pity really, he was looking forward to shoving the kid out of the way or maybe giving his ear a savage tweak. That would teach him to keep his nose out of other people's business. Too many questions, the kid was full of them, always wanting to know why his precious Nan had so many bruises on her arms. Everyone knows old people bruise easily. He grasped the wheelchair and spun it round roughly.

"Billy!"

Vera shouted a warning but Billy dare not take his eyes of the orlok. Whatever super-powers Billy possessed were growing stronger. It frightened him. He did not want to be different, not like this. Billy was used to being left out because Mum and Dad could not afford the designer gear other kids wore. He could put up with the sniggering and cruel taunts. Nan even made him laugh when she said, *'You all look the same in your birthday suits.'*

But Nan was gone and Billy knew he would never be the same as other kids. He just didn't know why. Now for the first time Billy was glad he was different, so was Buster.

The dream-monster was backing away shielding its eyes. Billy's anger broke against the creature in waves of light like the incoming tide driven by wild ocean winds. He was aware of Ryland but Buster was in mortal danger and Billy would not leave him to face the orlok alone.

It was too good an opportunity to miss decided Ryland. He would barge into the boy as he passed and send him sprawling. The ground was hard and with any luck the brat might break something.

"Come on Grandpa, time for your medication," said Ryland as he turned the wheelchair so it pointed straight at Billy.

Matron struggled to her knees her senses slowly returning to roost.

"Take him inside," she yelled, "it's time for his nap. "

"Why don't you take one," said Aunt Vera planting a foot on Matron's backside and shoving with all the force she could muster.

Matron hit the ground hard. This time she made no attempt to rise, her senses fluttering free.

"You viscous old hag!" shouted Ryland.

Forgetting Billy, he angled the wheelchair towards Aunt Vera.

"Grrrrrrrrrrrrrrr!"

Ryland stopped. A small white poodle stood in his path baring its teeth.

"Nice doggy," said Ryland backing away from the wheelchair.

The poodle followed, still growling.

"Call your dog off," he called to Aunt Vera.

Aunt Vera smiled.

"It's not my dog," she said.

"I'm allergic to bleeding dogs," said Ryland as he edged his way around Bella.

"Better keep your distance then," said Aunt Vera as she stepped lightly over Matron and walked towards the Gaffer.

The orlok reached the base of the tower and leapt. Its nails hooked between the stonework. Buster sprang but already the orlok was out of reach, clambering up the tower like a grotesque Spiderman.

"Time to leave," shouted Aunt Vera.

Thick mist shrouded the tower's summit. Billy watched until the orlok was lost from sight.

"Come on Buster," he said, "let's go."

"We'll have the police on you!" shouted Ryland as he struggled to get Matron to her feet but no one was listening.

From its lofty height, the orlok looked down as the Gaffer was helped into the car. He watched them drive away. Somehow the child must be stopped. The past must not be changed. What had been done must not be undone. It licked its wounds and plotted the child's destruction.

"Where are we taking him?" said Billy.

The Gaffer was snoring gently in the back seat of Aunt Vera's four by four. Colour crept slowly back into his cheeks as the air conditioner blasted a steady flow of hot air. Buster lay on the front seat licking his wounds. Before Aunt Vera could answer the Gaffer sat up and opened his eyes.

"Bad dream," he said.

He rubbed his eyes and peered at Billy.

"I know you. Where from?"

"Outside *The Hollies*," said Billy, "your son was going to dump you."

The Gaffer brightened.

"You stopped him. The old bat chased you away."

"She's a vampire," explained Billy.

"She's that alright," said the Gaffer his smile slipping.

"He dumped you after all then," said Billy.

"Nah, I volunteered," said the Gaffer.

Billy couldn't believe his ears.

"Why would you want to go and live with Matron?"

"Couldn't stay. I'm an embarrassment."

Billy didn't understand what '*embarrassment*' meant but it must be something bad.

"You the rescue party?" said the Gaffer.

Billy liked the sound of that.

"Yes," he said, "me, Auntie Vera and Buster."

The Gaffer nodded.

"Where you taking me?"

"Home," said Aunt Vera, "my home."

CHAPTER 36

THE HOUSE IN THE SACRED GROVE

The phone rang. Mum and Dad jumped. Mum recovered quickest.

"Hello . . ."

Mum placed her hand over the mouthpiece.

"It's Billy. . . Where are you?"

Pause.

"Why are you in Aunt Vera's?"

Mum rolled her eyes.

"You rescued the Gaffer from Matron's. . . you what!"

She turned to Dad.

"They've only gone and. . ."

"I heard you," said Dad taking the phone from his wife.

"Billy give the phone to Auntie Vera. . . Vera, what's going on?"

Mum folded her arms, tapped her foot and glared at her husband.

"What. . .now?" said Dad.

Mum raised her eyebrows. Dad ignored her. He replaced the phone slowly a troubled look in his eyes.

"For goodness sake Raymond, what's going on?" said Mum.

"We have to go over Vera's," he said.

"Why?"

"I'll explain on the way," said Dad grabbing his coat.

The four by four snaked its way between rugged hillsides climbing towards the Brecon Beacons that lay beyond. Scattered villages, snuggled against the foothills below, shrank rapidly until they were hidden from view. Great swathes of forestry covered much of the mountain peaks. Some had been cleared leaving behind scruffy patches like a week's growth of dark stubble. Rounding a sharp bend the car turned left onto a rough forestry path. The tyres crunched on gravel startling a flock of rooks into a loud protest as they wheeled and circled overhead. Billy had been this way before.

Mr. Groucutt was not a fan of the great outdoors. He preferred spelling tests in the classroom. It was warmer and his class were confined within four walls even if there were no bars on the windows. Unfortunately, being the only male member of staff Mr. Groucutt was often called upon to accompany classes on field trips. As the mini bus rattled along the uneven forestry trail Mr. Groucutt attempted to share some local knowledge.

"Did anyone notice anything unusual about the stones we passed earlier on?"

"There was loads of them," said Spencer Coombs.

Mr. Groucutt waited for a more helpful answer. None came.

"They were part of an old Iron Age settlement," he explained.

"Did you used to live there sir?" said Rhys Rowlands.

Some of the girls giggled.

"A bit before my time Rowlands," said Mr. Groucutt.

"What about dinosaurs, was they a bit before your time as well sir?"

Spencer Coombs was deadly serious. Cue laughter all round. Mr Groucutt conceded defeat. They drove on in silence and Billy imagined grim Roman legions tramping through the forestry while fearful Iron Age settlers huddled inside their stone homes. Without warning the bus crunched to a halt.

"Have we broken down?" squeaked Kayleigh Williams.

"Is there a shop?" said Brooklyn Hopkins.

"I'm not getting off," said Ross Tudor, "these woods are full of werewolves and stuff. I seen one!"

"Why are we stopping?" said Mr. Groucutt who wanted to get this trip over as soon as possible.

The driver who was also the guide stood up.

"People have lived on these mountain tops for thousands of years," she explained.

"Like *The Abominable Snowman*?" suggested Spencer.

"We are going to visit a place that was sacred to the Iron Age people who lived here. Do you know what '*sacred*' means?" inquired the Guide ignoring Spencer.

"Somewhere special where God lives," said Billy.

Nan always went to chapel every Sunday before she became ill and they knocked it down. *The Hollies* had once been a chapel. It was still special to Billy because Nan lived there.

"Very good," said the Guide, "Iron Age people had lots of sacred places where they believed their gods lived. Trees and water were especially important."

"We've got a hot tub in our garden," said Emlyn Gregory.

Everybody groaned.

"It's believed Druids performed religious rituals in groves of oak trees to honour their gods. Some historians think they even sacrificed people."

The Guide fell silent giving children time to conjure gory images of bloodthirsty Celtic ceremonies.

"Who'd like to visit an ancient oak grove," she said at last.

"Will them Druids be there?" said Kayleigh Williams her voice quavering.

"No," replied the Guide smiling, "they've long gone."

"I bet their ghosts haven't," said Ross Tudor.

"Shut up boy," barked Mr. Groucutt, "you've got ghosts on the brain."

"Two hundred yards down this track is the site of the oldest remaining oak grove in South Wales," the Guide told them. "It's on private land and we are the first school group to be allowed to visit, so best behaviour please."

Cheers from the boys. Silence from the girls.

A sense of nervous excitement took hold of the group as if they had just boarded a scary fairground ride and were waiting for it to jerk into life.

True to her word after two hundred yards a large stone wall appeared. The trees on the other side of the wall were different from the surrounding pine forests. The branches were thicker and spread wider, the leaves broader and a darker shade of green. They drove through large iron gates that had been left open. The wrought ironwork caught Billy's eye.

Nan had once shown him a picture of St Michael fighting the Devil. St Michael had wings and stood on a creature that looked half man half snake. St Michael held a flaming sword in his hand ready to strike.

"Did he kill it?" Billy asked his Nan.

"No," she said, "the Devil was banished from Heaven."

She must have noticed Billy's confusion.

"You know," she explained, "like when somebody has been very naughty and your head master makes them stay away from school for a bit."

Nan made it sound like the Devil got off lightly. He wouldn't mind being banned from school for a bit.

"How long did he get?" Billy asked.

"Eternity," said Nan.

Billy was shocked.

"He must have been really naughty."

"He was," said Nan laughing.

Whoever made the gate was an artist or something because they made a picture out of the iron as a centre piece. It was like the picture of St Michael only the angel didn't have wings and the creature looked different too. It had a large head with pointed ears. Its hands were outstretched to protect itself from the angel's sword. Billy noticed the fingers were long with nails like hawk's talons.

They tumbled out of the bus into a tangle of gnarled and ancient trees. Everyone fell silent even Spencer Coombs.

"Can you feel how special this place was?" said the Guide.

There were no stupid comments and no mention of ghosts. There was no need. The past brushed against them whispering long forgotten secrets in their ears.

The oak trees formed a circular clearing smothered in yellow primroses and bluebells. No one ventured forward, it would be like walking on freshly fallen snow.

"It's lush innit Billy?" said Brooklyn Hopkins. "Look at all them flowers."

Billy wasn't looking at the flowers. In the centre of the clearing two figures shimmered in the haze like faded holograms. They flickered in and out of focus but Billy knew one of them. It was the Red Lady. She seemed to be crying. She did a lot of that thought Billy. The other figure was also a woman, shorter and dumpier. The woman was trying to comfort the Red Lady. The Red Lady lifted her head and for a moment she was as real as Brooklyn Hopkins who was still wittering on about flowers and stuff. The Red Lady looked straight at Billy who felt his cheeks flush with shame. She had given him a letter to deliver and he had let her down.

"Why you blushing Billy?" said Brooklyn moving closer.

Billy quickly took evasive action. When he looked back into the clearing the Red Lady and her companion were gone.

"Five minutes and back on the bus," shouted Mr. Groucutt.

"If I had a boyfriend I bet he'd give me flowers like them," said Brooklyn staring at the bluebells.

Billy quickly moved further away towards the safety of some thick undergrowth. Through packed leaves he glimpsed a large building but he couldn't make out what it was. He squeezed between dense bushes to get a better view. All he could see was a window set in a stone wall. A face appeared, Billy could just make it out.

"What you doing Billy?" whispered Brooklyn who seemed bent on giving Billy's shadow the elbow.

"Look," said Billy "there's somebody in the window watching us."

Brooklyn pushed a little too close to Billy but the face had gone.

"Perhaps it's a ghost," she said, "I'm going to tell Ross."

Brooklyn rushed off but Billy knew it was not a ghost. He knew who it was. The face in the window was Nan's.

The four by four turned off the track and through the iron gates. The wrought ironwork was just as Billy remembered it but now he could give the creature a name. Orlok! But if the angel wasn't St Michael who was it? The creature was real. It existed inside and outside his dreams. If the creature was real didn't it mean the angel was real too? What then was it doing on Aunt Vera's gates? Billy couldn't believe this was where Aunt Vera lived. As they drove up a grassy track behind the ancient grove Billy had questions burning inside him like hot coals.

Gnarled oak trees lined the way. Interlocking branches formed a twisted canopy splintered with pale shafts of winter sunlight. At the end of the grass track a neatly cut lawn stretched up to Aunt Vera's house. House! It was a cluster of towers and pointed turrets of differing sizes, a castle out of a fairytale. Billy would have been disappointed had he known it was a '*folly*', the creation of a wealthy and eccentric coal owner with a love of local history. He had built it as a home for the family he employed to caretake the Sacred Grove.

"Home sweet home," said Aunt Vera. The car ground to a halt outside the entrance. Aunt Vera yanked at the handbrake, "Let's get indoors. I need to dress Buster's wounds."

"Am I going to live in a castle?" said the Gaffer.

The air conditioning had worked its magic.

"I'll explain everything when we get inside," said Aunt Vera.

The room Billy found himself in was round like the turret. There were no windows. Within a large recess set in the wall a log fire blazed. Facing the fire arranged in a semi-circle were six deeply padded wing backed chairs. In the centre of the room stood a rectangular table that looked as if it had been carved whole from a massive oak tree.

"Get on the table," Aunt Vera told Buster.

Buster climbed up painfully and Aunt Vera began to examine his wounds.

Billy and the Gaffer sat in two of the armchairs. They studied each other closely.

"You were Nan's boyfriend," said Billy but the Gaffer looked confused.

"Who's Nan," he said.

"Her name was Emma, she was my Nan."

The Gaffer leaned forward.

"You're him," he said, "the boy in the desert."

Billy remembered the dream that wasn't a dream. A thought struck him like a piece of Mr. Groucutt's chalk. Was it possible he could travel through time like Dr. Who? Buster yelped in pain and Billy's thoughts flew back to the Gaffer.

"Where's Emma?" said the Gaffer.

Billy hesitated, not wanting to upset him.

"She's gone, is she?" said the Gaffer reading Billy like a book.

"Yes," he said, "she was staying in *The Hollies* like you."

The Gaffer stared into the fire for a long time. That would explain the picture in the drawer.

"She's better off now then," he said at last.

Although it hurt Billy knew it was true. He wondered if he would ever be able to forgive his parents.

Buster cried out again and as Billy turned to see what was happening something sharp poked him in the ribs. He reached inside his coat and

345

felt the Red Lady's letter. On impulse, he had decided to bring it with him when they left to rescue the Gaffer. Now Billy thought he knew why.

The Gaffer confirmed something Billy had begun to suspect. He could travel through time, although he didn't quite know how. He guessed that would come with practice like learning your tables. On his last visit to Aunt Vera's he saw the Red Lady in the Sacred Grove. A thought slipped into his head. What if he had been meant to bring the letter? What if it was still possible to do what the Red Lady had asked, no commanded.

The Gaffer snored gently and Aunt Vera was too busy applying ointment to Buster's wounds to notice Billy slip away.

Outside the wind greeted Billy with a mournful tune plucked on the skeleton branches of naked trees. He hurried down the track that led to the Sacred Grove wishing Buster was running beside him.

There were no flowers just a bare expanse of grass around which the great oaks huddled. Billy had the feeling you sometimes get when you enter a room and people stop talking as if the sudden quiet was somehow your fault. All that he could hear was the wind playing tag through the trees. Billy thought twice about stepping into the clearing. It was a special place and he felt like someone who had turned up to a party without an invitation.

Startled by the sound of a car spluttering through the gates a group of grumpy jackdaws rose flapping from the trees. Billy guessed who the car might belong to. He stepped into the clearing.

Aunt Vera looked up as the door closed gently behind Billy.

"You can get up now," she said.

Buster heaved himself off the table.

"Still hurts," he growled.

"Thanks to all that thick fur it's hardly a scratch," said Vera. "Stop behaving like a cubling. Now go quickly. When the child enters the Sacred Grove, wait a few heartbeats then follow. Go!"

Buster padded across the room bursting out through the doors.

"What an earth does the woman think she's playing at?" said Mum.

Dad kept his eyes on the rough mountain track and said nothing.

"She's going to get a piece of my mind that's for sure. I told you she was batty. Who in their right mind would want to live on top of a windswept mountain?"

No comment from Dad.

The house peeped at them through the bare trees.

"I mean look at it for goodness sake! The woman must think she's some sort of fairy godmother."

Dad sighed.

"Raymond wait, is that Billy."

A small figure flitted through the tree trunks. Although Mum could not get a clear sight she was certain it was her little boy.

"Probably," said Raymond, "you know how he loves trees and things. He's safe enough up here."

Mum grunted.

"About as safe as Hansel and Gretel," she said.

The car stopped outside the main entrance to Aunt Vera's castle. Mum and Dad got out and walked towards oak doors that reminded Dad of a giant spear head. The next moment they were forced to jump aside as the doors flung wide open and Buster sprang out nearly bowling them over.

"That bleeding animal," said Mum, "he'll be the death of us yet."

They watched Buster disappear through the trees.

"Gone after Billy, I expect," said Dad.

"At least the police haven't beaten us to it," said Mum.

They stepped inside.

Light from the flames of a huge log fire danced across the stone walls. There were no windows and as far as Mum could see the room had no corners. In front of the fire six large armchairs formed a semi-circle. Someone sat in one. Dad walked slowly towards the occupied chair and stood over it. He was quiet for a moment.

"It must be the Gaffer," he said it so quietly Mum could barely hear him.

"Your father," said a voice.

Mum and Dad spun around.

Aunt Vera was standing at the head of a massive wooden table. The firelight played red across her face and the image of an ancient pagan priestess about to perform some terrible nameless ritual surfaced in Mum's mind. All the words Mum had lined up to do battle with Aunt Vera beat a hasty retreat.

"What's all this about?" was all Mum could muster.

"Sit down," said Vera, "I will explain."

"It had better be good," said Mum rallying her forces.

They sat in the armchairs beside the snoozing Gaffer.

"Why six armchairs?" said Dad.

"When Billy and Buster return we will be complete," explained Vera, "then we hold our council of war."

"Council of war!" repeated Mum as she stood up. "I told you she was bonkers Raymond. I'm off to find Billy and then we're going home."

"That might not be possible," said Aunt Vera.

CHAPTER 37

THE DUCKING STOOL

Buster weaved with surprising grace through thick woodland until the clearing was in sight. Billy was poised on its edge as though preparing to plunge into a pool of deep water. Buster hid behind a large oak and watched.

Taking a deep breath Billy stepped into the clearing. A sudden shock rippled through his body as his feet sunk through solid ground. He blinked. He was standing in water that lapped his ankles. A large hand gripped his shoulder and hauled him backwards.

"Take heed boy," said a voice, "you be not wanting to share the waters with a witch."

The Sacred Grove had vanished. Instead he stood on the bank of a large pond. Rushes grew along its sides while the shallows were carpeted green by masses of marsh pennywort over which dragonflies hovered and skimmed in the mid-day sun.

A crowd of people stood around the margins of the pond chattering excitedly in a way that made Billy think of parents at Sports Day waiting to cheer their kids to victory. The same excited sense of expectancy filled the air but these people were gathered together for a darker purpose. Billy thought he knew what.

On the far bank stood a wooden structure that looked like an enormous see-saw. One end of the see saw dangled over the water. A crude chair had been attached to it. Billy knew what it was. He had Googled a picture of it after the school visit to Miskin Manor where Selwyn had explained its grim function. Billy was staring at a real ducking stool.

A murmur rippled through the crowd growing louder with every passing second.

"The witch is come," cried a woman standing near Billy.

The woman looked as if she had just stepped out of a history book. They all did. Truth was, it was not the crowd that had stepped out of the past but he who had stepped into it, right up to his neck.

"Not so high and mighty now are you Mistress," shouted another.

Voices raised in anger were drowned by a rising crescendo of jeers and howls. The roar of a hungry beast. A small party was approaching. Billy raised himself onto his toes but he was jostled and buffeted by the crowd. He stumbled backwards into something solid and furry. He turned half expecting to see a wild beast looming over him with slavering jaws and red eyes. What he saw was Buster.

"T'is the witch's familiar," cried a woman.

The people in front of Billy turned around. When they saw Buster, they drew back.

"Careful child, that creature is most likely spawn of the Devil," said a large man with rotten teeth.

"He's my cat," said Billy.

Those closest to Billy moved away muttering. Some crossed themselves and whispered prayers against the *Evil One*. A space opened around them.

Billy and Buster moved closer to the pond and peered over a large clump of bulrushes. A woman dressed in a white linen nightgown was being dragged towards the pool by two burly men. A third man walked before them. At first Billy thought it was Colonel Pritchard. He wore fine clothes and a large hat with a plume. All eyes turned towards him.

"That be the new steward, Robert Courtney," said a woman. "They say he saved the Colonel's life."

Billy stared at Robert Courtney. Even from far away he could sense he was a very bad egg indeed. Buster growled deep in his throat. But it was not Robert Courtney who drew everyone's eyes.

"Look, the Witchfinder himself," shouted the man with rotten teeth.

A hush fell as a tall figure draped in a black cloak and cowl rode into view astride a black house. A wide brimmed hat shadowed the Witchfinder's face as he hunched forward in the saddle.

"They say he be ravaged by the pox," whispered a woman. "That be why he doth keep his face hidden."

Billy knew the real reason. He was staring at the *'nameless horror'*.

The woman in the white nightgown was forced to her knees as the crowd bellowed. Robert Courtney raised his hand. The mob fell silent.

"Good folk, you have gathered today to witness the trial of this woman charged with witchcraft and devilry."

An angry roar greeted Robert Courtney's words.

"Burn her, burn the witch," someone screamed.

The cry was taken up by others and just as a smouldering bonfire catches the wind the crowd was suddenly aflame.

"Let no man say we did not give the witch chance to confess her sin and beg mercy of her Maker," shouted Robert Courtney.

The noise died a little but Billy could still feel the angry heat of those around him.

"We've got to do something Buster," he whispered.

Buster growled. Billy suddenly felt like when he stood in the school yard watching helplessly while Ellis Kinsey and his gang beat up some poor little kid. What could he do, he was only a little kid himself?

Even as the thought entered his head he knew it was a lie. He was not just a little kid, he was different, very different. The most frightening thing was he didn't know how different. That's what really scared him.

The two men manhandled the woman in the nightgown into the chair. Every time she cried out in pain the crowd cheered. Once she was bound tight the chair swung out over the water.

"Confess your sin witch," said Robert Courtney.

The woman shook her head.

"I am not a witch," she said as she struggled to free herself.

"Do it," said Courtney.

Seizing one end of the ducking stool the men thrust it upwards and the woman was lowered into the water. Her screams excited the crowd but as her head disappeared under the surface people fell silent.

Billy watched in horror. It seemed an age before Robert Courtney gave the signal to hoist the stool. When he did, the woman rose out of the water coughing and spluttering. Weeds covered her head and shoulders and her eyes were shut tight.

"Confess," said Courtney.

Still gasping for breath, the woman shook her head.

"Again," said Courtney.

Once more the stool was lowered into the water. Billy watched bubbles rise to the surface and shuddered. He could not swim and dreaded having his face covered with water. Now he shared the woman's distress.

"Leave her alone," he shouted but his voice was drowned by a rising tide of hate.

Billy held his breath until he thought he would burst.

"Up," said Courtney and the chair broke the surface just as Billy released his breath.

This time the woman's matted head was bowed. She was retching and trying to gulp air at the same time. Robert Courtney waited until she could sit up and gaze across the pool. What she saw was a sea of twisted angry faces hurling abuse as if words were stones.

"I will ask one last time Mistress Penfield," said Robert Courtney raising his voice, "is Satan your master?"

'*Jemimah Penfield, my one true friend*'.

Billy recalled what the Red Lady had written.

"No," said Jemimah Penfield and with great effort raised her head, "it is you who are the devil. You and the creature that stands beside you."

She blinked to clear her eyes and gaze for one last time on the trees and sky. Molly wondered if she died would it be her or Jemimah Penfield's lifeless body they would drag from the pond. Then she saw it. There could be no mistake. The great cat Rowan, Lord of the Angelis, had sent to protect her babies was standing on the farthest bank of the pool. What could this mean? Fear and hope struggled inside her.

"May God have mercy on your soul," said Robert Courtney.

A chill passed through Billy as he heard those words. Courtney was going to drown Jemimah Penfield. He must do something, but what? The chair was lowered slowly into the water.

"What are you talking about," said Mum springing to her feet. "What's not possible?"

Aunt Vera said nothing.

"Billy's in the garden. I saw him as we drove in."

"It's a bigger garden than you might imagine," said Aunt Vera.

"Me and Raymond will find him, then we're going straight home."

Mum looked at her husband but he gazed into the fire and did not answer.

"Raymond?" said Mum becoming alarmed.

She turned to Vera.

"He is in the garden, isn't he?"

"He is and he isn't," said Vera.

"Stop doing that!" said Mum. "Where is Billy?"

"He's gone to rescue his great grandmother," she said.

Mum stood.

"Right Raymond, I've had enough. I'm taking Billy home."

Mum stormed off to look for Billy without glancing back. Dad got up to follow then hesitated. He looked at Vera.

"It's begun, hasn't it?" he said.

"Yes, it's begun," said Vera.

A Word About Locations

'The Pit of Shadows is set partly in a South Wales valley. The valleys were created during the Ice Age by huge glaciers gouging deep furrows in the earth like a potter's fingers in wet clay. The discovery of coal in the latter half of the nineteenth century impacted dramatically on the rural communities. In 1851 the Rhondda Valley boasted less than 1,000 inhabitants. Sixty years later a census recorded the population as 153,000. This phenomenal growth was replicated to lesser degrees across all the valleys. If the Klondike was famed for its gold then anthracite became the black gold of the South Wales Coalfields. Almost every village in every valley boasted its own pit.

Today nature has reclaimed her own. The mines are gone and so has much of the culture that surrounded them. There is still a strong tradition of male voice choirs linking to a lost heritage but they are also in decline. Valleys children now learn about their past by visiting tourist sites like Big Pit, Blaenavon or the Rhondda Heritage Park, Trehafod. Billy's grandfather was a miner but his world is as alien to Billy as that of cosmonaut on a space station.

The Miskin Manor where Billy encounters the Red Lady is based on Llancaiach Fawr Manor House near Caerphilly. This is a truly magical place where children are transported into the past without the aid of ghosts, although the manor is reputedly haunted. There is a Miskin Manor in the Vale of Glamorgan that also has an interesting history but is now utilised as an hotel and conference centre.

Crawsay Castle does not feature much in this book but will play a more prominent role in the next novel 'A Dark Forbidding Place'. It too is based on reality. Cyfartha Castle in Merthyr was the home of the wealthy ironmasters, the Crawshays. I have taken the liberty of relocating it above the valley where Billy lives and allowing it to fall into almost terminal decline. Cyfartha Castle is a thriving tourist attraction in Park, Merthyr Tydfil. Merthyr, once recognised as the capital of Wales, was lit day and night by huge furnaces that fired the steel industry. The Blaenavon Ironworks bear witness to the ferocity of the furnaces that helped power the Industrial Revolution. As the coal industry prospered so Merthyr fell into relative decline. The ports of Cardiff and Barry reaping the fruits of a black and bitter harvest.

Prehistoric and Iron Age sites lie scattered throughout the valleys. Gorsedd stones, Stone Age wooden posts, standing stones, cairns, Roman camps, Iron Age hillforts and settlements abound. Oak trees were sacred to the Celts and Aunt Vera's house stands near an ancient grove on top of the Rhigos mountain that looks towards the Brecon Beacons. The house itself is modelled on Castell Coch that lies above the village of Tongwynlais, near Cardiff. Its appearance is that of a medieval fairy tale castle but is in fact a far more recent construction funded by a wealthy Victorian, the 3rd Marquess of Bute. It stands on the site of an early Norman castle. Again, I have relocated it without the inconvenience of having to move it stone by stone.

Places to Visit

The South Wales valleys include: Gwendraeth, Amman, Loughor, Tawe, Dulais, Vale of Neath, Afan, Llynfi, Garw, Ogmore, Rhondda, Cynon, Aber, Ely, Taff, Taff Bargoed, Llwyd, Sirhowy, Ebbw and Ebbw Fach.

Rhondda Heritage Park: http://www.rctcbc.gov.uk/EN/Tourism/Rhondda HeritagePark/Home.aspx

Big Pit: https://museum.wales/bigpit/

Cyfartha Castle: http://www.visitmerthyr.co.uk/attractions/cyfarthf a-park-museum.aspx

Llancaiach Fawr: http://your.caerphilly.gov.uk/llancaiachfawr

Blaenavon Ironworks: http://cadw.gov.wales/daysout/blaenavonironwor ks/

Castell Coch: http://cadw.gov.wales/daysout/castell-coch/

The Welsh Folk Museum: https://museum.wales/stfagans/

There are many more places of interest to visit in the valleys but this list relates to locations in 'The Pit of Shadows'.

'A DARK FORBIDDING PLACE'

Part 2 of the Billy Angelis Series. Available Summer 2021

CHAPTER 1
GOD'S JUSTICE

Billy had never seen anyone die before. He had been there in the dream when Nan left for good but that was different. Nan slipped through his fingers like a helium balloon and drifted out of sight. The woman on the ducking stool was not going to drift anywhere. As the crowd gathered around the pond howled, she gagged for breath and tried to speak.

"I will ask one last time Mistress Penfield," said Robert Courtney raising his voice, "is Satan your master?"

"No," said the woman and with great effort raised her head, "it is you are the devil. You and the creature that stands beside you."

The woman gazed across the pond as though wanting her last memory to be of sunshine and blue skies. Her gaze fell upon Billy and Buster and her eyes widened. Buster growled.

"May God have mercy on your soul," said Robert Courtney.

For more information visit:
https://www.facebook.com/billybookseries/

ABOUT THE AUTHOR

Phil Rowlands is a retired headteacher turned author from South Wales He has written several books for children and adults as well as educational programs. Discover more at:
www.talesfromwales.net

www.ingramcontent.com/pod-product-compliance
Lightning Source LLC
Chambersburg PA
CBHW060346180626
46813CB00011B/40